Dan Wakefield
UNDER THE APPLE TREE

"A nostalgic re-creation of what life was like on the small-town home front. . . . The territory will be instantly recognizable to anyone who has read *Summer of '42.*"
—*The Washington Post*

"Vividly evokes the flavor, the innocence, and the ignorance of a decade gone by." —*Booklist*

"A slice of America. . . . Dan Wakefield has done it again. This is a quietly explosive book. It's a part of America, like apple pie and Pabst." —*The Alabama Journal*

"*Under the Apple Tree* takes on the question of our relationship with the revered past and the problem of the proper balance between innocence and the American experience, and dramatizes them in a palpable and charming mix of seriousness and entertainment. . . . But finally, it's Artie's discovery of the realities of sex and trust and betrayal . . . that gives Mr. Wakefield's engaging period study . . . its vigor and verisimilitude."
—Alan Cheuse,
The New York Times Book Review

UNDER THE APPLE TREE

A NOVEL BY

Dan Wakefield

A DELL BOOK/SEYMOUR LAWRENCE

A SEYMOUR LAWRENCE BOOK
Published by
Dell Publishing Co., Inc.
1 Dag Hammarskjold Plaza
New York, New York 10017

To Helen Brann

I

1

THE hero came into the kitchen with a lurch. Bacon popped in the skillet like shots, and he grabbed his side, wincing.

"They got me," he groaned.

"Redskins or Germans?" the hero's kid brother asked.

"Whiskey and women," Dad said, "if I know Roy."

Mom waved a homemade biscuit stained with strawberry jam.

"It's Sunday morning! That goes for all of you!"

"Water," moaned Roy, as he bent his head and turned on the faucet.

Artie the kid squeezed his eyes shut, picturing the way his big brother had looked the night before, in his glory. Wearing the black and gold colors of Birney High, Roy led the Bearcats to one more win in their still undefeated sea-

son of 1941, vanquishing the dread invaders, the red-clad
Demons of DeKamp. Pivoting and hooking, faking off defenders and dribbling the ball behind his back, Roy had
seemed like a god.

Now he looked more like a refugee from a Bowery Boys
movie.

He had on the T-shirt and Jockey shorts he had slept in,
and a pair of dirty white sweat socks. When he finished
slurping the water from the tap he straightened up, wiped
an arm across his mouth, and scratched under one armpit.
His face was pale and stubbly.

Dad looked up from his sunnysides and shook his head.

"Name of God. You look like Death warmed over."

"No wonder," said Mom. "He came home with the birds
again."

"Party after the game," Roy mumbled.

"I can smell it," Dad said. "The booze, and Beverly Lattimore's bear grease perfume."

Mom took a deep breath and waved her hand in front of
her nose.

"Why don't you buy the poor girl a nice little bottle of
'Evening in Paris'?"

Roy made a rumbling belch and went to the icebox.

"Is everyone starting in on me now?"

"Try sitting down at the table for a change," Mom said.
"Join the family."

Roy yanked the quart bottle of milk out and tipped it to
his lips, gurgling.

Artie knew he had to act fast, like the Green Hornet
disarming his enemies, or the morning would go down the
drain. He stared into his bowl of Hot Ralston (the cereal
Tom Mix guaranteed gave you "cow-boy en-er-gee") so his
folks couldn't read his face when he told the fib.

"If you let Roy have the car today, he's taking me up to
Devil's Foothills to hunt for the Phantom Caveman."

As soon as he said it Artie braced himself for the possible thunderclap that God might strike him down with for telling a lie, especially on Sunday, but nothing happened. Artie figured God understood it was only a "white lie," or at worst a "gray" one, since it was not for his own good, but only to help out his brother. They had cooked up the story the day before, so Roy had a good excuse for getting the car.

Mom puckered her lips and made a long, high whistle.

"Will wonders never cease," Dad said.

Artie glanced quickly back and forth at his parents' faces to see if he could read the verdict.

Each one looked as inscrutable as Charlie Chan.

"So does this mean yes or no?" Artie asked.

He tried to make his voice the way Mom called "nonchalant," which meant you couldn't care less. Roy was doing a good job of it, pretending he wasn't even listening to them while he slapped big gobs of Peter Pan on a piece of Wonder bread.

"The Phantom Caveman," Dad said. "First time I heard of him, I knocked the slats off my cradle."

"Well, he's back again," Artie said. "I heard at the barbershop they saw these strange, amazing footprints in the snow—and at night, there's this weird, mysterious blue light in the hills."

Roy scraped a chair back and sat down at the table, gobbling his peanut butter sandwich.

"The mystery to me," said Mom, "is Roy all the sudden finding time for his brother."

"Dammit, you're always harping on me to do stuff with him."

"I suppose it has to be forty miles away in the next county," Dad said. "On a wild goose chase."

"In this weather," Mom said.

Roy shrugged, stuffed the rest of the sandwich in his

mouth, and went around the table to give Artie a friendly biff on the shoulder. Actually it stung a little, but Artie didn't flinch.

"Sorry, old buddy. Would have been a great adventure up there, tracking those weird footprints through the woods."

"Aw, please?" Artie said, pleading to both his folks.

Dad rolled his eyes to the ceiling.

"Oh, carry me home to die," he said, like he always did when things seemed crazy to him.

Mom sighed.

"If they drop us at church?"

"All right," Dad grumbled. "At least they can wave at it when they go by."

"Shazam!" Artie yelled, and Roy grabbed him out of his chair and swung him like a sack of potatoes.

"But I want you home for supper," Mom said. "And Roy has to hit the books tonight."

Dad nodded, and aimed a finger at Roy.

"If you don't have the car back by dark, Roy Garber, you might as well join the Army."

Mom got up to get the bacon, and brushed her hand lightly against Dad's cheek as she passed.

"Don't even joke about the War, Joe."

"It's not ours, anyway. 'There will be wars, and rumors of wars.' "

Roy set Artie down and slapped him on the rear.

"We're off—like a herd of turtles in a snowstorm!"

Roy charged out of the room with Artie in hot pursuit.

The car crept around the corner after leaving Mom and Dad off at church and then Roy shifted into first and hit the gas.

"Wahoo!" Artie yelled.

They barreled down the street and screeched around a

corner, burning rubber like regular gangsters. The town was Sunday empty, and Artie pretended the people were all inside behind their davenports cowering in fear of the renegade outlaw brothers in their getaway car.

Roy hit the brake, the car skidded and spun in a circle, then slowed, and moved on steadily, safe and droning.

"Is that *all*?" Artie asked.

"I got to pick up the guys now. Where you want to be dropped?"

"Who all's going with you?"

"Wings and Bo."

Wings Watson and Bo Bannerman were part of the Bearcat starting five, along with Roy, not as great as he was, but real big dogs, all-'round athletes and helluva-fellas.

"Can't I come along—if I keep my trap shut?"

"Artie, you're not old enough."

"I'm going on eleven."

"You got to be sixteen or they won't let you in."

"It's not fair."

"Sure it is. You wouldn't even like her."

"*Everyone* likes Bubbles LaMode—you said so yourself!"

"Not *everyone*. Girls don't. Or wouldn't. And guys got to be old enough. To appreciate her."

"By the time I'm sixteen, she'll be dead, probably."

"Not Bubbles. She'll still be bumpin' and grindin'. Where you want to be dropped?"

"Home, I guess."

"I'll pick you up at the drugstore at five. Okay? And we'll say we followed what looked like the Phantom Caveman's footprints all afternoon, and we built a fire, and cooked hot dogs."

"How 'bout we say we caught a glimpse of him—we could see his beard, and this big fur robe he was wearing?"

Roy shook his head. "Stick to the footprints. And throw

in about the fire and the hot dogs, it's sort of like camping. They'll like that."

"Hey, Roy. Will you answer me something honest?"

"Don't I always?"

"Sometime will you really take me to hunt the Phantom Caveman?"

They pulled onto their street and Roy took a long glance at Artie, like he was sizing him up. He didn't say anything till he pulled the car up in their driveway and yanked the gearshift to neutral.

"Artie, when you're old enough to see Bubbles LaMode, you'll be old enough to drive. Right?"

"In about a million years."

"Well, when you're old enough to drive, and you got a real hot date, what you do is, you drive up to Devil's Foothills, and say you want to see if there's any sign of the Phantom Caveman being back in these parts. Then you park."

"Then what?"

"Then you 'do what comes naturally.' "

"What about the Phantom Caveman?"

"He'll never bother you. Okay? Now I got to get going or we'll never make it to Moline in time for the show."

Roy stamped on the gas pedal a couple of times, racing the motor in urgent bursts, but Artie didn't get out of the car.

"What if the girl doesn't want to 'do what comes naturally'?" he asked.

"Don't worry. She will. She's just got to pretend she doesn't."

"I bet Shirley Colby wouldn't."

Roy slammed his fist on the dashboard.

"Dammit! How come you always got to bring *her* up?"

"How come you always hit something when I do?"

"You're crazy!"

"Am not! Last time I said 'Shirley Colby' you kicked a tree. Remember? We were walking along Main, you were carrying your team bag—"

"I remember I told you then and there she's an Iceberg. You get it? Now 'that's all she wrote.' "

Roy mashed the gas pedal down to the floor and the car rocked and shivered with the roar.

"Hey, Roy! I won't ever mention Shirley Colby again if you play some pass with me now!"

"I'm gonna be late!"

"You wouldn't have got the car if I didn't tell the fib about the Phantom Caveman!"

Roy took his foot off the gas and pressed his head against the steering wheel, closing his eyes.

"Jesus wants me for a sunbeam," he said.

"Does that mean yes?"

Roy took a deep breath, raised his head, and switched off the ignition.

"One long one," he said. "That's all."

"Wahoo!"

Artie ran in and got the football in less than a shake, tossing it to Roy and then getting into scrimmage position with one knee and one fist on the ground, ready to spring.

"Okay," Roy sighed.

"No! You gotta *say* it!"

It wasn't any good without the ritual, the barked command of the quarterback.

"Go out for one!"

The simple, traditional signal of passer to receiver, like familiar magic, sent a tingling thrill through Artie, as always, and he leaped ahead, legs and arms pumping, running now not across his own snow-covered front yard but an autumn green gridiron, lined with straight white chalk stripes that marked the way to the goal, the field surrounded by cheering throngs whose roar was the very sound of glory. Artie jerked his head back over his left shoulder, saw the quarterback set, feeling the laces of the ball like braille, cocking his throwing arm and sending the spiral like a spun bullet through the clean air to strike the receiver in the pit of the stomach. Artie grunted at the impact but held, clutched, the ball, the victory, as he slumped breathless to the ground with the crowd's acclaim sweetly stinging his ears. He lay there, panting, as the fans' roar faded in the blast of the starting car and the quarterback, behind the wheel, fled.

2

ARTIE sat alone in the center of the universe.

Without anyone telling him so, Artie felt in his bones that his own hometown of Birney, Illinois (Pop. 4,742—Moose and Odd Fellows—Welcome!) was the focal point that the rest of the world spread out from in all directions, and the circular, white wooden gingerbread Bandstand in the middle of the Town Square was the center of Birney, and therefore of everything. He had learned in school that "the population center" of the U.S.A. was over in Elvira, a hundred miles or so to the southwest, but he figured that was just the "geographic" center, the way the North Pole on the map was only the "geographic" North Pole, but not really "true north," which was where the *magnetic* pole was located. He reasoned that if Elvira was the "population center" of the United States (and therefore, by definition, of the world and the universe), Birney must be the "magnetic" or "true" center. He never asked anyone about it; it was something he just knew.

When he squeezed his eyes shut he could picture the Town, fanning out from the Square, and beyond it fields and farms and woods, and beyond that cities, oceans, and foreign lands. If you went to the east you would hit New York and then the Atlantic Ocean, and across that, Europe, where everyone spoke different languages, except the English, who had kind of funny, high-falutin accents, but were brave and clean, like us, and were fighting the dirty Germans who didn't play by the rules but bombed whole cities of men, women, and children by the dark of the night. If you went to the west you hit California, and down at the bottom of it, Hollywood, where poor Shirley Temple had to live and grow up without ever seeing real snow, but on Christmas her parents put cotton all over the yard to make it *look* like a White Christmas. If you kept walking west from Shirley Temple's cotton-covered lawn you would fall into the Pacific Ocean, or, if you had a boat, and kept sailing west, you would come, inscrutably, to the lands of "the East," where the tall, trustworthy, yellow Chinese people, who were our friends, were fighting the short, bloodthirsty yellow Japanese people, who were our enemies. When Artie got his mind as far as the coasts of China and Japan, to the west, or England and Germany, to the east, he saw flames, as he had seen them in the newspapers, magazines, and newsreels about the War, the burning and bombing of cities and villages, the dead and bleeding bodies of soldiers in uniform and refugees in rags. He was glad to be able to blink himself back and be in Birney, "Home of the Bearcats," where life went on like it was supposed to, with people mostly behaving themselves, working and playing ball and listening to the radio after supper and going to church on Sundays, like God intended.

Artie felt God was usually watching over him, and glad of it, but today he hoped the Almighty was busy looking after the refugees in the flaming cities at the far edges of the earth, so He wouldn't notice or mind about anyone who happened to skip Sunday School in Birney, Illinois. If God's attention were elsewhere, it would also mean Ben Vickman wouldn't get any points on his scorecard in Heaven for being in Sunday School today, as he surely was. Vickman had won the Good Attendance medal, and was out to add new bars on it that hung from a little chain and made him look like some kind of old-fashioned French General. Vickman was mainly a good guy, but Artie was tired of him lording it over everyone because his Dad was a Doctor, and anyway, he didn't want to wait till Ben got out of Sunday School and went home to change to his messing-around-in clothes before thinking up something neat to do for the rest of the day.

Artie was in the mood for something more adventurous, anyway. He stood up from the floor of the Bandstand, feeling he had somehow "centered" himself in the scheme of the universe, and trotted off toward the little clump of shanties across the railroad track where Fishy Mitchelman lived. Fishy could do about anything he wanted, since his Dad flew the coop to join the Merchant Marine. His Mom, who liked everyone to call her Trixie, painted ladies' fingernails at the Birney Beauty Shop, and didn't much care what her son did as long as he didn't call her "Mom." Lots of mothers didn't like their kids to even associate with Fishy, but Artie's Mom actually liked the guy and was always feeding him cake and cookies, trying to fatten him up. He was a year older than the kids in his class, and a lot wiser in the ways of the world, which he learned about from spying on Trixie and her boyfriends, and hanging around with guys on his side of the tracks who did wild stuff like hopping freights to Chicago and getting tattooed. In return for Fishy's wisdom of the world, Artie helped him do his homework sometimes, writing up whole essays for him, but spelling some words wrong on purpose so it wouldn't look suspicious.

Fishy came to the door with a bag of potato chips he was eating, which was probably his breakfast.

Trixie was lying on the couch wearing a pink nightgown and reading a movie magazine.

"Whatcha doin'?" Artie asked.

"Lookin' for what's cookin'," Fishy said, and grabbed his coat.

"Don't do anything I wouldn't do," said Trixie, without looking up from her magazine.

Artie was glad to get out of the place. It smelled like boiled cabbage and perfume.

"We can't mess around in town," he said out of the side of his mouth as they crossed the railroad tracks. "I'm supposed to be up in the Devil's Foothills with Roy, hunting for the Phantom Caveman. Actually, him and Wings Watson and Bo Bannerman went to Moline to see Bubbles LaMode, so I'm helping cover for 'em."

"*Fish-ee!*"

When he said it, Fishy rolled his eyes around in his head like Barney Google. That was his trademark. So many things seemed strange, or "fishy" to him, and he said it so much and googled his eyes around that way, that everyone called him that, except for teachers, who called him Monroe Mitchelman, and thought he got his nickname because he liked to fish, which was really a laugh, since he'd never be able to sit still long enough to wait for a bite.

When they went by Old Man Bittleman's black Buick, Fishy stopped, screwed off the silver radiator cap, tossed it up in the air, twinkling, caught it, and stuffed it in his pocket, then walked away whistling, right in broad day-light, like nothing had happened.

"Why'd you do *that*?" Artie asked.

"If we wanna play broomstick hockey, that'll be the puck."

"Great idea!" Artie said, looking back over his shoulder to see if Old Man Bittleman was coming after them with a shotgun. He joined in whistling with Fishy, trying to look natural, like he hadn't just been an accessory to a crime.

They found an old, stubby broom in the alley behind Main Street, and Fishy swiped a garbage can lid to use for the goalie to defend with, and went out to Skinner Creek for the game.

When Fishy got tired, Artie built a fire, and they sat by it singing the popular song at the top of their lungs:

> I don't wanna set the world on fi-er,
> I just want to start a flame in your heart . . .

Fishy said he had something that would make them even hotter.

Artie tried to look excited instead of scared.

Fishy slowly drew from the pocket of his pants a small, brownish booklet. Not a real book, or magazine, but a special kind of thing on rough paper that Artie immediately recognized as something called a "three-by-five." It was called by its size, which was three inches high and five inches wide. Artie had only seen the outside of them before, and was not sure he wanted to see the inside.

Fishy opened it to the first page.

There was a cartoon drawing in black and white of Pop-eye the Sailor Man, and his skinny girl friend, Olive Oyl. In the regular comics in the Sunday paper Popeye smoked a pipe and had a tattoo on his arm and ate spinach to make himself strong. Olive was thin as a rail and had her hair in a bun and no chin but Popeye loved her anyway. Artie liked them, Popeye and Olive. They were funny and familiar, like friends.

Fishy turned the page, and his breath came faster, smelling of stale potato chips.

There was a picture of Popeye unbuttoning his pants, and Olive Oyl pulling her skirt up.

On the next page, Popeye pulled his thing out of his pants.

Fishy's potato chip breath came heavier as he turned the pages, showing Popeye sticking his thing into Olive Oyl, who looked scared but seemed to like it at the same time, just the way real girls were supposed to, and Artie made himself pretend to be excited, saying "hubba-hubba-hubba" right along with Fishy, whose eyes were now tilted and glazed like a moron's.

Fishy got up and went behind some bushes and came back pale and slack in the face, and Artie, who didn't want to show he felt sickish, suggested they go to Damon's Drugs and get some rainbow Cokes, he would even treat. It was still a couple of hours till Artie was supposed to meet Roy there, but he figured they could just hang around and look at the comic books.

They were sipping their rainbow Cokes, made from every kind of syrup at the fountain, and Fishy was tapping his hands on the table in time to "The Chattanooga Choo-Choo" playing on the radio.

Whatcha say boy—is that the Chattanooga Choo-Choo?
Track twenty-nine, oh brother gimme a shine. . . .

Suddenly the song stopped and the radio crackled.

The voice of a man who sounded like a minister, deep and doomlike, said they were interrupting this program to report that the Japanese had attacked Pearl Harbor, the

American Naval Base in the Pacific. The Japs had bombed American ships and the American Army Post without any warning, killing American sailors and soldiers.

The regular program resumed, picking up the rest of "The Chattanooga Choo-Choo."

Nothin' could be finah—
Than to have your ham and eggs in Car-o-lina . . .

Artie felt dizzy, like someone had spun him around with his eyes closed. He blinked, and looked at Fishy.

"Fish-*ee*," Fishy said in a low voice, not even googling his eyes around.

Mr. Damon, the druggist, came out from behind the fountain and took off the white apron he wore, like maybe he was going to get a gun or a pitchfork and go join the fighting.

"This means war," he said.

Artie stood up. His throat felt dry.

"*Roy*," was all he could say.

He grabbed his coat and ran.

The streets were the same, as if nothing had happened. Artie thought maybe everyone would run outside, rally with their neighbors, and decide what to do. Then he realized lots of people might not have heard yet, they might not have had their radios on, so they still were enjoying the peace and quiet of Sunday afternoon without even knowing their country had just been attacked. He wondered if maybe he should yell out the news as he ran, like Paul Revere warning that "The British Are Coming," but it didn't seem the right thing to do without a horse. He cut across the Hixons' front yard at the corner of Main and Sycamore and charged right through their scraggly hedge of bushes, figuring anything goes in Wartime. Farther down Sycamore, he saw the first sign of his country preparing. Old Man Syvertson, bundled up in his mackinaw and scarf and earmuffs, was hanging the American flag from his front porch. Artie touched the first two fingers of his right hand to his brow, giving the Cub Scout salute, as he passed.

"The Japs attacked Pearl Harbor!" Artie shouted when he burst into his house, but he realized before he was finished that his folks had heard the news.

Iva Tully, the widow who lived next door, was standing in the living room.

She had beat him to it.

As if that weren't enough, she ran to Artie and hugged him, pressing his face against her stomach.

"Thank God *he's* too young," she said.

"Mrs. Tully just brought us a nice peach pie," Mom said.

"Only half of one," the widow said. "It was all I had in the house."

Mrs. Tully always took pies and cakes to people in time of emergencies—funerals, weddings, illnesses, epidemics, and, evidently, Wars.

"Thanks," Artie said, wriggling out of her woolly grip.

Mrs. Tully patted him on the head and sniffled.

Dad came up and took her by the elbow, gently, and led her to the door.

"We sure do want to thank you, Iva."

He closed the door behind her and sighed.

"Old vulture."

"Now, Joe," Mom said. "She means well."

"Listen," Artie said, "does Roy have to go fight the Japs?"

"Where *is* he?" Dad asked.

Artie turned around as he took his coat off.

"Uh, he'll be right along."

"I didn't hear the car," Mom said.

She went and peeked out the window at the empty drive.

Artie flung his coat on the davenport and hurried into the kitchen, trying to think as fast as he could. Now that it was too late he realized maybe he should have stayed put at Damon's Drugs and waited for Roy to show up at five like they planned, but he figured in Wartime all other plans were canceled and everyone rushed right to headquarters, which was home. He was sure Roy would zoom right home when he heard the news, but what if he hadn't even heard? Would the owner of the Roxy Burlesque walk right on the stage while Bubbles LaMode was bumping and grinding and tossing her clothes away and announce that the Japs had attacked Pearl Harbor? Maybe the owner didn't even know himself, maybe they didn't even have radios in Burlesque House offices. Maybe Burlesque Houses didn't even have offices. He hadn't even stopped to think about it. He sure wasn't going to ask his folks. Even in Wartime, he wasn't going to betray his brother. Any more than he already had by rushing right home without him, anyway.

Mom and Dad came into the kitchen and Artie yanked open the icebox, pretending to rummage around for something.

"Artie?"

"Son!"

Artie grabbed a dried-up biscuit left over from breakfast and stuffed it in his mouth. He slammed the icebox door shut and turned around to face his folks, chewing like mad.

"We want to know where your brother is," Dad said.

Artie pointed to his mouth and made a sound like "Mmmf."

The biscuit tasted like sawdust.

"Of all times," Mom said, "this is no time for fooling."

Artie nodded.

"Like I said, he'll be right along."

"He didn't take you," Dad said.

"He did so! He took me for a ride! A really neat one!"

"He took us all for a ride," Dad said. "As usual."

Mom plunked herself down at the kitchen table.

"The Phantom Caveman," she said. "I should have known."

"Well, we were going to do that, but then Roy had to do some important stuff with Wings and Bo."

Dad started getting real red in the face and slammed his fist in his palm, but then he took a deep breath and sat down. Whenever he started flaring up like that he took the deep breath, and instead of getting mad he got philosophical. When he got philosophical, his voice had more of a downstate drawl.

"That Roy," he said, "would rather climb to the top of a greased pole and tell a lie, than stand at the bottom and tell the truth."

"I'll perk some coffee," Mom said.

Roy wasn't home by suppertime, so Artie and his folks went ahead and ate the Sunday leftovers. It was one of those meals with long stretches when all you heard was everyone chewing, and then all the sudden there'd be a whole flurry of talk.

"Those boys," Mom said. "They couldn't just go and join up, could they?"

"No," Dad said, "it's Sunday."

"How about Monday morning?" Artie asked.

"Lord sake, keep your pants on," Dad said.

Mom stabbed a piece of ham and just looked at it.

"They'll still just be boys on Monday," she said.

Dad put his hand gently on her arm.

"Roy is nineteen years old," he said.

"He's still in high school. He hasn't even graduated from high school."

"We can't blame that on the Japs," Dad said.

Mom sighed, and got this faraway look.

"Geometry," she said. "It's still a mystery to me. I passed it, but I see how someone could flunk it."

Dad blew on his coffee.

"Geometry wasn't all Roy flunked last year," he said.

Mom stuck the piece of ham in her mouth and spoke loud and cheerily as she chewed.

"No use crying over spilt milk!"

Dad made a kind of grunt and sipped his coffee.

After a while Mom cleared the table and brought in Iva Tully's pie for dessert.

Dad took a bite and nodded, smiling.

"Say what you will about Iva Tully, she can bake a pie."

"Well," Mom said, "let's count our blessings."

Artie spoke up, wanting to help.

"The best thing is," he said, "Roy's almost six feet tall."

Mom and Dad stared at him.

"I mean, no Jap in the world is big enough to beat him."

Mom burst out crying, and Dad got up and put his hand on her shoulder.

"All I meant was," Artie said, "it's a blessing that Roy is so tall and the Japs are so short."

"Finish your pie," Dad said to him.

After supper they sat around the radio in the living room and listened to the War bulletins. The news got worse and worse, as reports of all the American ships that sank and the men who went down with them grew. It was awful, but Artie figured it didn't prove a thing about the Japs being better fighters; it just showed how sneaky they were to attack on a Sunday without any warning or declaration of war.

The radio said F.D.R. was busy writing a speech he would say to an emergency session of Congress tomorrow, but Eleanor was going to talk to the nation.

Mom gave Dad a look.

"I want to hear this, Joe."

Dad threw up his hands like a surrender sign.

"And no remarks, please," Mom said.

"Did I make so much as a peep?"

"Thank you."

Mom went over and turned the radio louder.

The one thing she and Dad disagreed about was F.D.R. And of course Eleanor. Not to speak of their dog, Fala. Dad complained that Mom thought F.D.R. "hung up the moon," and everything he did was right. Mom believed F.D.R. was the greatest President since Lincoln and wasn't afraid to say so, which made a lot of people in Town think she was kind of an oddball. Some of them thought so anyway because she wore her hair in a single braid (some people called it a pigtail) and went around most of the time in dungarees and a pair of low blue Keds tennis shoes. Artie thought she was neater than any other Mom and was proud that everyone knew she was smart as a whip, whether they approved of her or not. If she hadn't gotten married and had kids, she'd have probably been a librarian or schoolteacher.

When Eleanor came on, Mom sat right next to the radio, like she wanted to be right beside her. In her high voice and the accent Mom said was dignified and Dad thought was phony Eastern, she spoke to the women of America.

"I have a boy at sea on a destroyer," Eleanor said. "For all I know he may be on his way to the Pacific; two of my children are in coast cities in the Pacific. Many of you all over the country have boys in the Service who will now be called upon to go into action; you have friends and families in what has become a danger zone. You cannot escape anxiety, you cannot escape the clutch of fear at your heart, and yet I hope that the certainty of what we have to meet will make you rise above those fears."

Mom took out her handkerchief and rubbed her eyes, which were already red.

Eleanor finished off by saying, "I feel as though I were standing upon a rock and that rock is my faith in my fellow citizens."

Mom turned the radio off then and blew her nose.

Dad got up and went over to rub the back of her neck.

"Tomorrow's still a school day, son," he said to Artie.

Artie nodded, knowing this was one time it wasn't right to mess around about staying up late. He gave Mom a kiss on the cheek and hugged Dad around the waist and went to his room.

When he got under the covers, Dad came in and sat on the edge of the bed.

"You'll remember this day the rest of your life," he said.

"Yes, sir."

Usually he didn't call his father "sir," but now that the War was on, it seemed like the right thing to do.

Dad clapped a hand on his shoulder, gave it a squeeze, and went out, closing the door.

Artie closed his eyes but he couldn't sleep. He wondered where Roy was and what he was doing, wondered if he and his buddies had driven right on to Washington, D.C., to march right up the White House steps bright and early in the morning and offer their amazing athletic skills as Birney Bearcats to President Roosevelt himself to help fight the Japs. Maybe Bubbles LaMode had gone with them, to volunteer as an entertainer who would boost the morale of the troops.

Artie said his prayer, asking God to bless America, and forgive him and Roy for pulling the wool over their par-

ents' eyes by fibbing about the Phantom Caveman. Artie
couldn't help wondering if maybe he'd gone to Sunday
School that morning and come right home to do his schoolwork, the Japs might not have bombed Pearl Harbor and
the War wouldn't even have started! But then he realized
that was crazy. As sneaky as the Japs were, they couldn't
have found out that he and his brother had violated the
Sabbath in Birney, Illinois, and even if they knew, they
wouldn't have cared. Nothing was sacred to the Japs, not
even God or America. Artie squeezed his eyes shut, knowing he'd need his sleep to be strong for the trying times
ahead.

A black armored tank with the sign of the Rising Sun on
the side roared down Sycamore Street, pulling right into
the Garbers' driveway with a sudden throb of the engine,
then stopped. A shot rang out . . . .

". . . have to slam the door?"

Artie woke to his father's voice, which did not sound at
all philosophical.

"All present, 'counted for!" came Roy's voice, wild and
slurry.

"Shhh! Your brother's asleep!" hissed Mom.

Artie threw back the covers, set his feet on the cold
floor, and got down on hands and knees. He moved stealthily to the bedroom door, reached up and opened it, then
crawled out along the hall to the head of the stairs. From
between the posts that held up the banister, he could peer
down into the living room, but from where he crouched, all
he could see were legs and feet.

Mom and Dad's legs were stiff; Roy's were wobbly.

"Where have you been—or can you remember?" Dad
asked in a cold, even tone.

Roy's feet made little shuffling moves, like he was trying
to keep his balance. His voice came out in a cracking sing-
song:

A bunch of the boys were whoopin' it up
In the Malemute Saloon . . .

"That's enough," Dad said.

His feet took a step closer to Roy's.

Roy's feet shuffled back, then planted themselves apart, defiant, "Went for a little spin is all," he said sullenly.

Mom's right foot began to tap.

"No more car," she said, "not till you graduate."

Roy made a croaking kind of laugh.

"School's out!" he said. "War's on!"

"You straighten up and speak like you should to your mother," Dad said.

Sassing Mom was one thing Dad was not ever philosophical about.

Roy's legs stiffened and he clicked his heels together.

"Atten-*hut*!" Roy called out like a Drill Sergeant.

Dad took a step nearer to him.

"Get smart with me and I'll clean your clock," Dad said, "and don't think I can't still do it."

Mom's feet moved quickly between Roy's and Dad's.

" 'If you can keep your head when all about you,' " she recited, " 'Are losing theirs and blaming it on you . . .' "

Roy hiccuped, and said in a slurry voice, " 'What's more, you'll be a man, my son—' "

His legs suddenly wobbled, and his body slumped over them.

Hands reached down.

"Let's get him to bed," Dad said.

"Gently now, Joe. Gently."

Artie swiveled on his knees and made for his room.

Grunts, falls, muffled moans, stumbling on the stairs, sounded through the pillow that Artie pulled over his head as the body of the fallen hero of last night's victory (it now seemed long ago, in another season) was hauled to its bed.

Artie knew if Roy went to War he would be a real hero on the battlefield, just as he had been on the gridiron and the basketball floor of Birney, but heroes in War could get wounded or even killed, and the other side of glory was not just defeat but death. Artie tried not to think about it, but his mind went out to those imagined far edges of the world where the soldiers and refugees ran and fell and this time the flames were brighter and closer; now he understood they were not just the backdrop to War, the bright decoration of battle.

They were real.

3

EVERYONE from first grade right up through high school assembled in the auditorium to hear F.D.R. on the radio. Over the urgently crackling airwaves that famous voice, with its top-dog, Eastern accent, told the boys and girls, the teachers and coaches of Birney, the way things were, in no uncertain terms.

"Yesterday, December 7, 1941—a date which will live in infamy—the United States of America was suddenly and deliberately attacked by naval and air forces of the Empire of Japan ..."

Artie got goose bumps, thinking of a whole *Empire* attacking his country; beside him, Ben Vickman made a hissing sound.

"I ask the Congress declare that since the unprovoked and dastardly attack ..."

That was a good word for the Japs—*dastards*.

". . . a state of war has existed . . ."

It was official now. The President had said it.

War.

Mr. Goodleaf, the Principal, stood up in the center of the stage when the speech was over. As befitted the occasion, he was wearing his uniform—the black and gold outfit with epaulets and braid that denoted his position as Director of the Band. Everyone stood as he led them in singing "The Star-Spangled Banner," "America the Beautiful," and the Birney Bearcat Fight Song.

Artie looked around the big room as he sang at the top of his lungs, and felt proud. His brother and the other big athletes stood against the wall, wearing their sweaters and corduroys, some with their hands on their hips or stuck in their back pockets, loose and ready for anything, players and winners who were ready and willing to fight for their home, their school, their country. No Empire of dastards could ever defeat them.

The four varsity cheerleaders bounced onstage in their streetclothes and led the Victory yell:

> Fight em, team, fight em;
> Beat em, team, beat em;
> Beat em fair, beat em square;
> Beat em, team, beat em!

Shirley Colby, as always, bounced higher than the rest, her dark hair flying, her taut calves, sheathed in nylon, shimmering.

Artie looked over at his brother looking at Shirley, and after the din of the cheer subsided, Roy doubled his fist and led the jocks in the unofficial, favorite, "Cemetery" cheer:

> Hit em in the teeth,
> Kick em in the jaw,
> Cemetery, Cemetery,
> Rah rah rah!

The auditorium roared.

Mr. Goodleaf got up again and called for order. He said now everyone should return to classes, and study as hard as they could to help win the War. He said there would be basketball practice in the gym and band rehearsal in the auditorium after school as usual. Then he said he wanted to see Roy Garber in his office.

There were hoots and whistles as everyone turned to look at Roy, who grinned and clasped his hands over his head like a champ.

"Your brother's in for it now," Ben Vickman said ominously.

"Like fun," said Artie.

He didn't believe Mr. Goodleaf had it in for Roy just because he led the "Cemetery" yell; that was the least the Japs deserved. What worried him was that Mr. Goodleaf had somehow found out about Roy and the guys going over to Moline to see Bubbles LaMode on the day the Japs attacked Pearl Harbor, but there wasn't anything unpatriotic about it since they didn't know it was going to happen. Maybe he found out they got drunk, though, which was breaking training, but why would he only call Roy when Wings and Bo were along too? Maybe Roy was the only one who got drunk, but even if that was true, his own buddies wouldn't have ratted on him. Maybe it wasn't anything bad at all, but just the opposite, like Roy being picked for some secret mission in the War because he was such a terrific athlete.

On the gravel schoolyard playground at recess, Artie

forgot to worry about Roy because Ben Vickman got all the kids stirred up about their Dads.

"If my Dad has to go in the Army he'll be an officer," Vickman bragged.

"Just 'cause he went to college don't make him any officer," Blimpy Ottemeyer said.

"Not 'cause he went to college, dopey," said Vickman. " 'Cause he's a *Doctor* is why he gets to start out at least as a Second Lieutenant."

"Fish-*ee*," said Mitchelman.

"Sounds more like the German Army if you ask me," Artie said. "We're a *democracy*."

Vickman gave Artie a little shove.

"You wait and see when your Dad is just a Buck Private," he said.

"Dumbo! My Dad knows so much about cars he'll probably be the Captain of a Tank Battalion!"

Actually, it never occurred to Artie that his Dad might have to go in the Army, since he figured he was too old to fight, but he wasn't about to tell Vickman that.

"Guys who just put gas in the tank are Buck Privates," Vickman said.

"Oh, yeah? My Dad can put gas in a tank with his eyes closed, you dope. What he really does is fix every motor of every car they got made!"

Artie gave Vickman a shove this time.

"So he's just a grease monkey!" Vickman said, and poked Artie in the ribs.

"You callin' my Dad a monkey, you dope?"

Artie poked Vickman.

"Monkey see monkey do!" shouted Vickman, and kicked Artie in the shin.

Artie kicked him back, and Vickman punched him one right in the nose.

Artie jumped him and they wrestled to the ground. The

other kids gathered around and the girls started screaming. Miss Mullen came and broke it up and when Artie stood and brushed himself off, there was blood on his shirt. Vickman had given him a nosebleed, but he really didn't care, and if anything, he was kind of proud. After all, it was Wartime.

Wanda Swanley started crying.

Artie pulled himself up straight, dabbed his handkerchief at his nose, and fell in beside Wanda, wanting to comfort her.

"Heck, it's nothing," he said very manfully, "just a little nosebleed."

"Who cares?" she sobbed.

"So how come you're crying?"

"My Dad's a mailman," she wailed.

"So what?"

"He'll have to be a Private in the Infantry!"

Ben Vickman's stupid bragging was ruining morale.

When school was out Artie delivered his paper route faster than he ever had in his life. He pretended the folded papers were hand grenades, the neighbors' front porches were enemy gun emplacements.

As soon as he finished he sped to the gym, to try to find out what Mr. Goodleaf had wanted with Roy. Maybe the Army had sent out a call for the best athlete in every high school in the country to form a crack team that would parachute behind the enemy lines and score a quick, unexpected victory right at the start of the War that would turn the tide of battle.

Roy wasn't at basketball practice, which meant something really big was up.

Artie took off for Joe's Premium, his Dad's filling station on Main Street, where Roy hung around sometimes to help pump gas or just to put pennies in the peanut machine and talk to the men who stopped in to shoot the breeze with his

Dad. Just as the ladies liked to sit around and gab at the Beauty Shop, the men of the town talked politics and business and crops at the filling station. It was warm in the little office where spark plugs and other kinds of auto parts were for sale and it smelled reassuringly of grease and machinery, the odors of he-men.

Dad was king here, ruling with his honorably oilstained hands, rags coming out of his pockets like cowboy kerchiefs, emblems of expert work, worn jaunty, like the Premium cap with "Joe" stitched above the bill, tilted back firm on his big curly head. He was patching an innertube and talking to Mr. Marburger, the Hoover Vacuum Cleaner Salesman, who was sitting in the old rocking chair by the peanut machine, slapping a folded evening paper on his leg.

". . . spotted some of 'em right over San Francisco," Mr. Marburger was saying.

"Excuse me," Artie said, "but has Roy been around?"

Dad looked up from the innertube, squinting.

"He's not at practice?"

"Well, he wasn't, but maybe he had something else to do. A lot's going on."

Mr. Marburger reached in his pocket and offered Artie a penny.

"Peanuts, on me?"

"No, thanks, I got to find Roy."

"If you find him, you tell him I want him to be at that table at suppertime," Dad said. "War or no War."

"Sure thing."

Artie started to go and then he remembered what Ben Vickman said, and looked at his Dad again.

"Say, Dad, if you have to go to War, will you get to be an officer?"

"If I have to go, it will mean we're down to the last pitchfork and peashooter."

"Huh?"

Dad shoved the innertube away and stood up, wiping his hands.

"I was too young for the last one, and looks like I'm too old for this one, son."

Mr. Marburger slapped the newspaper hard into his palm.

"The 'Last One,'" he said with a grunt. "'The War to end Wars.' That's what they told us."

"They forgot the Good Book," Dad said. "'There will be wars, and rumors of wars'!"

"Goddamn politicians," Mr. Marburger said, and then smiling at Artie added, "excuse my French."

"Well, I got to get going now," Artie said. "Don't take any wooden nickels."

Artie headed straight for Skinner Creek.

There was a spot there where Roy liked to go to be alone, to think and skip rocks or maybe just sip from a half-pint bottle of whiskey he sometimes fitted in his hip pocket. Artie was proud Roy had showed him the place; it was one of those times when his brother was being great to him, like big brothers were in movies, teaching you how to bait night-crawlers on a hook, or the way to place your hand along the laces of a football to throw a good spiral pass. Those were the times Artie loved his big brother, and mostly made up for the other kind of times when Roy would get him down and tickle him until he couldn't breathe, or throw a basketball right in his gut so hard it knocked the wind out of him, or worst of all, the time Roy had to stay home to baby-sit Artie instead of going out to a party and made Artie, who was only five, listen to the scariest pro-gram on the radio, "The Hermit's Cave," not letting Artie stick his fingers in his ears to shut out the fiendish laugh of the horrible Hermit—*yee-hee-whoo-ha-ha-ha-heeeeeeeeee!*

Those were the times Artie could have killed his big brother, bashed in his head with a brick, but of course he wasn't big and strong enough; he only could kick at his shins and Roy would just laugh and lift him in the air and swing him around like a sack of potatoes.

But Artie got over it every time and Roy would do something great again, so if ever he got into trouble and Artie could help, he would do anything on earth for the guy.

Like now.

Roy was sitting on his special rock, sipping from a half-pint of Four Roses, his big shoulders hunched against the cold.

"How they hangin'?" asked Artie.

He had learned that from listening to Roy and the other ballplayers when they got together at Joe's Premium to shoot the shit and eat peanuts out of the penny machine after practice.

"Kid," said Roy, "I hope this thing is over before you're old enough to have to go."

Artie was relieved. At least whatever had happened, Roy was in one of his real big-brother-in-the-movies moods, protective and wise.

"Heck," said Artie, feeling manly, "I'd like to get me one of those yellow-bellied Japs."

Roy put his arm around Artie.

"It's not all glory, kid," Roy said. "The truth is, War is Hell."

Artie was thrilled, his brother telling him how life really was, his arm around him, just like a scene of two brothers in a movie except for the powerful whiskey smell of Roy's breath when he spoke his words of wisdom.

"Is that what Old Man Goodleaf wanted?" Artie asked. "To talk to you about the War?"

Roy took an extra gulp of the booze.

"In a way."

"Do they want you to do something? For the War Effort?"

"Nobody's telling me what to do. I made me my own decision, by God."

"What?"

"I'm going to enlist."

"When the season's over, or what?"

"Tomorrow. Going to Moline and sign up."

"Before the *Henshaw* game?"

"It's just a game, kid."

"But it's the Big Game!"

"No game's bigger than Freedom."

Artie felt ashamed for putting sports before Freedom.

"Is that what Old Man Goodleaf said?"

"Dammit, you little twerp, you think I don't know which end is up without some jerk like Goodleaf telling me?"

Roy took his arm from around Artie, swigged down the last of the half-pint, and threw it at the frozen surface of Skinner Creek where it broke, like the warm and wonderful mood of brotherly camaraderie. Roy stalked off and Artie trotted after him, head down, like a shamed spaniel.

Later Artie learned—along with everyone else in school, and then in Town—that Roy got so mad because Old Man Goodleaf had called him in to tell him he was flunking Chemistry and English, and he'd have to do the whole semester over again, like last year, which meant he'd be ineligible for all sports, starting with the big Henshaw game next week.

Roy blew up at the supper table when the folks said they thought that was why he wanted to enlist right away instead of waiting till June. Of course now they knew he'd go to War, along with the other boys in Town; not even Mom would have dreamed of trying to get him to shirk his duty. If your country was at War, you fought for it, unless you were some kind of jerk or crazy person. The only question now was when.

Artie stood up for Roy's decision to go right away.

"High school doesn't even count compared to Freedom," he said.

"Eat your brussels sprouts," Dad said.

"Okay, but if I was old enough, I'd enlist right away too, just like Roy."

"Thank Heaven you're only ten," Mom said.

"Going on eleven!"

"By the time you're of age," Dad said, "this whole mess will be over."

Roy gnawed a piece of his drumstick and waved it at Dad.

"Not unless guys like me hurry up and get the job done."

Dad pointed his fork at Roy.

"The job you're supposed to get done first is earning that diploma."

"Diplomas aren't going to stop the Japs."

"Neither are you, single-handed."

"The War will wait till June," Mom said, "and then you could go off a high school graduate."

Roy suddenly pushed back his chair, jumped up from the table, and pointed at the ceiling.

"There it comes! It's got the old Rising Sun painted right on the wings, and its guns are blazing. It's a Jap Zero, coming in for strafing, coming right at me in my foxhole. I haven't even got a bullet left, but wait—hey—what's this?"

Roy pretended to pull something from his hip pocket, look at it, then wave it toward the ceiling or the "oncoming plane."

"I've got my high school diploma to save me! Take that, you dirty Jap, I got the hex on you! The powerful diploma-rays are zapping up at you like out of Flash Gordon's gun and you're bursting into flame!"

Artie giggled, and Roy looked around, pleased.

"All right, boys, you've had your fun, now finish your supper," Mom said.

Roy saluted and sat back down.

"Make all the fun you want," Dad said, "but the Japs won't be giving out the jobs when this thing is over, son. And the people who do won't hire you because you were a hero. They forget fast. I remember from the first one. A few weeks after the boys came home, the parades were over, and everything back to normal, nobody cared about the war or what anyone did in it, except for the politicians puffing up their records to try to get elected. It'll be the same way again, and you can take that and put it in the bank."

Roy took a slug of his milk and began to sing, loud and off-key:

> Over there—Over there—
> Send the word, send the word
> To beware—

"Everyone who finishes their brussels sprouts," Mom said, cutting off the song, "gets mince pie for dessert."

Roy made a little belch and rubbed his stomach.

"Good! I need all the mince I can get."

Roy winked at Artie, who giggled wildly, not sure what Roy meant but sure it must be a dilly.

"Oh, carry me home to die," Dad said.

Roy hitched into Moline the next morning before anyone was up. When he came home, he was different.

It wasn't just the G.I. haircut he got right after he enlisted, making his face seem bony and stark. It wasn't a uniform because he didn't have one yet, and he wouldn't even report for induction for another couple of weeks. The really different thing was his attitude. There was something real calm about him now, a feeling of high purpose, like the guy who was going to enter a tough kind of monastery where they only had bread and water and couldn't talk to anyone but God. Roy was preparing himself, like getting in shape for football except in the mind and soul instead of the body.

Instead of going off on a toot when he came back from joining up, Roy hung around Joe's Premium pumping gas and helping out Dad and shooting the breeze with the guys who dropped by to talk about the War. Wings and Bo came around after basketball practice, having Cokes and peanuts and saying how they envied Roy getting a head start on them, but they figured they'd better wait till June. They seemed to treat the new Roy with a new kind of respect, as if he were set apart from them now, beyond them, off in a more important world than the one they had shared of sports and girls and messing around. Artie was proud, and he stuck by Roy every minute he could, wanting to help keep up his morale before he went off.

The only one who didn't respect the new Roy was his old girl friend. Roy never really went steady with Beverly Lattimore, he never gave her his gold basketball on a chain to wear around her neck, and sometimes he went off with other adoring girls after ball games, but mostly he took out Beverly, and everyone knew they did the dirty deed when they parked out at Skinner Creek after dances and parties.

Beverly was known for her red hair and temper that matched, but Artie was really shocked when she marched right up to Joe's Premium after school and started in on Roy while he was lying under Old Man Bittleman's Buick with only his legs sticking out, checking the exhaust pipe.

"You can't fool me, Roy Garber," she said. "You're running away."

"Hi, Bev," Roy said from under the Buick.

"You're not any hero, you're a coward!"

"Hey!" said Artie, who was leaning against the Premium pump, sort of standing guard over Roy, but Beverly didn't even look at him.

Roy scooted out from under the car, looking up at Beverly real calm, and not even saying anything. That seemed to get her even more riled up.

"You're running away from Chemistry and English!" she shouted. "And *me!*"

Roy stood up slowly, wiping his hands with an oily rag, and instead of getting ticked, like he would have done before he changed, he spoke very quietly.

"I'm sorry you don't understand, Beverly."

"I understand, all right! It's a two-bit grandstand play is what it is, so you can keep on being a star even though you're ineligible!"

"Hey!" Artie shouted, but no one paid any attention to him.

Roy smiled at Beverly, sadly, like you'd look at a person who meant well but didn't have enough upstairs to understand you, and he turned his back and walked away from her like she didn't exist, and Artie looked around and she didn't. Beverly Lattimore was gone, as surely as if she had only been a drawing of chalk on a blackboard and Roy had simply erased her.

That night after supper, instead of going out with the guys or getting a date, Roy stayed home to sit around with the rest of the family in the living room and listen to Fibber McGee and Molly on the radio. They all stared at the big wooden arch-shaped radio like it was a stage and you could actually see Fibber and Molly, which you did but really in your mind, like you pictured the Lone Ranger or Ma Perkins or all the other people you had never actually seen in person but knew what they looked like from what they said and did in their stories on the radio.

When Fibber was over and the Longines Wittnauer Hour came on playing music, Mom said with just a little bit of sarcasm in her voice, "Well, Roy, going into the Army seems to suit you. All the sudden you don't have so many ants in your pants."

"Who said I was going in the Army?" asked Roy, real casual.

"You mean you didn't really enlist?" asked Dad. "It was all hot air?"

"I didn't enlist in the *Army*," said Roy.

"Well, I wish you'd have said so," Mom said, sighing. "I always felt the Navy was safer. I'd rather think of you being on a nice clean ship with regular meals instead of crawling around in some muddy trench."

"Being on a ship with enemy subs all around is just as dangerous," Roy said, "but anyway, I didn't enlist in the Navy."

Dad tossed the paper off his lap.

"Well, what the Sam Hill did you go and join, the French Foreign Legion?"

"No, Dad," Roy said very calmly and proudly, "the United States Marines."

Artie jumped and yelled joyfully.

"Hurray—'the Fighting Devil Dogs'!"

His mother dropped her darning and said, "Goddamn," which was even more shocking than Roy joining the Marines.

"Now, Dot," his father said, "it'll be all right."

"He's always had to hog the limelight," his mother said, meaning Roy but not looking at him or anyone else, just staring at the wall, "and now it'll end up getting him killed."

"Jesus, Mom," Roy said, "you sound almost like Beverly Lattimore."

"Don't add insult to injury," his mother said. "Everyone knows the Marines are the first to go in and be killed."

"You've got it all upside down, Mom," Roy said. "The Marines are better trained than any other fighting men, so they have a better chance to survive."

"Hogwash," his mother said.

"Now, Dot," his father said, picking up her darning for her, "it's true the Marines are trained to be a crack outfit. They don't just throw green kids into the front with broomsticks."

Artie started marching around the living room singing the Marine Hymn:

> From the Halls of Montezu-u-ma,
> To the shores of Tripoli . . .

Roy went over and put his hand on his mother's shoulder.

"Come on, Mom. As long as I was going to do it, I wanted to be with the best."

"You wanted to wear that fancy uniform with the red stripe down the pants, that's what you wanted."

"For God's sake, Mom."

Roy was starting to crack and be like his old self.

The lines in his face were tightening, but his father put a hand on his arm.

"Your mother has a right to be upset, Roy. It's only natural."

Roy eased up, nodding, and Artie continued his march around the room, singing with patriotic fervor and pride:

> First to fight our country's battles,
> And to keep our honor clean,
> We are proud to wear the ti-i-tle
> Of United States Marine!

Even though Roy was a changed man, you still could have knocked Artie over with a feather when his older brother made him the offer.

"How'd you like to take in a movie?" Roy asked Artie, like it was the most natural thing in the world. Actually, the only time Roy took Artie to the movies was on his birthday or when his parents started nuzzling each other and gave Roy the money to take himself and Artie to the Strand so they could be alone in the house, though they didn't say that was the reason.

"What movie's on?" Artie asked, suspicious.

"A Bob Hope, I think. Or maybe it's the new Roy Rogers."

"So how come you wanna go if you don't even know?"

"Look, you don't want to go to the movies, have us a little popcorn, maybe go by Damon's for a sundae afterward, it's no skin off my teeth. Forget it."

Roy started walking away and Artie reached and tugged at his sleeve.

"I didn't say that. I just wondered how come."

"Never knew you had to have a 'how come' to go to the movies."

"Okay, that'd be great. Just you and me, huh, after supper?"

"After supper, sure. Listen, you wouldn't mind if Shirley Colby came along?"

"Shirley Colby! What's she got to do with it?"

"I thought you liked Shirley Colby. Thought you said she was probably the prettiest cheerleader in U.S. of A., never mind Birney High."

"Yeah, but you told me she was just an Iceberg."

"I said that?"

"Lots of times."

Roy shook his head, smiling not at Artie but at himself,

or rather the way he used to be before the War changed him.

"I guess I was still such a kid then I thought the main thing in life was making out."

"What is it then?" Artie asked. "The main thing in life?"

He was getting confused.

Roy slung a brotherly arm around him.

"There's better things. Higher things. You'll learn, someday."

Artie felt uncomfortable, and slid out from under his brother's arm.

"I thought Shirley Colby wouldn't go out with you," he said.

"She wouldn't. Won't. She doesn't believe I've really changed. But she did say she'd go out with *us*. You and me, pardner."

Roy did a fast shuffle, took a boxing stance, and landed a soft left at Artie's shoulder.

"Okay," said Artie, "I get it now."

It was like he'd be the chaperone, so Shirley would think she was safe.

"There's nothing to 'get,' ole buddy," said Roy, still dancing around him, throwing little taps of punches. "We're all just going to have us a good time."

"Ha," said Artie.

Roy dropped his boxing stance, and looked sternly at Artie.

"Shirley's a decent girl and I respect her," he said, "so don't go getting wise about it."

Artie walked away, embarrassed and confused. He had just begun to find out he'd soon be old enough to try to make out with girls, and doing it was the most exciting, terrific thing in the world, along with playing varsity football and basketball. Now before he was even old enough to try making out, Roy was making it sound like that was just kid stuff. Artie felt like a jerk.

The only time Roy acted nervous after joining up was waiting outside the movie for Shirley to show up. He lit a cigarette, and then after just a couple of puffs he dropped it to the sidewalk and mashed it out with his foot, like he was trying to scrunch out some kind of killer bug.

"How come we didn't pick her up at her house?" Artie asked.

"I told you, it's not a real 'date,' numskull."

Roy jerked Artie's stocking cap off and rubbed his knuckles over Artie's skull real hard so it hurt, but Artie gritted his teeth and didn't yell. Then Roy stuck the cap back on him.

"Besides, her parents are weird about things."

The Colbys were real snooty, even though they lost their big bucks in the Crash and had to sell the fabulous house on the hill that looked like some kind of mansion in *Gone With the Wind*. Now they just lived in a regular frame two-story with an old-fashioned gingerbread front porch on Pine Street. Some people claimed they got even snootier when they had to move to Pine, and looked down their noses at their neighbors. Shirley wasn't snooty, though; everyone said she was just "reserved" because she was always so quiet and polite, but she always smiled and spoke to everyone, and proved she wanted to be a part of things when she went out for cheerleader. She turned out to be about everyone's favorite cheerleader, even though—or maybe because—she didn't really seem like the others. Even when she jumped up high and spread her legs wide at the end of a cheer, there was something ladylike and delicate about her. She reminded Artie of a princess disguised as an ordinary high school girl.

A minute or so before the start of the movie she came around the corner, looking serious and beautiful. She was wearing a nice plaid coat and had on stockings and loafers. Shirley never wore bobby sox, or skirts and sweaters, but came to school in dresses or jumpers with blouses and always the stockings and loafers or real heels, like college girls or ladies wore. She had on a white scarf that matched her mittens and a furry white hat that came down over the line of her dark bangs.

When Roy saw her, he looked like a pinball machine when somebody put a nickel in.

In the movie, Artie sat next to Roy who sat next to Shirley. Shirley had offered to sit in the middle of Artie and Roy but Artie had hurriedly made some dumb excuse about how he liked to sit on the aisle, because the idea of sitting in the dark next to Shirley Colby, her knees and boobs only inches away from him, her perfume that smelled like essence of honeysuckle making him dizzy, would have been too much to take, so he sat next to Roy, with Shirley a seat away. Still, though Artie laughed and looked at the movie, from the corner of his eye he kept watching to see if Roy would try to make out with Shirley. Once, when there was a big laugh, Roy real casual slung his arm on the armrest of the seat between him and Shirley, but Shirley kept her hands in her lap and Roy never reached for one, much less a knee. Either he was playing it real cool, or he actually had grown into some mysterious wisdom about other things being more important than making out.

At Damon's Drugs after the movie Artie had a double-chocolate malt, Shirley had a cherry Coke, and Roy had a cup of coffee, black without cream or sugar. It was part of his new grown-upness, Artie guessed.

"Before Pearl Harbor," Roy said, "I guess I was living in a dream world. I kept pushing the War out of my mind, like it wasn't real. Just something you saw in the newsreels."

"I guess a lot of us did," said Shirley.

"I sure did," said Artie, wanting to get his two cents in. But Roy and Shirley didn't even seem to hear him. They were staring at each other's eyes as they talked, like they were hypnotized or something. Maybe this was the thing that was more important than sex. Hypnotism. It seemed like before you got around to learning one thing there was a new one you had to figure out that was even more complicated.

"The trouble with me is," Roy went on, "I pushed everything out of my head that was really important."

"Lots of people do," said Shirley.

"You don't," Roy said.

"You don't really know me."

"I'd like to. I mean, I'd like to know your mind. What you think about things. I feel like I've just started thinking myself, for the first time in my life, and I feel this goddamn —excuse me—this real deep urge to talk about it with someone. Someone who has their own values, real standards."

"You never seemed to be interested in things like that."

"That was before Pearl Harbor."

Artie sucked up the last of his malt, making a noise with his straw, and went to look at the magazine rack. He couldn't stand that hypnotizing stuff going on with Roy and Shirley.

Roy made Artie come along when he walked Shirley home, though Artie couldn't figure why since Roy and Shirley were still in their hypnotism state and Artie felt like a fifth wheel. Roy stopped when they got to Shirley's house, not even going to the door with her where he might have tried for a smooch good night, but just stood and looked at her eyes and said he had never enjoyed anything so much as their talk and he had so much more to say to her he wondered if she'd take a walk with him tomorrow after school. Not a date, just a walk, a chance to talk about serious things.

Shirley said yes.

Real life went on, like the Henshaw game, and the Packers played the Bears for the pro Western title, and they even had the Rose Bowl, but it was switched from California to the stadium at Duke University in Durham, North Carolina, so the big crowds that came to such a historic event would not be endangered by attack from Japanese bombers who might make a raid on the West Coast. You knew it was Wartime even though you were listening to a ball game on the radio, because the sportscasters, patriots like everyone else, never mentioned the weather anymore —like whether the playing field was muddy or frozen—so that Jap and German spies could not pick up vital information for possible surprise attacks. The whole country was on the alert, Artie included.

When the family saw Roy off on the train for Boot Camp in Quantico, Virginia, no one but Artie seemed to notice that Shirley was wearing Roy's old silver ID bracelet. It hung significantly but loosely from her left wrist. Artie figured Roy didn't have time to get some links of the chain taken out so it would fit her better. There wasn't time to think of all that stuff during War. The main thing was, she was wearing it.

Roy had never gone steady because he was too busy playing the field and Shirley had never gone steady because she was too pure and didn't want to get that serious about a boy but now suddenly because of Pearl Harbor they had come together—only to be torn right apart by Roy going off to the Marines.

Just before Roy swung aboard the train he kissed his mother and hugged his father and went into a long, movie-passion slurparooney with Shirley and when that was finally over and lipstick was smeared all over Roy's mouth like a wound, Roy knelt down and biffed Artie one on the shoulder, and whispered, pointing his thumb to Shirley standing stoically behind him, "You take care of her while I'm gone, ole buddy."

Artie gulped and nodded, and when everyone had waved off the train and it had disappeared into a dot and then nothing, Shirley, pale and beautiful, took one of Artie's hands in her own as they walked back with his folks to the car.

Artie couldn't speak. Shirley's hand was cold but it seemed to burn his own. He did not let go and run, he walked straight ahead, chin up, heart pounding at a million miles a minute, shoulders squared, eyes forward. He did not even care if other kids saw him walking like this holding Shirley Colby's hand and make fun of him. He would do his duty.

This was War.

II

1

THE shadow of a Messerschmitt slipped across the moon.

Or was it a dive-bombing Stuka?

The aircraft spotter adjusted his binoculars, squinting. His hands were cold but he held them steady. From his rooftop position he commanded a sweeping view of the terrain. Bare skinny branches of winter trees cast menacing shadows against the snow. The small rows of houses and the long fields beyond were silent, hauntingly still. The spotter fought back the urge to sniffle, fearful of betraying his position.

He lowered his binoculars, wiped his eyes, blinked, and craned forward, certain he saw a darkened wing move swiftly over the moonlit landscape.

The sound of a motor groaned in the distance.

The wing and the motor might mean an enemy aircraft.

But now the wing was gone and the motor coughed and chugged, from over on Old Route One. The spotter had to admit, disappointed, that the motor was probably the truck of some farmer.

But what about the wing?

It might have been a Japanese Nakajima 96.

On the other hand, it might have been a crow.

The spotter reached into the pocket of his mackinaw and took out the pack of Enemy Aircraft Identification Cards that showed the silhouettes of Jap and German planes. His fingers, stiff with cold, let the pack slip, and half a dozen cards went floating off the roof, lazily drifting down like black and white leaves of winter. The spotter scrambled to grab the cards and almost toppled from his perch. It was a close call, like you had to expect at any minute during Wartime.

"Artie, will you come down from there? It's past your bedtime!"

The spotter sighed, pulling the mittens his mother made him wear from the pocket of his mackinaw and putting them on before climbing back into the house through his bedroom window. The mittens hampered his ability to focus binoculars and so he never really wore them on duty but pretended to his mother he did. It wasn't lying, it was part of being patriotic and protecting women—especially mothers—from all the things about War they didn't understand.

With Roy away at Marine Boot Camp in Quantico, Virginia, Artie was serving as an Assistant Junior Air Raid Spotter. Good Americans everywhere, from Brooklyn to Hollywood, were fighting on the Home Front in order to do their part, and Artie was proud to be one of them, helping protect his own hometown against attack from Japs or Germans.

At first there was wise-guy, defeatist talk around Town that Birney, Illinois, was safe from the War, being almost in the middle of the heart of America. Sure, these shirkers had to admit there were German subs off the East Coast and everyone knew New York might be bombed; a Jap sub had actually tried to shell an oil plant in California, and enemy planes had been spotted over San Francisco, but the scoffers laughed and said there wasn't any threat for a small farm town like Birney, in Illinois.

Like fun!

The wise guys were laughing out of the other side of their mouths when the Illinois Civil Defense put out a pamphlet that Mr. Goodleaf brought to school for everyone to study that showed how "Chicago can be bombed." There were maps that showed how via the polar air route, Chicago was actually closer to Nazi-occupied Norway than New York City! And if the Nazis were going to bomb Chicago, they were sure as shooting likely to drop a few on All-American towns like Birney, only a couple of hundred miles away, just to try to demoralize the heart of America.

After Artie climbed down from his spotter's perch on the roof and into his upstairs bedroom window, he went to the kitchen and gulped a hot Ovaltine Mom had ready for him, and then went to bed but not to sleep. Under the covers, with his secret miniature flashlight the size of a fountain pen, he studied the article he'd clipped out of *Life* magazine with instructions for identifying enemy planes.

Under the silhouette of the Jap Nakajima 96, the *Life* article said, "If you see the full front view (above, center) you should throw yourself flat on the ground, against possible machine gun fire. . . . If you will memorize these planes, you will doubtless save yourself a great many unnecessary alarms."

He wondered if he ought to practice throwing himself flat on the floor, but then he heard his mother's footsteps and clicked off the flashlight, tucked the *Life* article under his pillow, and pulled the covers over his head. The black silhouetted shapes of enemy planes, Jap and Nazi, swooped and soared through his mind, vicious as vultures but doomed to defeat because of the vigilance of all Americans, including himself, Artie Garber, a soldier of the Home Front, and his brother Roy, in training to be a United States Marine.

Safe and sound, he slept.

When Artie went to Damon's Drugs now he didn't waste his time with the comic books. He flipped through the real magazines, looking for stuff about the War. The most exciting thing he came across since the article in *Life* about spotting enemy planes was an editorial in *Collier's* about what to do if real-live Jap or German airmen bailed out in your own hometown. Artie took the *Collier's* and sat down at a table to study it more carefully. He was going to order a cherry Coke to sip while he reread the crucial instructions, but he realized the price of one would pay for half of a dime War Stamp, so he asked for a glass of water instead, and bought a penny bubblegum ball to go with it. Goose bumps rose on his arms as he read again the advice to Home Front patriots: "It may come to pass, as has been predicted, that enemy airmen will fly over here occasionally during the war, drop bombs on important industrial spots, then bail out, let their planes crash, and give themselves up. In case such things do happen, we'd like to put in an earnest plea now, to any civilians who may reach these airmen instead of police or soldiers, not to obey the human impulse to lynch them, shoot them, or kick to death."

Artie could see it all happening in a flash:

Him and Fishy are out at Skinner Creek playing broom hockey with a radiator cap, when they notice a flash of white silk in the woods. An enemy parachute! Alertly, they hold up their brooms across their chests like rifles at the ready. Artie pockets the radiator cap for possible use as a lethal, grenadelike weapon, and he and Fishy stealthily slide across the ice toward the dangerous enemy. Moving within a few yards of the white silk mound, which is moving and shaking with something alive underneath it, Artie cries out, "Come out with your hands up, or prepare to meet your maker!" The white silk is suddenly thrown aside and up from the ground springs a short, stubby, Japanese Zero pilot, his face the color of, dark lemonade, his buck teeth protruding like fangs. He reaches for the revolver in his holster but before he can draw, Artie whips the radiator cap from his pocket and hurls it at the dirty, slant-eyed Son of Nippon. The Jap falls backward with a gurgling cry as the improvised missile strikes him on the brow and Fishy leaps upon him, pinning the little demon to the cold ground, shouting as only Fishy would at such a moment, "Gonna hang your yellow balls from a flagpole, fooger!" The Jap screams "Banzai!" and lunges upward, grabbing Fishy's neck with clawlike little monkey hands. Artie springs to the rescue, beating the Jap to submission with his broomstick. The two young patriots tie the enemy's hands behind him with cord from his own parachute, and Fishy starts kicking him to death, but Artie restrains him. "This is a democracy," Artie explains. "Even this dirty yellow dog deserves his day in court!" Fishy, after planting one more kick in the Jap's belly, agrees to abide by the principles of democracy, and the two brave citizen-soldiers march the prisoner into Town as people pour out of stores and houses to cheer as the captured airman is led to the altar of American Justice.

Artie took a big gulp of his water, folded the *Collier's* to the page of editorials, and got up to show the vital defense information to Fishy, who was huddled in a corner by the magazine rack. Fishy had not yet shown a lot of interest in keeping up with the War, but was still poring over the pages of demoralizing sex publications like *Peek* and *Titter*, which showed pictures of half-dressed women whose mouths were always puckered in a way that looked to Artie as if they were just about to whistle or spit.

When Artie went up and tapped him on the shoulder, Fishy was engrossed in the pages of *Wink*. His eyes were focused like ray guns on a picture of a woman wearing a frilly black bra with matching panties, a garter belt as complicated as the straps of a parachute, and black shoes with heels like daggers. Artie just stole a quick glance at the picture, which made him feel queasy.

"Hey, Fish," he said, "I got something real important to show you."

Fishy only made a kind of grunting sound, and his eyes remained fixed on the picture like it was a map of hidden treasure he was trying to memorize.

"I said I got something to *show* you!"

"Better'n *this*?" Fishy asked, his gaze still burning on the page of the magazine.

"I mean something real," Artie said. "Important."

Fishy sighed, stuck the *Wink* back in the rack, and said, "Foog."

Artie started reading from the *Collier's* editorial in an urgent, Wartime whisper. Fishy squinted as he listened, like he was trying to get it, but it really was too complicated, like one of those math problems about how many acres of crops Farmer Brown would have if he planted a third with potatoes and the rest with wheat and it rained seven months of the year except on Thursdays. When Artie finished he looked eagerly at Fishy, hoping at last his pal's patriotism would be aroused.

"*Well?*" Artie asked.

"What?" Fishy looked blank.

"Well, what would you do if you caught one?"

"Bluegill, croppy, or bass?" Fishy asked.

"Not fish, you dope, enemy airmen! Japs parachuting down in the woods to spy and sabotage us! Would you lynch him, shoot him, or kick him to death? Or would you just tie him up and take him to jail so he could have a fair trial?"

"Kick him in the old crotcherooney," Fishy said.

"*Collier's* says you shouldn't, even though it's a human impulse. You got to restrain yourself."

"Foog."

Fishy plucked the *Wink* from the rack again and flipped back to the picture he'd been memorizing.

"Don't you even give a darn about the War?" Artie asked. "I mean, if everyone stood around looking at stuff like that, the Japs'd beat us easy. Germans, too."

"Show 'em this, they'd be too busy beating their meat," Fishy said, shoving his right hand in his pocket.

"You boob!"

Artie flung down the *Collier's* in disgust and stomped out of the drugstore, knowing it was no use counting on Fishy to help in the War Effort. He was through with that jerk for the Duration.

Walking home briskly in the bracing cold, Artie felt suddenly surprised and proud that he had used that word in his mind—*Duration*. It was a new term, one of the many new things brought on by the War, from songs and slogans and uniforms even to new meanings of words. "The Duration" meant for however long it took to win the War, like when you said you shouldn't use a lot of sugar or gas for "the Duration." Artie vowed he'd find a new friend for the Duration, a real red-blooded patriotic kid who would help him carry on the work of the Home Front, and maybe even join the Marines with him if the Duration was still going on when they got to be eighteen. Fishy Mitchelman would never get in the Marines; even the Army might turn him down. They probably had tests that would show he thought too much about sex to be able to fight good.

Priority.

That was another important new word Artie learned from the War. With so much going on and everyone having whatever they did for the War Effort added on to their regular life, like work and school, people had to figure out what things were most essential and give them "priority," which meant top billing, or 1-A classification.

Artie's own priorities included schoolwork (you had to be smart to fight the enemy), his paper route (the more money he earned, the more War Stamps he could buy), writing letters to Roy with clippings from the sports page to keep up his morale, keeping watch from his rooftop position as an Assistant Junior Air Raid Spotter, cheering up his folks so they wouldn't be blue all the time with Roy off at Boot Camp, and last but not least, maybe in fact most important of all, "taking care" of Shirley Colby like he promised his brother he would.

2

On the days Shirley had cheerleader practice after school, Artie sped right to the gym when he finished his paper route and walked her home, carrying her books. In the late blue afternoon light, with lamps coming on in the windows of houses, they strolled down the quiet sidewalks, talking about the War, and Roy.

"What's his favorite breakfast?" Shirley asked.

Artie's mind raced to come up with the best answer. He would never in a million years have revealed that Roy glommed huge blotches of peanut butter on Wonder bread and gurgled milk straight from the bottle without even sitting down at the breakfast table, since it might make him seem like a screwball. Bacon and eggs was the normal thing to have, but it almost sounded *too* normal, like Roy was no different than any other Tom, Dick, and Harry. Artie tried to think of what people in movies had for breakfast, lovey-dovey husbands and wives in vine-covered cottages with sun streaming in through the gingham curtains, but the only thing that popped into his mind was Jimmy Cagney squishing the grapefruit into the face of that pretty blonde he was mad at, and he realized grapefruit was a lousy answer since it might make Shirley think of the same thing. Artie himself had switched his breakfast loyalties from Tom Mix's Hot Ralston to Quaker Puffed Wheat because it was "the cereal shot from guns" and that seemed better than "cowboy en-er-gee" in time of War, but it didn't sound like the sort of thing a girl would understand. Then all of the sudden the right thing for Roy to like for breakfast came to Artie in a flash.

"Wheaties," he said.

"Wheaties?" Shirley asked, like she was checking to make sure.

" 'Breakfast of Champions,' " Artie said proudly.

Shirley smiled, hugging her arms close to herself, like she was holding this new information with tender protection.

"*Wheaties*," she said dreamily.

She began to hum.

Artie figured she was in the mood to sing now. On their walks, they usually ended up singing a song together, but Shirley didn't like the fighting tunes that were Artie's favorites, like "Good-bye Mama, I'm Off to Yokohama," so he learned all the words to the sad-sweet kind she liked the best. He started crooning her favorite, even though his voice always croaked on the high notes, and Shirley joined in.

There'll be bluebirds over
The White Cliffs of Dover
Tomorrow just you wait and see.

There'll be love and laughter
And Peace ever after
Tomorrow when the world is free . . .

When they finished, she always had tears in her eyes, and Artie never said anything. It was like keeping quiet after a prayer. The walks with Shirley made Artie feel special, almost like he was in a movie about the Home Front of America, him being Mickey Rooney the kid brother, and Shirley being Claudette Colbert only younger, the beautiful girl who was keeping the home fires burning for her guy.

The walks were wonderful, but Artie thought they weren't enough. He thought Shirley ought to be more in his own family, and finally he got up the nerve to ask his folks how come they never had her over for supper.

It was the night Mom made her special hot chili that you put on top of spaghetti and ate with cornbread and cold milk and custard pie for dessert. Maybe because it was Roy's favorite meal that Mom forgot and set four places at the table and then when she saw what she'd done she sat down and cried. Dad rubbed the back of her neck and jollied her up, and after everyone got to stuffing themselves with chili and feeling good again, Artie came out with his question.

"How come we don't have Shirley over for supper sometime?"

Mom and Dad gave each other a look.

"We hardly even know the girl," Mom said, which wasn't like her at all.

"But you should! She's Roy's girl now!"

"If we'd had all of Roy's girls here for supper," Dad said, "we'd have fed half the state of Illinois."

"But this is different!"

"Wartime doesn't make *everything* different," Mom said.

"That's the same custard pie, and you've hardly touched yours."

"Roy never gave a girl his ID bracelet before."

"Artie," Dad said, "an ID bracelet is not a five-carat engagement ring."

"But that'll be next. You do this first."

"Time will tell," Mom said.

Artie pushed his pie away.

"Fish-*ee*, if you ask me," he said.

Mom looked at Dad and said, "Joe?"

Dad sighed and put down his fork.

"All right, son. The fact is, we don't want to be out of line."

"That's right," Mom said. "The Colbys are—funny."

"You mean snooty?"

"Don't go putting words in our mouths," Dad said.

"But Shirley isn't that way at all," Artie said. "She's just real quiet, and serious."

"I'm sure she's a very fine girl," Mom said.

Dad nodded.

"And we'll probably get to know her better when Roy comes back from Boot Camp."

Artie shrugged, then played his ace, acting as nonchalant as possible.

"Too bad we can't have her before then so she could read us the long, terrific letters Roy wrote to her, telling how he's doing at Boot Camp and all."

Mom's mouth fell open.

"*Letters?*" she asked.

Dad grunted.

"Roy writing a postcard would be like me writing *Gone With the Wind*."

"Well, I guess Shirley inspires him. Like in the Coty ads?"

"What's perfume got to do with it?" Dad asked.

"The Coty ads in the magazines now, where they show the guy in the Army, and the girl waiting for him, and it says 'His duty to serve—hers to inspire.' "

Dad rubbed his forehead and closed his eyes.

"Oh, carry me home to die."

"Please, Joe! I don't want to hear that when boys are dying."

"Sorry, Dot. Artie's got me coming and going."

"All I said was Shirley must be inspiring Roy, since he wrote her this long letter about how he is and what he's doing and everything."

"You win, Captain Midnight," Mom said. "Does Shirley like chicken and dumplings?"

"I think it's her favorite," Artie said.

"For supper, Thursday night," Mom said.

"Oh, carry me—"

Dad stopped, and cleared his throat.

"Carry me back to ole Virginny," he said instead of the other one.

It was what he would say now when things seemed crazy to him for the rest of the Duration.

Artie was pretty nervous walking Shirley home from cheerleader practice. He knew darn well she'd like to come to supper at Roy's house, but he didn't know for sure how she'd like bringing his letter along to read to the folks.

"You get any more letters from Roy?"

"Oh, no, I'm sure he doesn't have any time. He must have stayed up all night to write the one he did. I read it over and over before I go to bed."

"I guess it's a real good one."

Shirley got the kind of look on her face like she did that night after the movies when she and Roy seemed to be hypnotized.

"I never knew what was inside him before. Because

of—well, the things he did, I thought he was shallow."

"Oh, no, he's real deep," Artie said loyally.

Shirley looked at him with her hypnotized expression.

"Just think. You're his brother."

"Heck," Artie said, like it was nothing, and grabbed hold of a tree branch and snapped it back.

"You must know more about him than anyone else in the world, except for your parents, of course."

Artie thought maybe Beverly Lattimore knew some stuff about Roy that he and his folks didn't know, but he wouldn't have said that even if Japs put bamboo sticks under his fingernails and set them on fire.

"They'd like you to come have supper with us Thursday."

Shirley stopped in her tracks.

"Are you sure? It was their idea?"

"Cross my heart and hope to die. Mom's even making chicken and dumplings."

"Oh, I don't want her to go to any trouble."

"Heck, she *wants* to. After all, you're almost part of the family now."

"Is that what she said? Your mother?"

"Well, I don't remember the exact words, but it's what she meant, I could tell."

Shirley gave him a bear hug.

"Oh, Artie!"

She let him go and stepped back, beaming at him.

"Can I bring anything?"

Artie looked down at his shoes.

"Yeah. I told 'em you would."

"What? I'm not even a very good cook! What in the world did you tell them I'd bring? Nothing like a cake, I hope—I'm a flop when it comes to baking."

Artie looked up at the sky, like he was trying to identify an enemy aircraft.

"I told 'em you'd bring your letter from Roy."

"Artie Garber!"

"Well, they haven't gotten any, themselves."

"That letter is highly personal!"

"Isn't there any regular stuff in it? I mean, like about the food, or how he likes bayonet practice or something? You could just read a part like that."

Shirley looked like a bee had stung her.

"Bayonet practice," she said.

They walked the rest of the way in silence, without even singing "The White Cliffs of Dover."

Shirley sat very erect at the table, eating her chicken and dumplings in tiny bites, looking beautiful in her blue cashmere sweater. The trouble was, everyone coughed more than they talked. It was like being in the infirmary.

"There's this neat new song," Artie burst out suddenly. "I don't know all the words yet, but the first part goes like this: 'We're Going to Find a Fella Who is Yella, and Beat Him Red White and Blue . . .' "

"Not at the table, we're not," Mom said.

"Well, it's patriotic," Artie said.

Mr. Garber cleared his throat.

"There's all kinds of patriotism," he said. "I like mine on the quieter side."

"You like Kate Smith," said Artie. "She's not so quiet."

"You won't catch her singing about beating people black and blue," his mother said.

"Not black and blue—red, white, and blue," said Artie.

"These dumplings are scrumptious," Shirley Colby said.

"Please have more," Mom said.

"Oh, no, thank you, I couldn't take another bite, I've stuffed myself so."

"I hope you have room for some rhubarb pie," Mrs. Garber said.

"Well, just a little," said Shirley. "I'm sure it's wonderful."

"I bet ole Roy would like to be here now," Artie said. "I bet he doesn't get chicken and dumplings and rhubarb pie in the Marines."

"We don't know that for sure," Dad said. "He hasn't got around to writing us yet."

"I just hope he's getting enough to keep him going," Mom said.

"Oh, I'm sure he is," said Shirley.

"Did he tell you that?" Mom asked eagerly.

"Well, not exactly," said Shirley, patting her napkin at the corners of her mouth.

"Artie tells us you got a letter from Roy," Mr. Garber said.

"Oh, yes! I brought it along."

"How thoughtful!" Mom said.

"That was really neat of you, Shirley," said Artie.

Shirley gave him a dagger look as she bent down and picked up her purse from beside her on the floor. She took out a long envelope, and a fat sheaf of folded pages. There must have been six or seven pages in the letter, written by Roy! Artie's parents leaned forward, like they were going to reach for the letter. Shirley held it close to her chest, tight, like she was afraid the pages might fly away.

"We'd sure appreciate hearing some of it," Dad said.

"Oh, of course," Shirley said. "Let me just see if I can find anything that would be of any interest to you."

"Anything at all," Mom said.

"Well," said Shirley, "he says here—"

She stopped talking and started to blush, then quickly put the first page in back of the others.

"Well," she went on, "he says it's real cold over there in Virginia, and he's simply exhausted when he gets to bed . . ."

"Roy said 'simply exhausted'?" Mom asked.

"In so many words, he does. I was just trying to sort of sum it up, more or less."

Shirley took the next page and the next and put them in back of the others.

"Oh—here's a good part!" she said. She read from the letter: " 'There are guys here from Brooklyn, Texas, and even Maine. Some of them have pictures of their girls, but none of them—' "

Shirley stopped and went on to the next page.

"None of them what?" Mom asked.

"Oh, that was just sort of silly. There's a real good part, though, that I'm trying to find."

Shirley went through to the last page, then took a deep breath of relief.

"Here it is—listen to this."

"We are," Dad said.

Shirley read from the letter, with great feeling, like it was a recital in English class: " 'I'm proud to be part of this great outfit that has made its mark on history from the Halls of Montezuma to the Shores of Tripoli. No matter what the cost in sweat, blood, and tears, it will all be worth it to know that I am playing a small part in making my country and my loved ones safe for democracy.' "

"That's us!" Artie said. "His 'loved ones'!"

Shirley quickly folded the pages of the letter, stuffed them back in the envelope, and stuck it in her purse.

"That's Roy, all right," Dad said.

"That's all?" Mom asked.

"Well, all that's really interesting."

"If that was the interesting part," said Mom, "the rest must have been the stock market report."

Shirley burst out crying. Dad stood up, and Mom went over and put her arms around Shirley.

"I'm sorry, dear. There, there. We're all just a little on

edge. Heavens, we ought to be happy Roy wrote you so many pages, whatever they say."

"It's the God's truth," Dad said. "That's more than he wrote through all the high school he had."

"See?" Artie said. "Shirley inspired him. Just like the girl in the Coty ad."

Shirley stopped crying, and turned her moist red eyes toward Artie, confused.

"What girl?" she asked.

"In the Coty ad. Where it says 'His duty to serve—hers to inspire.'"

Shirley burst out crying again.

"Oh, carry me—" Dad said and then paused, adding with a sigh, "back to ole Virginny."

Mom stood up and smiled, making her voice sound real chipper.

"Let's have the rhubarb pie!"

3

ARTIE figured Shirley was part of the family now that she had cried at their supper table, and he turned his War Efforts back to the part he'd been neglecting, which was finding a serious patriotic friend to replace Fishy Mitchelman for the Duration.

Artie discovered his man the day the *Bearcub* came out.

The *Bearcub* was the four-page newspaper published once a semester by the grade school kids of Birney, with articles about stuff like the 4-H Club and the School Rhythm Band, essays on Citizenship and Weather, and poems, mostly by girls. The biggest surprise of the new *Bearcub* was a poem by this quiet little guy who was new in town, Warren Tutlow. The poem went like this:

American soldiers, Marines and Sailors
Over the whole world through

Will shed their blood in sleet and mud
To make things safe for you.
So get your Home Front fighting going,
Watch out for booby traps,
Save scrap metal and Buy those Bonds
And we'll slap the Jap right off the map!

Artie looked over at Warren Tutlow when he finished reading the poem, and realized Mom was right when she said, "You can't tell a book by its cover." There was Tutlow, this scrawny little towheaded kid with glasses as thick as Mason jar bottle caps, a kid you'd never want to choose up for in a ball game. You'd never guess that on the inside he was a red-blooded, tough-minded person who burned with the fever of patriotism.

Artie waved his hand in the air and Miss Mullen called on him.

"I think we should all give a hand to Warren Tutlow for his patriotic poem."

Everyone turned toward Tutlow and most people clapped and whistled. All except Ben Vickman, who waved his arm back and forth like he was trying to stop a runaway horse.

"He didn't even make up the last line himself. He stole it right out of the War Stamp book!"

There were gasps of breath, and the tips of Tutlow's large, protruding ears turned red.

Artie knew that Vickman was twisting things around because he was jealous. The truth was, the War Stamp books that were passed out to all the kids in school had stirring slogans to make you angry and one of the pages said "Slap the Jap Right Off the Map" and showed these pictures of ugly, monkey-faced Japs with their fang teeth dripping blood, so you'd want to buy the dime War Stamps to paste over them and cover them up. Once you filled the

whole book with dime and quarter stamps it was worth
$18.75, and if you waited till the War was over to cash
it in like you were supposed to, it was worth a whole $25!
Artie figured it wasn't "stealing" to use the slogan from the
Stamp book in a poem, it was helping more people get
stirred up about the War, and he said so.

"Warren Tutlow wasn't 'stealing' to put that in his poem.
He was helping the War Effort, so more people would
know about slapping the Jap right off the map. That's what
I call using the old bean!"

The other kids were relieved that one of their classmates
wasn't really a poetry thief, and most of them spoke up
with "Yeah" and "Right" to show it was okay by them.
Even Miss Mullen said, "I believe Artie Garber is one hundred percent correct," and Artie, encouraged, spoke up
again.

"If you ask me, we ought to make Warren Tutlow the
Poet Lariat of the Class."

"Poet Laureate," Miss Mullen corrected, "and I think
that's a fine idea."

Artie led the applause, happy to see Ben Vickman
slumping down in his seat, defeated.

In the schoolyard at recess Tutlow came up to Artie and
said, "Hey, thanks."

"Shoot, I was only doin' the right thing."

They both kicked at some gravel, and then Ben Vickman
walked up to Artie and asked, right out of the clear blue
sky, "What kind of Gas Ration sticker has your old man
got?"

"He's got a 'B' sticker, what's it to you?"

A "B" sticker meant you were doing something important enough to get more gas than people whose work had
nothing at all to do with the War Effort and only got an
"A" sticker. Since Artie's Dad had to go out sometimes to
help people get their car started, he needed the extra gas.

"Well, my Dad's got a 'C' sticker, cause he's a Doctor!" Vickman bragged.

A "C" sticker meant that the work you were doing was so important you could get about all the gas you wanted.

"Maybe so," Artie said, "but your Dad's no Lieutenant in the Army like you claimed he was going to be."

"That's what he'll be if they ever call him up to go in."

"Fat chance," said Artie.

"Darn tootin'," Tutlow piped up in Artie's defense.

Vickman screwed up his face in an ugly sneer and leaned close to Tutlow.

"Oh, go write a poem," he said.

Tutlow looked him right in the eyes, and without even blinking he said right off the bat:

> Roses are red,
> Violets are blue,
> Hitler stinks
> And so do you!

Artie let out a real hee-haw, and all Ben Vickman could say was, "Aw, your father's mustache," which didn't have anything to do with the price of eggs, and he slunk away.

Tutlow invited Artie to come over to his house after school.

Artie was really impressed to find out that Tutlow not only read the War stuff in the magazines, he clipped it out and pasted it into a scrapbook with a picture of Old Glory on the front.

Tutlow had stuff in his War Scrapbook that even Artie had missed. The most exciting thing of all was an article from *Life* magazine about this bunch of farmers out in Tillamook, Oregon, who were organized by a blind veteran of World War I to defend their homes and families against enemy attack. There were pictures of the farmers with their guns, crouched behind tree stumps. The article said: "They are prepared to defend their heritage with bullets and frontiersman's lore. Sworn to die fighting if need be, they plan to hide their dairy herds deep in the woods, to combat forest fires started by incendiary bombs, and to harry the invader who dares penetrate their trackless timberland. To a man, they are dead shots."

When he finished reading the article, Artie looked at Tutlow and said, "My Dad has a twenty-two rifle he goes hunting with. And I got a BB gun."

"Well, I got a BB gun," said Warren, "but I think all my Dad has is a blackjack."

"A blackjack?" Artie asked, impressed. "How come?"

"He says if anyone ever tried to break in the house and rob us, it's better to be able to bang him one on the bean than shoot him full of holes. Then, when he's out cold, you can call the police."

"That's really neat," Artie said. "What's your Dad do?"

"He's an Insurance Man. Sells Farm and Life."

"Wow," said Artie.

He didn't know exactly what it meant to sell Farm and Life, but it sounded pretty important. Maybe dangerous, too, if Mr. Tutlow had his own blackjack.

"I bet if you bopped a Jap on the head with a blackjack," Tutlow said, "you might really kill him instead of just knocking him out, since he'd be so small."

"Heck, yes," Artie said. "A blackjack would be a sort of different kind of secret weapon than a rifle or BB gun for killing Jap invaders if they tried to take Birney."

Tutlow nodded, and both boys vowed to ask their Dads if they could start up an armed group of men like the ones in Tillamook, Oregon, to defend their own town.

Dad was underneath a Studebaker when Artie went over to the station to ask about getting him to help organize a group of armed men to stave off parachute attacks from the

Japs or Nazis on Birney, Illinois. All Artie could see was Dad's legs and feet sticking out from under the car which was really okay, maybe even best, since Artie was kind of afraid his Dad might think the whole thing was weird and give him one of those "Now, son" looks or come out with one of his philosophical sayings like, "You don't get anything done by running around like a chicken with its head cut off."

"Who are these fellas with guns?" Dad asked when Artie explained the whole thing.

"Farmers, out in Tillamook, Oregon. They were organized by this blind veteran from World War One."

"Well, far as I know, we don't have us any blind veterans from World War One here in Birney."

"Aw, come on, Dad," Artie said. "You don't have to have one of those. It's even better if the guy in charge isn't blind, if you ask me. So he can see the parachutes dropping."

Dad scooted out from under the Studie, stood up, looking at Artie real serious now, as he wiped his greasy hands with the greasy rag.

"Son," he said, which meant it was going to be serious, "those fellows out in Oregon, they're right near the Pacific Ocean, where Jap subs are sneaking around, so they have some call to get their guns out and be on the ready, but it's just not the same for us here right smack in the middle of the country."

"What about the airplanes? What about Chicago is closer to occupied Norway on the polar route than New York City and we're right below Chicago?"

"If the wind blows one down here from Chicago, you let me know and I'll go and grab the twenty-two."

"Heck," said Artie, "it's not the same."

His Dad fished into his pocket and handed Artie a penny.

"Here, go put this in the peanut machine."

Artie turned and went in the office part of the station,
but he didn't get peanuts. He would save the darn penny
and put it toward a ten-cent War Stamp. He would also
figure out a way that he and Warren Tutlow could do more
for Civil Defense instead of just waiting around for their
Dads to go grab their guns and blackjacks when the enemy
was already landing in the Town Square.

Mom came in the house humming, carrying a bag of
groceries. She walked in the dining room, screamed, and
dropped the bag.

The bodies of Artie and his friend Warren Tutlow were
lying face down and motionless under the dining room
table.

Artie looked up and asked, "What's wrong, Mom?"

"What on earth are you doing under there? I thought
you were dead."

"For gosh sakes, we're practicing," Artie said.

He and Tutlow crawled out from under the table and
started gathering up the spilled groceries.

"This War has poisoned everything if boys have to practice being dead," Mom said.

"We weren't dead, ma'am," Tutlow explained. "We were
practicing what to do in an Air Raid."

"Haven't you even read the CD Air Raid pamphlet?"
Artie asked his mother.

"What pamphlet?"

Artie scrambled up and got the pamphlet, which was
lying on top of the table that he and Tutlow had been lying
under.

"It says the safest place in an Air Raid is at home," Artie
said, scanning the pamphlet. "You should go to the center
of the house and lie down under 'a good stout table.' That's
what we were doing."

"Well, you gave me a scare."

"You should know this stuff too, Mom," Artie said, and

proceeded to read from the pamphlet. " 'You most likely won't be hit or trapped, but if you are, you can depend on rescue squads to go after you.' You're supposed to remember to 'answer tapping from rescue crews.' "

"Just don't go around tapping when I'm not expecting it, please," Mom said.

"Also, you're supposed to stay away from windows, Mom. You should know this stuff."

"I know enough to duck if the bombs start dropping. I don't have to read a pamphlet."

"Listen to this," Artie said, and read from the pamphlet again: " 'You can lick the Japs with your bare hands if you will just do these simple things . . .' "

" 'With your bare hands'!" Mom shouted. "Let me see that thing."

She took the pamphlet from Artie and looked at it, shaking her head, then starting to nod, like she'd found a part she agreed with.

"I hope you remember this part, boys," she said, holding up a finger while she read: " 'Do not be a wise guy and get hurt.' "

"Aw, Mom," Artie moaned.

"It says so right here in the pamphlet," she said, and took the groceries to the kitchen.

4

THE change in Roy when he came back from Moline after enlisting was small potatoes compared to the way he had changed when he got back from Boot Camp for his furlough before being shipped overseas.

Now he wore the uniform of the United States Marines. Artie used to think that nothing in the world was more big-time and glorious than the uniform of the Birney Bearcats, which only went to show how wet behind the ears he had been before the War. The gold and black uniform of the Birney football and basketball teams was only kid stuff compared to the forest green of the United States Marines.

It was not just the uniform that made Roy look different, but the body inside it. It seemed like he'd been issued a whole new physique to go with the new outfit. His spine

had been replaced by an iron crowbar, his chin filed and
sharpened, his shoulders yanked back and broadened like
some huge metal chains were pulling on them. Even his
smile was different. Instead of curling up at the corners, it
went across his face in a straight, military line.

His mother cried when she saw him.

His father puffed up, throwing his own shoulders back
and standing straighter.

Artie saluted.

Shirley Colby fainted.

It was right at the train station, and several people
screamed when Shirley swayed and started to fall but quick
as a whip Roy caught her, lifted her in his arms as easily
as picking up a rag doll, and carried her inside. Roy gently
laid her down on a bench and waved away the gathering
crowd.

"I'll handle this," he said, in his new, deeper voice of
command and assurance.

Everyone backed away, respectfully.

"Will she be all right?" Artie's mother asked in a whisper.

Artie cupped one hand over his mouth, and imitating the
resonant voice of the great radio newscaster H.V. Kaltenborn, he spoke in his mother's ear the thrilling new slogan
that covered so many Wartime situations, including this
one:

" 'The Marines have landed, and have the situation well
in hand.' "

Back home in the afternoon Roy took off his uniform
and got on his old brown corduroys and black and red
flannel shirt and white wool socks and saddle shoes, but
still, he was changed. It was like a new person had put on
the old clothes; it was not a scruffy high school kid who was
wearing them, but a fighting man in disguise.

In front of his mirror with the bedroom door closed,

Artie practiced looking like Roy. He had always wanted to look like Roy, ever since he could remember, and it got his goat when friends of his folks told him he looked like his Mom or Dad. "You're the spittin' image of your father," his Dad's pals would rumble heartily, while his Mom's buddies would coo that "You're your mother all over again." He liked the way his Mom and Dad looked, but he didn't want to look like either one of them. He wanted to look like his brother, and it made him mad that his own hair was so darn light, almost the color of straw, instead of nearly black like Roy's. He figured having dark hair was manly, and blond was for kids and girls. He used Brylcreem on his hair like Roy did, but it only made it gummy and slick instead of darker. He wished he was thin like Roy, too, instead of a little bit chubby, and in front of the mirror he tried sucking in his cheeks to look gaunt but he couldn't hold them that way for long. The one thing he really could imitate was the way Roy moved and walked, and he used to practice slouching and hanging loose, but now he threw his shoulders back and stood ramrod straight before the mirror, hoping to perfect a state of permanent "Attention!"

"Okay, troops, muster up!" Roy called before supper, holding a bag he'd brought back from Quantico, Virginia, that held presents for everyone. He gave his mother a gold and scarlet pillow with tassels that said on it "Quantico, Virginia, U.S.M.C." and had the emblem of the Marine Corps; his Dad got a real regulation Marine fatigue cap for wearing at work; and Artie got an official shoulder patch of Roy's own battalion! He wanted his mother to sew it right away over the heart of his best white sweat shirt, but she said it would have to wait till after supper.

"So what did you get Shirley Colby," Artie asked, and for a split second Roy looked embarrassed and blushy, but then he suddenly let out his old Hermit Caveman's laugh— "yee-hee-heeheh-heh-heh-whooooo!," poked his finger in

Artie's gut and said, "That's for me to know and you to find out!" just like he used to say, and right then he was like the old horsing-around high school guy he used to be, as if that guy was still inside him, hidden now by the U.S. Marine, and could pop out for a little while if he wanted to, like Superman changing back into Clark Kent the mild-mannered reporter when the occasion demanded.

Roy was asked to speak to the whole school at Auditorium the next day, and then he was all Marine again, somber and straight, his eyes dark and solemn and his mouth that thin military line. The Band played the Marine Hymn and everyone sang it like crazy, and then Mr. Goodleaf, resplendent in his bandleader outfit, came to the microphone to introduce Roy.

Ben Vickman reached across Caroline Spingarn to pinch Artie on the leg and whisper loudly, "Wonder if Old Man Goodleaf is gonna say your brother flunked Chemistry and English before he ran off to join up?"

Artie didn't even lower himself to answer that; he just made a face like he'd smelled a skunk, and shook his head sadly at the jealous little twerp like he really was sorry for anyone so stupid. Even better, Caroline Spingarn, who had rosy cheeks and reddish blond hair that turned under like June Allyson's, scooted away from where she was sitting on the floor so she was farther away from Ben Vickman and closer to Artie. She smelled wonderfully of Camay—"the Mild Beauty Soap."

Actually, Artie was really nervous that Mr. Goodleaf might say something embarrassing about the old Roy who was wild and got into all kinds of trouble back in his other, old life in high school that seemed about a million years ago now.

"We are here today," Mr. Goodleaf said into the microphone, "to hear from a young man we all know . . ."

Uh-oh, Artie thought, and crossed his fingers on both hands.

". . . a young man," Mr. Goodleaf went on, "who has just come through with flying colors the most rigorous physical and mental training of the world's finest crack fighting outfit, the United States Marines."

There were cheers and whistles and Artie yelled with relief, shaking his fists in the air.

Roy sat in his red and blue dress uniform on the auditorium stage beside Mr. Goodleaf like a statue in the park, immobile, stern, as if he didn't hear the words or the cheers, that those things didn't matter anyway. Artie bet that a Jap could have gone right up and put a samurai sword to his throat and Roy wouldn't even have flinched. Or Beverly Lattimore could have done a striptease on the stage, flinging her bra right onto Roy's lap, and not even his Adam's apple would have bobbed in his throat.

"As we all know," Mr. Goodleaf said, "our fine boys who will graduate this June are anxious to go into the Armed Forces as soon as they have their diplomas. One of our boys, in the sacred privacy of his own conscience that none has a right to question, decided he could not wait until passing that milestone, and chose to enlist immediately after the infamous sneak attack on Pearl Harbor. Now, he is about to be the first of the many brave boys of Birney who will risk life and limb to defend us all from the forces of tyranny. Let's give a hand to our own Roy Garber."

The noise was bigger than if Roy had just scored the winning basket with one second on the clock in the final game of the State Tournament.

Mr. Goodleaf waved for silence, and the crowd managed to control itself.

"Before I ask Roy—that is—Private Garber—to say a

few words to us, one of our own students has been inspired to write a verse that I think expresses a bit of what all of us feel. Would Warren Tutlow come up here, please?"

All eyes shifted and scanned the room, a murmur swept up from the crowd, and little Warren Tutlow stood up, pushing his thick glasses firmly back against his nose, and strode manfully to the stage. Artie was proud that old Tutlow had come through with one of his knockout poems just for Roy; he was a real friend and patriot.

Ben Vickman leaned across Caroline Spingarn and whispered:

> Roses are red, violets are blue,
> Roy Garber flunked English and chemistry,
> Boo hoo hoo.

There were hisses and "Shhhhs" all around, and Artie pretended he didn't even hear.

Warren Tutlow went up to the microphone that Mr. Goodleaf lowered to suit his size, and cleared his throat. He recited without even looking on the paper he had written it down on:

> From the Halls of Birney High School
> To the Shores of Tripoli
> He will fight our Bearcat battles now
> On land and on the sea.
>
> He will lick the Japs and Germans
> And come home to Victory,
> He'll get out of close shaves better than any barber,
> We know we can all depend on Roy Garber.

There were cheers and whistles and stomping on the floor, and a little girl in pigtails from the first grade, Nancy

Ann Ibbetsen, ran from the wings and handed Roy a bunch of paper daisies, curtsied, then ran off to laughter and applause.

Now, Roy moved.

He took the white Marine dress cap from his lap and placed it, along with the paper daisies, on his chair, as he stood and strode to the microphone, which Mr. Goodleaf adjusted upward.

Assuming the position of Attention, heels clicked together, Roy looked straight ahead, his jaw firm, his eyes focused on some faraway battlefield.

"Thank you," Roy said.

Artie felt goose bumps. It was just the thing to say.

"I want to thank all of you, teachers and students alike, for giving me the inspiration and morale to fight for all of you. The world is in flames, and it is the job of me and the other men of the Service to see that those flames never touch these shores. I have a family here. My own little brother is in the auditorium."

Artie bowed his head as he felt the eyes of others looking on him in awe.

"I have pride in my home and my country, and I will fight to the death to keep them—to keep you—safe for democracy. Whatever happens, you can be sure that I will uphold and honor the motto of the uniform I now wear—Semper Fidelis. Always Faithful."

Roy did an about-face and went back to his seat, as everyone rose and cheered and Mr. Goodleaf struck up the Band to play "God Bless America" and the sound shook the hall.

When the song was over, Roy marched down from the stage, through the crowd, and went right to where Shirley Colby was sitting. He held out his arm and she rose, putting her own arm in his, and as they walked off together the crowd parted, as it would have for Cinderella and the

Prince. Although he couldn't see it with his eyes, Artie had the feeling that Roy and Shirley were surrounded by a kind of halo of light, the invisible magnetism of love.

"Isn't it heavenly?"

"Huh?" Artie said, embarrassed at being caught in the middle of his own daydream.

Caroline Spingarn was leaning close to him, the sweet smell of the Mild Beauty Soap oozing from her every pore.

5

I T turned out that the secret present Roy had brought back to Shirley Colby after Boot Camp was nothing at all like the tasseled pillow he had got his mother, or any kind of souvenir of Quantico, Virginia, or Marine Corps stuff. He had brought her a shoulder patch of his outfit, just like the one he gave to Artie, but that wasn't the main thing by a long shot.

The main thing was an actual engagement ring.

It didn't have a diamond in it—Roy couldn't afford one of those—but it wasn't just a high school ring or Marine Corps ring; it was a regular kind that you bought in a jewelry store and it had a little gold heart on it.

Mr. and Mrs. Garber were kind of flabbergasted, but they pretty much said if that's what the kids wanted to do, it was their lives. Besides, it was Wartime, and everything

happened faster now. Artie's Dad lit up a cigar for the
occasion, and staring philosophically through a doughnut-
sized smoke ring said, "One generation cometh, and another generation passeth away." Mrs. Garber broke out the
fermented cider from its hiding place in the basement and
poured everyone a glass of it, including Artie (his first!),
and recited to Roy, "May you live in a house by the side of
the road and be a friend to man."

Shirley's parents didn't take the news so philosophically.
In fact, they raised the roof. They demanded to "have
the whole thing out" with Roy and his family, and for that
grim purpose invited the Garbers for supper. Except they
called it "dinner."

Mr. and Mrs. Colby had been the big dogs of the whole
town until the Crash came and wiped out the First National
Bank of Birney. Mr. Colby had been the president of the
bank and he lost his position as well as his personal fortune
that he got from his rich parents who owned a whole lot of
land that the railroad bought and they gave up farming for
Travel Abroad.

Kenneman Colby went to the University of Urbana and
belonged to what Artie's Dad called "Eta Piece-a Pi," but
that was just the name he gave to all the snooty fraternities.
Mr. Colby belonged to one of the snootiest, and married
this glamorous gal from the Quad Cities area, Marcelline
Huckaby, who was also in one of the snooty sororities and
came back to Birney to help her new husband be head of
the bank and lord it all over the ordinary people. After the
Crash when they had to sell the big family house on the hill
and move to Pine Street, they scrunched all their fancy
furniture and stuff into it. Mr. Colby took a small office on
Main Street and had a sign painted in gold on the window
that said, "Kenneman Colby, Investment Counselor." Actually, what he did was, he helped some farmers and busi-

nessmen balance their books and make out their tax forms.

For the big night of dinner at the Colbys, the Garbers got all decked out in their finest. Roy put on his Marine dress uniform with the red stripe down the blue pants, Mom donned the black dress with the dime store pearls and the run-down red high heels, Dad put on the blue serge suit with the white shirt and the tie with a hand-painted waterfall that he wore to funerals and Moose Lodge banquets, and Artie wore the brown wool Sunday School suit that made him itch like a madman, complete with the starched shirt and red knit tie that his Mom said was dashing, but gave him the feeling he was being slowly strangled. Artie had wanted to wear his Cub Scout uniform, but his folks said that wouldn't do for the Colbys.

Even Artie's torturous outfit that made him feel like the Mummy didn't impress the Colbys. Shirley's folks looked surprised and ticked off to see him there. "You brought the boy?" Mr. Colby asked, in a tone that would chill your gizzard.

"You said 'the family.' Artie's part of the family," Dad answered back.

"He's only a child," Mrs. Colby said, looking down her nose at Artie.

"I'm eleven years old on April eighteenth," Artie told her.

Shirley, who looked very pale in her black dress and hardly any makeup, came to Artie's side and took his hand.

"Artie's my very dear friend," she said, which made a lump in Artie's throat that almost choked him in the collar and tie.

"Very well," Mrs. Colby said, "won't you all have a seat, please?"

She reminded Artie of a mean governess in one of those English movies where everyone sat around making nasty cracks at each other. Her hair was pulled back in a bun and the collar of her plain blue dress was sealed with an old-timey brooch, like it was locking her clothes on for extra safety. Mr. Colby as per usual had a suit with a vest and a gold watch chain with his old fraternity emblem dangling from it. Artie bet the Colbys never washed the dishes together and nuzzled each other like his own parents did.

Dinner was chicken à la king, but Mrs. Colby called it "fricassee." Artie could hardly swallow, not only because of the strangling collar and tie, but also because the whole feeling in the room was what Fishy would have called "colder than a brass monkey's balls in the Yukon." For a minute, Artie felt kind of good about Fishy and sorry he didn't hang around with him anymore; he'd have given about anything for Old Fish to get a load of the Colbys. Then Artie figured he ought to keep his mind on what was going on, in case there was anything he could do. Mrs. Colby had told everyone where they had to sit at the table, and Roy and Shirley didn't get to sit next to each other. Once, Dad tried to bring up the Subject they were all supposed to hash out, but Mrs. Colby coughed and dabbed at her mouth with her napkin and said she thought it would surely be more appropriate to discuss such a delicate matter *after* dinner. That made Artie wonder why in Sam Hill they had to eat the dinner at all, unless it was some kind of strategy, like making the enemy weak from nerves before you attacked him. Roy and Shirley kept shooting these eye-balling glances back and forth, like prisoners of war trying to signal each other in the presence of the enemy. It made Artie think of the psalm where it said, "Thou preparest a table before me in the presence of mine enemies." He had always wondered what that meant, and maybe it was something like this.

Mr. Colby said he thought War Bonds were not only patriotic, they were a sound investment. Everyone agreed, and Artie told how he had already covered up four pages of his War Stamp book with dime War Stamps.

"Attaboy," Roy said, and managed to give Artie a nice wink.

"Laudable,'" Mrs. Colby said.

Then she went on about what a harsh winter it had been, and after everyone agreed with that too there was just quiet all around, until out of the blue Artie's Mom spoke up.

"All at once I looked and saw a crowd of daffodils," she said.

"Dot loves her poetry," Dad said proudly.

He would probably have patted her on the knee, except he hadn't got to sit next to her.

"I'm afraid I was spoiled by the Bard," Mrs. Colby said. "I can't seem to fathom contemporary."

"To each his own," Artie's Mom said brightly.

Then it was quiet again, right through dessert, which was chocolate pudding, but Mrs. Colby called it Moose.

Artie had to pinch himself hard on the leg and think about Japanese torture to stave off a giggling fit about the Moose.

Everyone "retired to the living room" as Mr. Colby put it, and they all got a glass of sherry wine except for Artie, who didn't want anything anyway except for a stick of the Doublemint he'd brought to chew for keeping his mind off the awful itching of the wool suit.

Mr. Colby hooked his thumb in the pocket of his vest and finally got down to brass tacks.

"I'm sure we would all agree," he said like a judge in a courtroom, "that any sort of formal engagement between these two fine young people would be precariously premature."

"If anything's 'precarious,'" Artie's Mom said, "it's my son going off to fight in a foreign war."

"I fully sympathize with you," Mrs. Colby said, "and I

lay the blame squarely on F.D.R., who solemnly promised that none of Our Boys would be sent overseas to settle other people's differences."

"That was before Pearl Harbor," Dad said.

"F.D.R. could have avoided Pearl Harbor," Mr. Colby said. "He let it happen just to stir up the kind of hatred that would plunge us into war."

"Horse manure," Dad said quietly.

"Really!" Mrs. Colby snapped.

"Excuse my French," Dad said, "but Franklin Delano Roosevelt is the President of the United States, whatever we may think of him."

"That is no less tragic for being indisputable," Mr. Colby said.

Shirley stood up, locking her pale hands together in front of herself.

"Roy and I are in love," she said.

"You're a child of seventeen," Mrs. Colby said.

Now Roy stood up, squaring his shoulders and putting his hands behind him like at the position of Parade Rest.

"I am nineteen years old and a Private in the United States Marine Corps. I am in love with Shirley, and she has accepted my engagement ring."

"Not with our permission," Mr. Colby said.

"Then I am officially asking you to grant such permission, sir," Roy said.

"Out of the question," Mrs. Colby said.

Shirley went to Roy and took his hand.

They stood together, like facing the firing squad.

"They certainly make a nice couple," Mom said.

"This is not a high school prom!" Mrs. Colby shouted.

"You are right as rain, ma'am," Dad said calmly. "This is Wartime, and young people have to grow up fast."

"My daughter does not have to grow up one whit faster

than God intended," Mrs. Colby said, "no matter what F.D.R. wants."

"She is going to graduate from high school," Mr. Colby said, "a recognized milestone on the road to maturity which, if I am correct, young Roy here has not yet passed himself."

"He enlisted is why!" Artie shouted.

"Children should be seen and not heard," Mrs. Colby said with a fake sweet smile.

"Out of the mouths of babes," Dad said, one-upping the old crow.

"I can still be engaged and finish high school!" Shirley said.

"One thing leads to another," Mrs. Colby said. "You could end up being a War wife, living in one of those tin-roof huts."

"*Quonset* huts," Artie corrected her.

"I only want Shirley to wait for me," Roy said, "until I get the job done and come back to finish my own education."

"She can wait without getting engaged," Mrs. Colby said.

"It's not the same!" Shirley shouted.

"Exactly our point, my dear," Mr. Colby said smugly.

"She already has my ID bracelet anyway," Roy said. "The ring is just the next step."

"High school mementos are perfectly acceptable," Mrs. Colby said.

"Is that some kind of rule out of Emily Post?" Roy asked her angrily.

"I'm happy to know you're aware of her existence," Mrs. Colby snapped.

"Mother!" Shirley cried.

"My son may not be a scholar, but he's always been a

gentleman," Mom said. "Roy, I mean. Artie is something of a scholar as well."

"If your son is indeed a gentleman," Mr. Colby said, "he will refrain from pressing his suit."

Suddenly Artie got this picture in his head of Roy in his underwear standing at an ironing board with his Marine dress uniform draped over it all wrinkled and Roy trying to iron it out when old man Colby comes rushing in and yanks the iron away, telling Roy he can't "press his suit."

"Hey, Roy, you can't *press your suit*!" Artie blurted out and this time even though he quickly tried to pinch himself hard and think of dirty Japs lighting straws underneath his fingernails he couldn't stave off the new laugh attack; this was a real blitzkrieg of laugh attacks, one that burst out with a howl and had him rolling on the floor with the tears running down his cheeks and stuff coming out of his nose.

"The child is possessed!" Mrs. Colby cried, which only made Artie's laugh attack all the worse, doubling him up with hysterics, sending him rolling across the Colbys' living room floor as he yanked at his collar for air, gasping and gulping between the wild giggles, seeing his contorted reflection in the mirror of Roy's glossy-shined black Marine shoes, which made his laugh even wilder, and then he heard the giggling spread to his mother and father and Shirley burst into sobs but it was too late to stop himself.

The next thing he remembered was hiccuping going back home in the back seat of the car and Roy saying disgustedly, "Jesus wants me for a sunbeam."

The next day Artie apologized and Roy swore he wasn't mad at him, so they horsed around in the backyard tossing the football and then Roy asked Artie if he'd like to learn some Marine judo tactics. Artie said sure, how did he do it?

Roy assumed a balanced stance of readiness and said, "Come at me like you've got a knife."

Artie pretended he had a knife in his right hand, raised it high and went rushing at Roy, when the next thing he knew he was flying through the air, his stomach in his mouth, and landed with a sickening thump on the hard ground.

Roy came over and looked down at him, his brows furrowed seriously.

"You all right, soldier?" he asked.

"Sure," said Artie in a whisper that was the loudest thing he could do, and Roy reached down and helped him up.

Artie never knew if the judo was to get him for having the laughing fit at the Colbys or just because Roy wanted to let him in on the Secrets of War. Whatever it was, Artie was relieved to know that if any dirty Jap came at Roy with a knife, the poor little Nip wouldn't stand a chance. Roy would just do the judo on him and flip him clear back to the Land of the Rising Sun.

6

Even though Shirley's folks wouldn't allow her to get engaged to Roy they didn't try to stop her from going out with him, and every night after supper Dad would toss Roy the keys to the car and he'd take off to pick up Shirley to go to a movie or drive. Artie figured there wasn't much driving, it was probably mostly parking, so they could neck each other up. Or maybe even do the dirty deed, except with Shirley it wouldn't be a dirty deed, it would be because of Love and real pure. Ordinarily a girl like Shirley wouldn't do it until she was married but now that the War was on even some nice girls did it with their boyfriends before they went overseas, since it might be the only chance they'd ever have to do it at all in case the guy was killed, which made it all right and even patriotic, since doing it would boost the fighting man's morale.

Except for the judo trick, if you counted that as something mean, Roy was real nice to Artie all the time, like he
was to everyone else, now that he was changed from a
black sheep into a U.S. Marine. He got up every morning
for breakfast, and instead of pacing around and glomming
down peanut butter sandwiches and milk, he sat at the
table and ate eggs and bacon and toast and coffee and juice
and even oatmeal, even thanking Mom for the great chow.
That's what Artie called his food now, too. "Chow." It was
lots more fun to think you were "chowing down" instead of
just eating. It was more like being in Wartime.

Everything went so fast Artie realized at recess one
morning that Roy's leave was more than half over and he
might never see him again till he'd helped slap the Japs off
the map and then knock the Nazis to kingdom come, which
might take a lot of months or even years. Artie decided
instead of going to Geography he would go and find Roy,
so they could do some more brotherly shooting the bull.
Roy walked a lot now. After sitting around and helping
Mom with the breakfast dishes, he liked to just stroll
through Town or out to his favorite rock at Skinner Creek,
mulling things over, until it was time to meet Shirley after
school. When the recess bell rang, instead of going back
inside from the schoolyard, Artie just sort of slunk around
the side of the building and walked on away, like it was the
normal thing. If you acted like what you were doing was
normal, people didn't usually ask any questions.

Artie just meandered on out to Skinner Creek, stalking
through the woods like a Marine on a mission, careful not
to snap any twigs or brush against crackly bushes that
might alert the enemy if any were around. He stopped
when he spotted Roy's rock, stiffening, not moving a
muscle.

Roy was there but so was Shirley, too, both of them
sitting under a big blanket. Evidently Shirley had the same

idea Artie did, that so little time was left she'd rather be spending it with Roy, even if it meant cutting classes. Artie didn't want to horn in on them, but he figured he might just go over and shoot the breeze for a while and then make himself scarce, when he noticed that Roy's pants and shoes, and Shirley's skirt and shoes, as well as her bra and panties, were lying on the ground by the blanket.

Holy Toledo!

Artie sank down to the ground and lay motionless, squeezing his eyes shut. He didn't want to be spying on his own brother and the greatest girl in the world; on the other hand, if he got up and started walking away they might see or hear him and *think* he had been there spying on them and figure he was nothing but a dirty little sneak with yellow Jap blood in his veins.

He couldn't see them now but he could hear them. He thought of sticking his fingers in his ears, but then if they got up to leave he wouldn't even know and they might walk right into him, thinking he'd been lying there all the time spying on whatever they'd been doing while they were doing it. He figured the best thing was just to lie still and listen till a part came that sounded like they had all their clothes back on and were just philosophizing.

"I never thought it would be like this," said Shirley.

"It never has been," Roy said.

"You don't have to say that."

"I'm only saying it because it's the truth. That's the only thing I can say now. The truth."

"I know there've been lots of others."

"They don't even count."

"Not even Beverly Lattimore?"

"Don't even mention her name."

"All right. Will you say mine? Will you tell me again?"

"Shirley Colby, I love you. With all my heart and soul, and the pride of the United States Marines."

"Oh, Roy."

There was heavy breathing now, and little moans and groans.

"Wait," Shirley said.

"What, my darling?"

"I want you to put it on first."

"Honey, I *always* put it on first, you know I wouldn't let anything happen. I just have to wait till the right moment."

"No, I didn't mean *that*. I know you do, darling. I know you're protecting me."

"What, then?"

"I meant the ring. I want you to put it on my finger, before we do it. So I'll feel engaged."

"We *are* engaged."

"I know we are in secret but when we're together we don't have to have it a secret, and it makes me feel better."

"You didn't have it on a while ago."

"I forgot. But I just remembered."

"Okay. Sure. Where is it?"

"I thought you always kept it in your pocket."

"I do. Damn. I'm sorry. It's cold out here."

"Hurry back under the blanket!"

"Whew."

"I'll keep you warm, darling."

"I know, sweet. Here. Let me have your hand."

"There. It's yours."

"Damn. Excuse me. I should have got a bigger size."

"I like that it's hard to get on. If it just slipped on and off, it wouldn't mean as much."

"*There*. Now. We're official."

"Engaged. To my fiancé, my love."

"Love me, Shirley."

"I do."

"Do!"

Now there was panting and little sighs and heavy hard

breathing and then Shirley was making little yelps and Roy was sounding like the Chattanooga Choo-Choo and Artie figured this was his chance to make a run for it, they wouldn't notice now if a panzer division roared through the woods with all guns blazing. Artie jumped up and ran, sprinted, pumping his arms and legs as hard as he could, hearing behind him a sudden high scream from Shirley and a strangled, barking roar from Roy that sounded like he'd been hit by a flying mortar shell.

The day they saw Roy off to War was wind-whipped, raw, and cold. March had come in like a lion and was going out like one too. Dad was warming up the car in the driveway and Artie stood facing the house with his Baby Brownie poised to get a snapshot of Roy when he came out the door. Mom came out first with a bag of sandwiches she'd made for Roy to eat on the train, and then Roy came out with his duffel bag and put his arm around her, and that's when Artie said, "Hold it!" and snapped the picture.

"Ready to roll?" Roy asked, and started for the car.

"Let's not forget anything," Mom said. "Are we all sure we got everything?"

It was like they were all going off on a family outing.

"I forgot something!" Artie shouted, and he tore back into the house. When he came back out with the football, Mom was in the car and Roy was standing next to it, taking a last look around, like he was trying to memorize how everything was. Artie tossed him the football. Roy looked at it for a moment, surprised, then he nodded, and said, "Go out for one!"

Artie turned and raced across the yard, leaning into the cold wind and pumping his arms and legs with all his might. He pivoted sharply at just the right moment as the ball came spinning from the leveled arm of the quarterback and struck him like a fist in the pit of the stomach, just right, and he reeled backward with it, holding on, completing the play, the connection. He would have that now, when Roy was gone.

At the train station, you could see everyone's breath when they spoke. Artie was glad it was cold, since he figured it would be a long time before Roy lived in bracing weather again. He was going to San Francisco to be shipped out, which meant he'd be sent to one of the million little dots of islands in the South Pacific to fight in steamy jungles where the Japs swung down from the trees like monkeys. They were tough little sons of guns all right, even General MacArthur was retreating from them on Bataan, but with new reinforcements like Roy he would soon be smashing back at them and cleaning them out of the Pacific like so many cockroaches.

"Be sure to write this time," Mrs. Garber said.

"On my honor," said Roy, saluting.

"Just a line, son," Mr. Garber said. "So we know."

Mr. Garber blinked then and turned away, into the wind.

Roy nodded, and then he took Shirley's hand and slung his other arm over Artie's shoulder and led them a little ways off from the folks.

"Me and Shirley got some 'sealed orders' for you, ole buddy," Roy said in a low, secret tone.

"You can trust me to the death," Artie said.

"We know," said Shirley, smiling through a mist of tears.

Roy reached in his pocket and slipped Artie something in a handkerchief tied with a knot.

"Put that in your pocket, and keep it somewhere safe, in your room or something, and don't tell a soul."

"My mother searches everything," Shirley explained.

"It's her ring," said Roy.

Artie nodded, keeping a straight face and not even

blushing to give away what he knew about the ring, how Shirley wanted to wear it when they did the thing.

"Thanks, pardner," said Roy, squeezing Artie's arm, "and keep an eye on the future Mrs. Roy Garber for me, huh?"

"Don't worry about us," Artie said. "We'll keep the home fires burning for you."

Roy made a funny face and spoke in one of those late-night radio announcer voices: "And keep those cards and letters coming in!"

Shirley threw her arms around him and they clinched, and then the train was coming and everyone crying and hugging and waving and Artie got off the last line, shaking his fist for Roy and shouting, "Give 'em gung ho!"

7

ARTIE felt a little weird pulling the little red wagon he used to play with as a kid right down Elm, but he figured anyone who wouldn't understand that it wasn't a toy any longer but part of the War Effort was a real dumbo. All the good guys in the class had got their old wagons out of their basements to use for collecting paper in the big scrap drive the school was having. With Roy gone off to War now, Artie felt he had to do everything possible to help on the Home Front, and he and Warren Tutlow had pledged to collect a thousand pounds of scrap paper for the drive. Artie was on his way to meet up with Tutlow and load a whole bunch of papers and magazines out of old Miss Morse's basement when who should pop out from some bushes at him but Fishy Mitchelman.

"Gonna give Caroline Spingarn a ride in your little red wagon?" Fishy asked with a leer.

"Not that it's any of your beeswax," Artie said, "but me and Warren Tutlow are collecting for the scrap paper drive and we signed up to get a thousand pounds."

"Won't get any thousand pounds on that little dinky-doo," said Fishy.

Artie gave him a real disgusted look and started pulling the wagon along up Elm, walking real fast.

Fishy fell in beside him, squinting his eyes.

"Old four-eyes Tutlow able to see good enough to collect?" Fishy taunted.

"Warren Tutlow's got more brains than you eat apple-sauce," Artie shot back.

"Foog," was all Fishy could reply. "Anyhow, any jerk at all can load paper around."

"So how come you don't?" Artie asked.

"I am. I'm comin' along right now and help."

"Well, it's about time you started doing something for the War," Artie said.

He didn't know if Warren would want Fishy coming along, but he hated to discourage the first sign of patriotism from the guy.

Fishy started marching, and singing at the top of his lungs, "Good-bye Mama, I'm off to Yokohama—"

Artie joined in, "For the red white and blue, my country and you . . ."

When they finished the song, Artie glanced at Fishy from the corner of his eye and said, "How come you said that about Caroline Spingarn?"

" 'Cause she creams for you," Fishy said.

"Foog," was all Artie could think to say.

Warren Tutlow didn't seem to mind Fishy coming along, but when they got to old Miss Morse's basement and started stacking up the magazines and tying them in bundles so they wouldn't fall off the wagon and fly all over

Town, Fishy stopped helping after a couple of minutes and went into a corner to look at the pictures of women in some old fashion magazine.

"Hey, Fishy," Artie said, "you going to help, or just stand around being a slacker?"

Fishy had already fixed his attention on one particular picture and was eyeballing it like he did the dirty magazine in Damon's Drugs.

"Hubba-hubba-hubba," he said in an unhealthy whispery sound.

Artie went over to see what he was looking at. It was an ad for some kind of cold cream, and it showed this sexy woman sitting on a beach wearing a real skimpy bathing suit.

"Is that all you can think about?" Artie asked.

Without even answering, Fishy ripped the page from the magazine, folded it neatly, tucked it in his pocket, and started up the stairs out of the basement.

"Hey, where you goin'?" Artie asked.

"Gotta go home and take a nap," Fishy said.

"You'll ruin your brains!" Artie shouted in warning.

Warren Tutlow finished tying a bundle of magazines and said, "Your buddy seems kind of fickle about doing stuff."

"He's not fickle, he's a sex maniac. Not my buddy anymore, either."

"Well, I guess you always find out who your real friends are in Wartime," Warren said.

"Bet your bottom buck," said Artie, and feeling a bond of battlefront comradeship, they hefted the stacks of magazines up the stairs.

Artie told Warren Tutlow he had to take an afternoon off from the scrap paper drive to attend to one of his other important Home Front duties, which was keeping up the morale of Shirley Colby, so she in turn could keep up Roy's morale out on the battlefront with her loving, true-blue, inspirational letters from home. Also, Artie wanted to be able to write Roy himself and give him a firsthand account of how he was keeping an eye on Shirley, and how she was keeping a stiff upper lip and her home fires burning for him.

There was an article in *Life* magazine Artie tore out to give to Shirley to help her in her own War Efforts, and he took it to her after cheerleading practice. Shirley sat down on the bottom row of the gym bleachers with Artie and read the part of the article Artie had underlined for her, which said: "Since kiss imprints are liable to smudge en route through the mail, best to let the lipstick dry as thoroughly as possible. Sometimes in order to get a better impression of their lips, girls apply a little cold cream on top and blend it carefully."

When Shirley finished reading it, she burst into tears.

"What's wrong?" Artie asked, afraid he had done something awful.

"I'm sorry," Shirley said, sniffing, then dabbed at her eyes with a dainty white handkerchief.

"No, I'm sorry," Artie said. "But why?"

"I'm terrible," Shirley said.

"Why?" was all Artie could say again.

"Because," said Shirley, biting her lip, "I don't want to kiss a piece of paper. I want to kiss *him!*"

Then she broke down sobbing again, and Artie felt like a heel, though he hadn't meant to do anything wrong. He wanted to make her feel better, but he couldn't put his arm around her or take hold of her hand or any stuff like that right in public and him just a kid, so he asked if she'd like to go to Damon's Drugs for a small lemon Coke. A small Coke was only a nickel, which was half of a dime War

Stamp, but Artie felt it would be well spent for the War if it would make Shirley feel better again.

Shirley blew her nose and then smiled and said that sounded just fine.

Shirley insisted on buying Cokes for them both, and Artie gave in, figuring it was all right because even though she was a girl she was older than he was, so it was kind of like having a big sister buy you something instead of a girl friend. Afterward Shirley wanted to take a walk, and Artie was glad; it was something he could do to help, walking with her out to Skinner Creek and talking so she wouldn't be sad and alone.

The sun was warm and reflected in the puddles from the rain the night before and everything smelled earthy and pungent, like it got just before things started to grow and get green again. It was a heady smell, like some kind of perfume except it was made by Nature instead of in factories.

They went right to the rock where Roy always used to go to think things out, which also was right by the place where he and Shirley had done it under the blankets that time and Artie was only a stone's throw away but they never knew it. Artie got a little nervous, worrying he might give away what he knew, like saying out of a clear blue sky, "I was here the time you and Roy did it under the blankets but I didn't look and I couldn't help listening but when you both started making all the noise I took off." It was scary just having that go through his mind in Shirley's presence, knowing he might get his wires crossed and blurt it out, and he had to concentrate hard on being sure he didn't give it away.

"Me and Warren Tutlow have collected seven hundred and forty-two and a half pounds of scrap paper for the War Drive," Artie said, trying to change the subject in his mind.

"Amazing," said Shirley.

"Not really, it's not really much of anything till we get a thousand pounds."

"A thousand pounds," she said.

Artie could tell she was a thousand miles away, or however far it was to one of those little dots of an island where Roy might be hurling a Jap over his head at this very minute.

"You really shouldn't worry about Roy," Artie told her. "If a guy comes at him with a knife, he knows how to throw him right over his shoulder. I know. He did it to me."

"I'm terrible," Shirley said.

"What?"

Shirley stood up, and folded her arms real tight across her stomach.

"I am," she said. "A terrible person."

"No, you're a wonderful person," Artie said. "If anyone said you were terrible, I'd gouge out their eyes with my thumbs. No one did, did they?"

"No."

"So how come you think so?"

"I know."

"I don't get it," Artie said.

Shirley bit at her lip.

"I shouldn't be talking to you like this," she said.

"It's okay. I like you to talk to me."

"I don't have anyone else to talk to about it. They'd think I was crazy."

"How come?"

Shirley sat back down on the rock, drawing her knees up to her chin and smoothing the skirt down over her legs. She was wearing stockings with her ballet slippers and the sun made glinting lights on the smooth silk of her legs.

"There are certain things a girl can do in Wartime that it wouldn't be right to do otherwise," she said.

"Sure," Artie said, figuring she meant the stuff she did with Roy underneath the blanket but naturally didn't want to come right out and say so. Knowing he sort of knew what she meant without her having to spell it out made Artie feel proud and wise.

"In Wartime, a girl should do her duty, if she loves a man, but she's not supposed to really be crazy about it."

"She's not?"

"Not any more than a man who does his duty by killing the enemy should actually *enjoy* doing it. Then he'd just be a killer, nothing more than an animal."

"I guess so," Artie said. "But I don't think you have to worry about that happening to Roy. I mean, I think he'll just kill off the Japs he has to, to get the job done, but he won't want to keep on killing people after we win the War."

"Of course not. By the same token, a girl should do *her* duty, and do it well, and be glad she had the right and privilege of doing it, but she shouldn't really *love* doing it, or she'd just be an animal herself, like the man who enjoys killing the enemy so much he becomes a killer."

"But you don't have to kill anyone. You just have to keep the home fires burning."

"They're burning all right."

"So everything's fine. You're doing your duty."

"I did," she said. "The trouble is, I want to keep doing it."

"Your duty?"

"I'm being a phony to call it that. Don't you see? 'Duty' is something you have to do even though you may not want to, and if you really love doing it, it can't be 'duty.'"

"What is it, then?"

Shirley squeezed her eyes shut, and hugged her knees to her chin.

"Sin, I suppose."

"But things that are a sin in peacetime, aren't a sin in war," Artie said. "Like killing is a sin if there isn't a war on, but killing a Nazi or Jap is something you have to do and it's good if you do. That's why they give guys medals who kill a lot of enemies. That's a guy's duty. But they don't give girls medals for doing *their* duty."

"If they did, I'd get the Congressional Medal of Honor."

"Well, I bet Roy'll give you all the medals he wins when he gets back home."

"I don't want his medals!" Shirley cried. "I want *him*!"

"You will," Artie said. "He loves you. As soon as he comes back, you'll have him."

"*If* he comes back."

"I swear he will."

"And *when* he comes back. Months? Years?"

"However long it takes to get the job done."

"That's easy for *you* to say."

"Heck no, it's not. He's my brother."

Shirley jumped up and started walking around the rock, shaking her head.

"Listen to me. I'm sorry. See how selfish I am? I really am terrible."

"You're not either," Artie said.

Shirley stopped, and stared off into the woods.

"What if something wonderful happened to you," she said, "something you thought would be nice, but turned out to be the most exciting and fabulous thing that ever happened to you, and you got to have it happen for a little more than a whole week, and then you knew you couldn't have it happen anymore for months or maybe years or maybe never?"

"I'd feel pretty punk."

"Oh, Artie," she said. "So do I. So do I."

The tears were coming down her cheeks, and Artie got it now, what she was telling him.

"I heard we got guys working on secret weapons," Artie said, "that'll end the War in no time and bring Our Boys back home. Maybe that's what'll happen, real soon."

"If it doesn't, I think I'll explode. Or just burn up inside. Maybe that's what I deserve. The fires of hell."

"Don't say that stuff."

"I'm sorry. I'm talking baloney. Forgive me? After all, think of all the other girls. Sweethearts. Even wives. They have to wait, too. If they can do it, I can do it."

"Sure you can. You just have to be real brave and tighten your belt."

"My belt?"

Shirley suddenly laughed, and then blew her nose, real hard. Artie stood up and tossed a rock into Skinner Creek, making a splash in the sunny green water. Then, without saying anything, he and Shirley turned and walked back through the woods toward Town.

Artie's eleventh birthday was April 18, and he got everything he wanted—and more. His parents gave him the official pair of Boy Scout semaphore flags, each one divided into a red and white triangle and sewn onto a stick, just like regulation Army or Navy or Marine Semaphore flags, and Warren Tutlow came over and looked through Artie's binoculars at Artie up on the roof making some of the new signals he had already learned by positioning the flags: he could do "V" which was for Victory, and also "SOS," and "Hi." When he learned the whole semaphore alphabet he'd be able to send entire messages clear across town to Warren Tutlow by signaling from his roof.

Shirley Colby came by to give Artie her present, which

was a purple label "Okeh" record of "We'll Heil, Heil,
Right in Der Führer's Face," and Shirley went downstairs
to the basement with him while he cranked up the old
Victrola and marched around the room making the Bronx
cheer "Heils" along with Spike Jones and the City Slickers
on the record. Shirley smiled a little, but she looked real
pale and even thinner than usual. Artie hoped she wasn't
going to waste away to nothing before Roy came marching
home.

Fishy Mitchelman dropped over and gave Artie a pinup
picture of Betty Grable that he had torn off a calendar at
Bob's Eats on Main Street.

Most exciting of all, after supper and the birthday cake
with eleven candles that Artie blew out with only one little
extra huff that his folks said counted as one huff so he got
his wish (which he wouldn't have told them on pain of
death), Artie went to the movies with Caroline Spingarn. It
wasn't actually a real "date"; kids in sixth grade weren't
allowed to have dates yet, but they could "meet" each other
at the movies, and that's what Artie and Caroline did. They
met each other at seven o'clock sharp in front of the Strand
and Artie bought tickets for both of them and they went
inside and sat together to watch Errol Flynn in *Desperate
Journey*. Artie thought about holding Caroline's hand, but
he kept feeling this presence behind him and Caroline, like
a lookout scout, and sure enough it turned out to be Mae
Ellen Spingarn, Caroline's older sister who was a Junior in
high school, who came to sort of keep an eye on Caroline
since it was her first time to meet a guy for a movie. Artie
was glad he hadn't tried to sneak his hand onto Caroline's
(Mae Ellen would have seen for sure), but anyway Caroline herself leaned close to him a couple of times, pretending to giggle at something but the real reason was to give
him a whiff of her Camay Beauty Soap smell, which really
knocked him out.

That night he studied his aircraft spotter cards with his penlight beneath the blankets, and then, after resisting for a long time and trying to think of serious stuff like the War, he took the Betty Grable pinup from the envelope Fishy had handed it to him in and he studied that with greater concentration than he'd ever been able to apply to the Messerschmitt or Stuka, memorizing every line and curve of the perfect body, imagining the wet red slurp of those fabulous lips on his mouth, sucked in the sight of the blond hair and the bare limbs stretching from the tight-fitting bathing suit, and found when he switched off his penlight that he had so well imprinted the picture on his mind that he could see it in every detail with his eyes closed and that vision made his cheeks grow hot and even more magically made his thing get big and hard till he touched it to see what was happening and touching it felt good so he did it more although he knew it was wrong and a dangerous thing to do, and for a while he tried to push the pinup picture from his mind and see the sweet face of Caroline Spingarn or the lovely, haunted eyes of Shirley Colby, but old Betty Grable kept popping back into his mind, looking over her shoulder at him with that come-hither smile, and his mind's eye traced down the perfect swell of her thighs and along down the calves and up again to the full, smooth, protruding behind, and the bare back and then the blond-capped goddess face and as Artie pressed himself to the thrill of it he throbbed in a way he had never done before, wiping out his mind for a moment in a terrifying mixture of pleasure and pain that left him limp and gasping. He was still dry but he knew something had exploded in him and that he would not be the same again. His thing had shrunk back to normal and he only hoped he hadn't done it any permanent damage.

The next morning Artie found out he had gotten his wish when he blew out his birthday candles. The radio said that

Colonel Jimmy Doolittle had led a bunch of B-25s on a bombing raid on Tokyo, revenging Pearl Harbor and scaring the devil out of the Japs by attacking their own hometown. This was the first sign the tide could be turning for America in the War. But everyone knew now it wouldn't be over easily or soon. The Japs, even though they were laughably short, were mean and tricky fighters, and they'd been preparing for War for years and years, while America was just beginning to roll its tanks and ships off the assembly lines. On the other side of the world, the Nazis were still goose-stepping all over Europe, and America was going to the rescue of the brave, clean English, who were led by old Winston Churchill and the valiant pilots of the RAF. Like the popular song said about beating the Germans, "We did it before, and we can do it again," but it was going to be a long, bloody battle.

People were beginning to settle in for the trials and deprivations of Wartime. In May, you had to line up to get Food Stamps for the rationing of most of the stuff that was good, like meat, butter, sugar, and eggs. Artie knew that Wartime sacrifice had really come home when Mom served up the first supper of liver, which wasn't rationed at all, and no wonder, the way the stuff tasted. When Artie complained, Dad just told him to put more catsup on it, and that way at least you could get it down.

All the guys in Roy's class joined up right after graduation. Bo Bannerman got in the Air Corps, and Wings Watson joined the Army. There was a big parade down Main Street for the boys who were leaving to defend America and save the world for democracy, and as the drums rolled and the bugles blared, Artie wished he were old enough to go himself.

Since that wasn't possible he did the next best thing and

planted a victory garden in the backyard. He dug the rows himself and spent his own money to buy the packages of Burpee's seeds for radishes, carrots, and his favorite vegetable, lima beans. There were never enough limas to make more than a couple of helpings for supper, and the carrots were kind of short and stubby, but the radishes came out great. Artie pulled them up proudly, washed the dirt off them, and put them on a plate at the supper table. Mom and Dad said they were the best radishes they'd ever had. Eating them made Artie feel good even though they didn't have much of a taste when you got right down to it; the thing was, radishes tasted so blah that it made you realize you were living in Wartime, and if worse came to worst and America's farms were destroyed by German incendiary bombs you could always survive on radishes from your own backyard till Victory came.

A couple of weeks after school started in the fall, Shirley came over to read to the Garbers Roy's first letter from the fighting front! The family got one letter all to themselves in the summer, scrawled in big handwriting that Mom said showed how tired Roy was, but Dad said it just meant Roy was trying to fill up the page and so was the same old Roy and they shouldn't worry about him. The only exciting part of it had been where the censors had inked out a word. Roy had said, "I got me a view of the ocean, but the nearest hotel is at XXXXXXXXXX."

But the letter to Shirley from the front was full of amazing, firsthand stuff about actually fighting the Japs! Of course, Roy wasn't allowed to say where he was, and when you wrote him it was just to the A.P.O. number in San Francisco where all the mail to the South Pacific went, but from reading the papers everyone knew Roy's First Marine Division was fighting in New Guinea, and Guadalcanal, and it was probably one of those places or maybe one of the smaller islands that wasn't even famous yet. The important thing was that he was really in the thick of it.

Shirley's voice cracked and the thin, V-mail stationery rattled in her trembling hands when she read from Roy's letter how the Marines were doing great but the fighting would probably take a long time because "it takes time to dig the little rats out of their holes. . . . If you look into the jungle you can't tell if there are three monkeys out there or three hundred . . . it's better to shoot a few coconuts than miss a Jap." Artie made Shirley read those "good parts" over so he could write them down and report them to his class at school, which made him sort of a hero himself, just because he was Roy's brother.

But that was nothing compared to the day Artie went to pick up the papers for his route just before Thanksgiving. The bikes of three or four other carriers were parked outside the shed where the truck dropped off the papers from Moline and Old Man Mosely counted them out and made sure all the routes were delivered and the money collected on time. The kids were huddled around Mosely reading something in the new paper, and when Artie came up everyone started cheering. There was a story in the paper that read:

FORMER BIRNEY STAR GETS 17 JAPS ON GUADALCANAL

A sharp-shooting fool who is as cool while picking off Japs as he was while sniping baskets for Birney (Ill.) High School was listed in official records today as one of the outstanding snipers in this jungle battle-field. He is Private Roy Garber, credited with seventeen Japs—all of them plucked out of trees with a Garand rifle. Close behind Garber is Private Charles Bailey of Swayzee (Ind.), with eleven. He got them all at one time.

Artie stuck a pin for Roy on the Battle Map of the South Pacific he had thumbtacked to the kitchen wall, right on the island of Guadalcanal. He prayed he would grow up faster so he could join the fight for freedom, and dreamed of being in uniform alongside Roy, the two heroic brothers risking their lives so the world could live happily ever after.

III

1

Artie was in uniform.

He stood at Attention along with more than two hundred other troops awaiting their orders.

"Right *hace*!" barked the Commander, and Artie pivoted on his right heel, snapping his left alongside it in the same rhythm as the rest of the disciplined ranks, all with chins up, shoulders thrown back.

"For-ard *harch*!" the command came, and Artie stepped ahead, his legs moving in unison with the hundreds of others, his chest thrust out and swelling with the pride of being part of this well-trained outfit.

"By the left flank—*harch*!"

As one man, the lines swung smoothly into lengthwise columns on command as they approached the reviewing stand, where among the uniformed officers stood the ven-

erable United States Senator Orville P. Hapgood, wizened
and wise, silver of hair and tongue, come to deliver an
inspirational Wartime message to the troops.

"Eyyyyyyyyes—*right*!" the command cracked forth, and
Artie almost threw his neck out of joint he snapped it so
hard to his right, where his eyes caught a glimmer of the
Senator himself, his silver hair tousled by the breeze, his
black suit and gray tie seeming like a kind of uniform of his
own.

When the troops had passed in review and assembled
again in formation the Commander put them at Parade
Rest and introduced the distinguished visitor.

"We of Camp Cho-Ko-Mo-Ko, Boy Scouts of America,
are proud to welcome the Honorable Senator Orville P.
Hapgood, who is here today to pay tribute to our work, and
spur us on to greater effort in the fight for freedom and
democracy."

In the hot sticky Sunday air, with only the sound of a
few buzzing horseflies marring the military stillness, Artie
concentrated with all his might. He wanted to remember
everything down to the last detail so he could write all
about it to Roy in his next V-mail letter. Everything was
happening so fast now it was hard to keep up with all the
exciting stuff going on in his own life and around the world.

Just before school was out for summer vacation the
Americans and British had routed the powerful panzer di-
visions of the Nazis in the desert of Africa, and Artie had
clipped out the headline about it that said "Axis Trembles
with Fear!" Out in the South Pacific, Roy and the U.S.
Marines had finally captured the key island of Guadalcanal, and were pushing back the Japs in those tiny dots of
islands on the Battle Map that Artie had thumbtacked up
on the kitchen wall. He stuck a red pin in whatever place
he thought Roy was fighting, and memorized the weird-
sounding names of places no one had ever heard of a year

ago and now were famous: *Rendova, Kolombangara, Vella Lavella, Bougainville.*

Some people thought the War might even be won by Christmas, which would make 1943 a red-letter year for Freedom as well as for Artie, who had joined the Boy Scouts on his twelfth birthday and put away the innocently bright blue kidlike uniform of the Cubs for the manly khaki outfit he wore today. The orange crayon marks on his bedroom door showed he had grown past the magic five-foot mark and now was tall enough to be in the Service! He only wished he and his uniformed comrades could march to San Francisco right now and board a ship bound for the Solomon Islands to reinforce Roy and his leatherneck buddies.

He tensed his muscles to resist the awful temptation to swat away the horsefly that had settled on the tip of his right ear, and watched in statuelike respect as Senator Hapgood stepped forward, stern and gray-faced, to address the troops of Cho-Ko-Mo-Ko. Artie wondered if the decrepit old guy would be able to talk loud enough, but he shouldn't have worried. Hapgood's crackling voice resounded clearly across the cow-pasture-turned-parade-ground, with words that would remain forever engraved in the hearts and minds of every boy who heard them, right to their dying day.

Before the unforgettable part, Hapgood praised the Scouts of Cho-Ko-Mo-Ko for taking a whole week off from their regular schedule of canoeing, knot-tying, making fires from their own wooden and leather-thong tools, and baking potatoes in the mud, to spread out across the surrounding countryside and collect scrap metal from every farm, in a drive that brought in 17,483 pounds of potential planes, guns, and ammunition for the War Effort. The boys knew from the ad clipped out of *Life* magazine and posted on the Pow-Wow Board just how directly this material could be transformed into fighting equipment: "7700 aluminum pans make a pursuit plane . . . 1 iron makes 2 helmets . . . 1 old tire makes 8 gas masks . . . 1 refrigerator makes 3 machine guns . . . 1 old radiator makes an aerial bomb . . ." and so on. Artie had hoped they could actually collect the 7700 pans to make a whole pursuit plane, but a lot of the farmers' wives were pretty chintzy about giving away the pans they cooked in even for a pursuit plane. The guys hoped anyway that the whole amount they collected would make a pursuit plane, even if a lot of it was rusty old car fenders, broken bicycle chains, beat-up shovels and teeth-bent rakes and battered cans instead of actual aluminum pans. The Senator didn't say anything about the pursuit plane, he just said the Scouts of Cho-Ko-Mo-Ko had made a "significant contribution" that would help Our Boys on the far-flung battlefronts of the world in the fight to save it from the dark night of everlasting infamy.

They had heard that stuff before, but none of them had ever heard anything like what the old Senator told them next.

"You boys are learning the lessons here that will make you the kind of brave soldiers who are fighting and dying for us right now," he said. "I happen to have personal knowledge that some of those soldiers who used to be Boy Scouts, just like you, and who learned the lessons of loyalty and courage from Scouting, were captured behind enemy lines and brutally tortured by the Nazis, who wanted them to tell the secrets about the strength and positions of the American troops. But these brave boys, these former Scouts, refused to betray a single secret to the enemy, even though the sadistic Nazis *beat their privates to jelly!*"

At that moment, as if it were part of a rehearsed ma-neuver, the right hands of more than two hundred as-sembled Scouts reached automatically to cover themselves protectively between the legs but then in iron discipline forced their hands back to their sides. Only one guy,

George Pendennis, actually grabbed his gonads with both hands and doubled over with an awful "Arggggh" sound coming out of him that everyone pretended not to hear because they were still at Attention.

The Senator went on for another couple of minutes about the stars and stripes, and the truths we hold self-evident, and this nation indivisible, under God, but no one heard or anyway remembered anything after the incredible words *"beat their privates to jelly."*

When the Commander dismissed the formation most all the guys went charging off to their cabins so they could hold on to their balls and screech and moan as they writhed around on their bunks imagining Nazis beating their privates to jelly. It was a million times worse than anything they ever had heard before, much worse than the supposedly true life story of the blacksmith in Decatur who was ready to slam down his huge metal hammer on a piece of iron on the anvil but he didn't notice that one of his balls had got loose from his pants and was lying on the anvil and he smashed the damn hammer down and crushed his own ball! But even if that was true, which lots of guys swore it was who claimed to know eyewitnesses of friends of the doomed blacksmith, just one accidental smash, no matter how awful and crushing, was nothing compared to a bunch of Nazi torturers methodically going at it until they had *beat your privates to jelly*.

Artie wanted nothing more than to run to his cabin and join the other guys in holding his balls and writhing around whooping and groaning, but the awful thing was—awful now, anyway, after what the old Senator had said in front of everyone—Shirley Colby had driven herself and Caroline Spingarn out to Cho-Ko-Mo-Ko to watch the Sunday Retreat parade along with other relatives and visitors and Artie had to go over and squire them around the place. They were already smiling and waving at him, so he couldn't even put his hands on his gonads just to check and see if they were all right, that they hadn't turned to jelly just from hearing the torture story. He was afraid if he even tried to do it on the sly, Shirley and Caroline would think he was playing pocket pool.

Artie forced a smile as he bravely went up to Shirley and Caroline, pretending nothing was wrong or different, hoping they would all agree without saying anything not to mention the horrible torture story. Artie escorted the girls to the Canteen, which used to be the Trading Post before the War, where he treated them to Mounds Bars and root beers but didn't feel like having anything himself but a stick of Spearmint from a pack already in his pocket. Artie chewed ferociously.

While they were on the porch of the Canteen, leaning on the rail overlooking the little creek called Old Tuscarora, which was supposed to be an Indian name meaning "Babbling waters," the Camp Commander, Harrison "Ribs" O'Mahoney, came up and started being real buddy-buddy with Artie, which he never had been before in his life until Shirley Colby showed up.

Ribs was a tall guy with a sunken chest and long arms and legs that sort of hung real loose on him, which was good for giving guys the knee or the elbow playing football and basketball. Ribs had just graduated from Oakley Central but the Army, Navy, the Marines, and even the Coast Guard turned him down because of a trick knee he had got in the Thanksgiving game with Geneseo, which gave him a slight limp that got even worse after all the Services rejected him, maybe because he felt ashamed or wanted people to know there was something really wrong with his leg instead of just a yellow streak down his spine.

"Pretty neat Retreat today, huh, Artie?" Ribs said, pretending he gave a tinker's damn what Artie thought.

"Sure," Artie said.

"These pretty girls here your sisters?" Ribs asked.

"Nope," Artie said. "This is Shirley Colby, and this is Caroline Spingarn."

The girls smiled politely at Ribs, and he flashed a real Pepsodent gleamer at Shirley.

"Friend of the family?" he asked her.

"I go with Roy Garber," she said, holding up her wrist with the silver ID bracelet on it. She had had some of the links taken out so it fit her now.

"Lucky guy, Roy Garber," said Ribs.

"If you call being out in the Solomons 'lucky,'" Shirley said.

"There's worse things," Ribs said, and with little spots of red coming out on his cheekbones he turned and limped away, worse than usual. Artie felt sorry for the guy, having to go around in nothing but a Boy Scout uniform when he was old enough for the real thing.

"I didn't mean to make him feel bad," Shirley said.

"That's okay," Artie said. "Ribs has a trick knee and all. That's what makes him feel bad."

"You'd think he could do *something*," said the practical Caroline Spingarn. "Couldn't he drive a tank at least? Sitting down?"

"You got to be a hundred percent, I guess," Artie said.

"At least he's working with boys," Shirley said. "That's a contribution."

"Well, it's nothing much when you think what happened to those boys who were tortured like they were and never gave away any secrets," said Caroline. "Ughhhh. *Jelly*."

"Excuse me," said Artie.

He knew he was going to heave his cookies and he ran off as fast as he could, hoping to make it in time.

"Where are you going?" Caroline called after him.

Damn her!

"To Old Wasacoma!" Artie shouted back.

A bunch of other Scouts walking to the Canteen broke up laughing, pointing at Artie and slapping their knees and yelping like a bunch of hyenas.

"Old Wasacoma" was the Indian name for the latrine.

Artie refocused his binoculars but he still couldn't see anything but green leaves.

"There it goes!" shouted Ribs O'Mahoney. "Look at the markings on the wings!"

That made Artie think of Swastikas and Rising Suns, or the Star of America or the Bull's-eye marking of the RAF fighter planes, and he lost all the concentration he was trying to muster to spot the bird.

"Okay, you guys," O'Mahoney said, "we saw one. That was a yellow-breasted nuthatch."

Ribs was leading a Bird Study Hike, and as usual, he kept spotting more and more kinds of birds you had to identify for Bird Study Merit Badge, even though Artie wondered sometimes if he really saw them. The thirty or so birdwatchers were either still squinting up in the air, or looking questioningly at Ribs.

"Okay, you guys," he said impatiently, "go on and write it down. 'Yellow-breasted nuthatch.' "

Everyone obediently wrote the name in their Bird Book, making it official that they had "seen" this species, since Ribs O'Mahoney told them they had. Artie wondered if the whole thing was really legal, or whether some National Bird Study Review Board might call him up before them to question whether he had really seen all those birds or only been *told* he had seen them, which might be cheating, but might be okay since a superior officer had given him the orders to do it.

Artie wrote down "Yellow-breasted—" and then he got all out of concentration again, thinking of *breast*, which made him want to check again to see if his gonads were all right. Ever since the famous "jelly" speech of Senator Hapgood, Artie had the awful suspicion that his tools had shrunk, maybe like they were practicing how to hide or retreat to escape the possibility of being beaten to jelly. It was hard to forget about, since now every kid in the Camp went around saying, "Look out, or I'll beat your privates to jelly!" and everyone snorted and wheezed and whooped, but even though they tried to act like it was funny, it was a nervous kind of funny. Artie knew his things were still there, he knew he could still pee all right, but ever since the speech he had not had anyone point at him in the morning and yell "H.O.!" because the towel wrapped around him for reveille lineup was sticking out in front of him due to a hard-on. In fact, the only guy he knew of who had had an H.O. for reveille lineup since the jelly speech was Ernest Maydap, who everyone figured was such a hick he didn't even know what his "privates" were.

At night after taps, Artie lay in his bunk and tried to play with himself to see if his thing could get hard anymore, but the darn thing just lay there like a worm. Actually, that wasn't a really fair test, since you had to be so careful not to make the bedsprings squeak or suffer the awful infamy of getting reported for jacking off in camp.

Breast—.

The unfinished word did not make Artie think of the nuthatch for Bird Study but of the pinup pictures he had, not just of Betty Grable but even ones he liked more now of Hedy Lamarr, Dorothy Lamour, and Lana Turner. Of course he hadn't brought them to Camp, that would have been un-Scouting, but he remembered them pretty darn well after all the scrutiny he had given them at night with his penlight under the covers.

"Gung ho—let's go for a grackle!" Ribs O'Mahoney said, and the band of birdwatchers straggled on up the hill after him, clutching their pencils and notebooks.

Without even thinking he was going to do it, Artie dropped his notebook. He got down on his hands and knees, like he was searching for it, and then when the last of the Scouts had moved out of sight, he stuck the notebook in his pocket and slunk off into the woods in the other direction.

The Cabin Row was deserted. Everyone was off spotting birds, tying sheepshank knots, portaging canoes, baking potatoes in mud, identifying poison oak, learning how to do artificial respiration, weaving bright-colored strands into lanyards for carrying whistles around your neck, and all the other healthy, useful, character-building kinds of things that Scouts were supposed to do at Camp Cho-Ko-Mo-Ko.

All except Artie Garber. He was slinking into his cabin in the middle of the day like a pre-vert. It was dark and silent inside, and smelled of a mixture of citronella oil, shoeshine polish, and farts. The second day of Camp the Renfro brothers, skinny Arnold and fat Bud, had held a farting contest, and tied at 237 farts apiece in succession, which not only broke the recognized Cho-Ko-Mo-Ko all-time record set by the legendary Earl "V.A." Beasley (he was so thin he was known as "the Vanishing American," or "V.A." for short) back in 1940, but also left an insidious, pungent odor that all the swabbings and airings-out that followed had been unable to completely get rid of.

Artie tried not to think about the smell, which was not the kind that got you in the mood, and climbed up on his bunk, the Upper Back Left. The Upper bunks were worst of all for trying to get away with any kind of fooling around on since the guy beneath you was bound to hear the slightest squeaking of bedsprings. "Bedsprings" made Artie think of the only other atrocity anyone claimed to have happened that was worse than the blacksmith who accidentally smashed his own ball (worse, that is, until Senator Hapgood gave his speech). That was the one about a guy in one of the cabins cleaning his Upper bunk for Inspection and unknowingly getting one of his nuts caught in a spring when the Camp Commander came in and called "Attention" and the poor guy jumped down from the Upper, leaving his ball there caught in the spring and ripping it off as he made the fatal leap to the floor.

Artie touched his own balls to see if they were okay and at least they were there, but felt real small and tight. His thing itself was the shriveled worm it had been ever since the Senator's speech. He touched it lightly with his fingers, massaging gently, and closed his eyes, picturing the pinup of Dorothy Lamour.

But nothing happened.

He figured he was more in the mood for a blonde, so he switched to Betty Grable, but she didn't help either.

Neither did Lana Turner.

Sweat was breaking out on his hands and on his forehead, not from the heat of illicit excitement, but the panic of being unable to make his thing respond to his mind. Maybe some nerve connection had been broken by the specter of the torturing Nazis!

Thinking of that only made things worse, though, and Artie realized he'd better get going soon or the guys would be coming back from the Bird Study Hike, spotting him in the act like a ruby-faced gooney bird.

Then he thought of this real sexy movie he had seen just before coming to camp, called *White Savage*, with Maria Montez, Jon Hall, and Sabu, the elephant boy. Maria Montez was the sultry "Princess Tahia," dressed in these slinky, harem-type outfits, with bangles and bracelets dangling from all over her. There was a scene where Jon Hall burst into her tent and real cool she dismissed her brawny bodyguards, saying, "You may go now. This may develop into a private matter."

Artie imagined himself instead of Jon Hall bursting into

the tent of Princess Tahia, and her telling the guards to get
lost so she could be alone with him. He was wearing a
Marine dress blue uniform, and he started removing the
snazzy trousers with the red stripe down the side. Soon he
and the Princess were lying on the silken pillows, writhing
in ecstasy.

It was happening! His thing was growing, pulsing and
throbbing. Princess Tahia was curing him of the dread
"privates to jelly" fear! Gratefully now as well as passion-
ately he lavished his kisses on her, at the same time moving
up and down on top of her as she squirmed with lust on the
silken pillows.

The bedsprings of the Upper bunk were squeaking in
rhythm to Artie's ravishing of Princess Tahia, and his own
hard breathing accompanied it with hoarse, rasping fervor.
He remembered in the midst of the passion to make sure his
thing was between his underpants and his Scout short
pants, so when the flood burst the telltale stain would not
be in his sleeping bag, where his dirtiest deed would be
discovered by his superior officer. He could hide his pants
and put on others, but he couldn't hide his sleeping bag,
which was turned inside-out and examined by the Troop
Leader at daily Inspection. The worst disgrace was to have
that milky stain in your bag, and some of the mean guys in
the troop had pulled what Artie thought was an awful trick
on this poor hick Ernest Maydap, who had hardly ever
been off his family's farm except to go to Scout meetings at
the local Grange Hall. The mean guys, led by the insidious
Roscoe Wittles, had taken some real cream from the mess
hall and poured it in a big spot in Maydap's sleeping bag
and rubbed it in, so at Inspection he got accused of spilling
his seed right in Camp, which was un-Scoutlike behavior.
Maydap had broken down crying, and later Artie tried to
comfort him and say it was a dirty trick, but he hadn't had

the guts to do it in public, he just said it to Maydap walking alone in the woods.

Artie didn't want to get the real stuff on his sleeping bag, so made that adjustment of his thing and was really going to town, about to explode, the spring-squawking and breath-rasping loud and uncontrolled when suddenly Artie heard another sound, the whine and slam of the screen door of the cabin, and just as he was bursting and flooding himself and Princess Tahia, he looked up to see Ben Vickman staring at him. Their eyes met for an awful moment of knowing, and Vickman turned and rushed from the cabin.

Ribs O'Mahoney was Camp Commander, but the actual Chief of Cho-Ko-Mo-Ko, the adult man in charge of the whole thing, like the Principal was in charge of high school, was Victor L. "Pops" Hagedorn. Pops was a large, shambling man who slicked back his thinning hair with Brylcreem, but always looked sloppy somehow in his uniform, the knee socks never straight, the neckerchief askew, the shirt always coming untucked out of his pants. The important thing was that everyone agreed Pops had a heart as big as all outdoors. He didn't have any kids of his own or even a wife but he was Father to the kids in his Latin class at Oakley Central, and in summers was Pops to the Scouts of Cho-Ko-Mo-Ko.

Pops had summoned Artie to a private pow-wow with him at Shagbark Hickory, which was the name of the Chief's cabin. Both the man and the boy sat in cross-legged Indian fashion on the floor of the cabin. Pops was filling his pipe, and as always, tobacco was spilling out and settling in flakes on his knobby knees. Artie wished he would hurry, knowing that Pops never really got to the point in a serious pow-wow until he had his pipe stoked up and burning.

Artie could already feel his own cheeks burning, knowing he was here because Ben Vickman had reported his dirty deed to the Chief. That was terrible, and Artie was totally shamed, full of the guilt he knew was his due, but still he was thankful that Ben Vickman hadn't squealed to the other Scouts. That would have even been worse, and Artie had to hand it to Ben for being a square shooter by keeping his trap shut to everyone but the Chief. On the other hand, going to the Chief just showed what a serious crime had been committed. It flashed through Artie's mind that the appropriate punishment for sneaking away from a Bird Study Hike to whack off in full daylight in a cabin of Camp Cho-Ko-Mo-Ko, B.S.A., might be for the culprit to have his "privates beaten to jelly."

When the Chief finally got his pipe stoked up, with the clouds of tobacco smoke curling around his head, he spoke more in sadness than anger.

"Artie," he said, "you know what you did was wrong."

"Worse than that," Artie volunteered with eagerness. "It was dirty."

The Chief nodded, looking wise and sorrowful.

"I'm sure you've read what the Scout Manual has to say on the subject."

"Yes, sir, many times."

It was true. There was a chapter in the "Health and Safety" part of the *Official Boy Scout Manual* called "Conservation," and although it didn't use any of the actual words like jerking or whacking off or whipping the puppy, it said that all boys got these "urges" sometimes, and when they felt such bad desires coming on them, they should take cold showers and long walks. It also recommended "hip baths," where the boy beset with lust sat in a tub of luke-warm water with his behind and his gonads soaking in the water and his legs hanging out over the edge. Artie had discussed this remedy with Warren Tutlow, but they started giggling, thinking how stupid they would look sitting in a washtub like that. And what if your folks came in and saw you, how were you to explain what the heck you were doing soaking your behind and gonads in a washtub of luke-warm water? Wouldn't it be a dead giveaway that you were full of evil thoughts that were so hard to control you had to resort to such extreme measures?

"And you've also read the part of the Bible, about how it's wrong to 'spill your seed'?" Pops continued.

"Yes, sir," Artie said.

He had always wanted to ask why it said the wrong thing was "spilling your seed on the ground," whether doing it "on the ground" was even worse than doing it on blankets or in a sleeping bag, but he didn't think this was the time to go into that.

"All boys have such desires," the Chief said sadly.

At least that made Artie feel normal.

"But they have to learn to control them," said the Chief.

Now Artie felt crummy again, realizing he lacked self-control, willpower, and other stuff that made you have character. Maybe he would end up a bum hopping freight cars and getting tattoos. He could team up with Fishy Mitchelman and ride the rails, doing odd jobs to scrounge enough money to buy some cheap wine and maybe a can of Spam to heat up for dinner on a Sterno stove.

"For your own sake," the Chief went on, "you must save yourself."

"I was already baptized," Artie said, "but maybe it didn't 'take.' "

"I didn't mean in the religious sense," the Chief said, "though of course that's important, too, and the strength of the Lord should be able to help you in exercising self-control. What I meant was, you should save yourself for when you get married."

"When I get *married*?" Artie asked, knowing that was quite a ways off.

The Chief nodded, his eyes misting over.

"Someday," he said, "you'll meet a nice girl. The 'right girl.' You'll want to settle down, and have children. Then you can use your seed in the way the Lord intended. Until then, for the sake of your future wife, as well as your own sake, you must try to save yourself."

"Until I get married," Artie repeated, wanting to make sure.

"Right now, it must seem a long way off, but the years fly by."

Years!

Most guys didn't get married till around twenty-one or so. That was nine years that Artie was supposed to go without spilling any of his seed. Was it because if you wasted too much of your seed you wouldn't have enough left over to make babies? He wanted to ask, but was afraid. He remembered how overpowering the dirty desire was when it came over him, and he figured if he had any chance of resisting it he would have to spend the next nine years of his life taking hikes, cold showers, and hip baths. He would have to practically spend every night sitting in a washtub of lukewarm water with his legs dangling over the edge. Then he thought of something even worse than waiting nine years.

"What if you never get married?" he asked.

The Chief clamped down on his pipe and coughed. Fiery ashes spilled out onto his bare knees, and he swatted at them like hornets.

"I didn't mean you, sir," Artie said quickly, "I just meant in general."

"The Lord finds different paths for all of us," the Chief said. "I have my own children. My wonderful boys. Hundreds of them, in class and at Camp, year after year. You are one of them, son."

The Chief, with his eyes all watery now, reached out and placed a sweaty palm on Artie's knee.

O God, Artie prayed in silence, *please don't let Chief Hagedorn be a pre-vert.*

Artie bowed his head and sat frozen, not even twitching a muscle. But then the Chief just gave his knee a couple of pats and took his hand away.

Artie breathed again.

"It will all work out, according to God's plan," the Chief said. "You will find, if you do your best to preserve yourself, God will sometimes help you, relieve you of excess, during your sleep, when His will and not thine be done."

It was okay to have wet dreams, then. Well, that was something, at least. Maybe it would make Artie get more sleep, knowing there might be a heavenly reward for it.

"Now," the Chief said, "I want you to put all this behind you and get out there for the rest of camp and throw yourself into Scouting with everything you have."

"Yes, sir!" Artie said, pulling his legs out of the Indian squatting position.

Artie figured he had lots to be grateful for. He had not been stripped of his rank of Second Class Scout, or sent home in shame, or made an example of, much less had his privates beaten to jelly. It was now up to him to spend the rest of Camp swimming and hiking and baking potatoes in the mud and all that good, healthy stuff, harder than any other kid in Camp, to try to make up for his dirty deed and so wear himself out that he wouldn't even think about it again.

The Chief, relighting his pipe, called out "Good Scouting!" as Artie charged out of the room and into the bright day.

That night after taps, Artie couldn't help worrying about how he was going to get through the next nine years without going crazy.

2

THAT September Artie started the seventh grade a[nd]
the Allies invaded Italy. American and British troop[s]
had finally hit the mainland of Nazi-held "Fortress
Europe." Our team was really on the offensive now!

Artie came home one day from delivering his pape[r]
route to find Mom and Dad in the living room, dressed u[p]
like it was Sunday. Their faces were so darn white it look[ed]
like they might have just given blood to the Red Cross.

"Whatsamatter?"

Mom's mouth opened but no sound came out, and [she]
shook her head and looked down at the floor.

"Roy," Artie said. "He's okay, isn't he?"

"God willing," Dad said.

He went and put a hand on Artie's shoulder.

"Billy Watson was killed."

"*Wings?* You mean Wings Watson?"

Dad nodded.

"At Salerno. Over in Italy."

"I know. In 'the ankle.' "

"Son, he was hit by a shell. It wasn't just in the ankle."

"No, I meant—"

Artie felt like someone had punched him in the gut, and it was hard to talk, the words coming out between gasps of breath.

"I meant 'the ankle' on—on 'the Italian Boot,' where we landed. Is where—Salerno—is."

He leaned against Dad and put an arm around him, holding on.

"Thousands of miles from home," Mom whispered. "Our Boys, dying."

Artie felt sick and scared at the same time.

He had known that lots of Our Boys would get killed _ding Italy, but that was the Price of Victory, so even _ugh it made him feel sad there was no use getting down _he dumps about it. He had thought of the casualty fig- _ in the War sort of like the opponents' score in a ball _me. It was bad if their score was high, but you didn't _nk of each number of the total as a real American guy _ was all the sudden dead. It was too hard to picture _ you didn't even know the guys who had changed into _d ng but numbers.

_w it was different.

_w it was Wings Watson.

_e could picture him, flying down the basketball _ leaping for a rebound; horsing around with Roy and _ the filling station, grinning and playing the peanut _e, giving Artie a friendly poke in the ribs, spitting _ the little gap between his front teeth.

_ now.

Where?

They didn't even have his body, or what was left of it, at the funeral.

The service was held in the living room of the Watsons' rickety old gray farmhouse a few miles from town. Sam Watson mostly raised chickens and his wife Eldora was known as "the Egg Lady" because she delivered fresh eggs to people in town. She and her husband stood gripping each other's hands by the table where they'd put the silver-framed picture of Wings in his uniform along with a vase of flowers. That was all there was of Wings at the funeral. The picture of him. He was smiling.

Later, his "remains" would come home in a box that no one was allowed to open. Some people wondered if the rule was really for "health reasons" like the government said or whether what was left was too awful to look at or whether it was only rocks and sand in the plain pine box, at least his family would have something to bury while all the time whatever was left of the real flesh and bones was some-where in the bloody foreign ground of a country shaped like a boot.

How come he had to go clear over there from Illinois?

That was just one of the questions that nagged at Artie's mind, even though he knew all the right answers about us having to save the world for democracy.

Even worse than those kind of questions were the ones about what really happened to a young guy who died. Somehow it seemed fairly natural for an old person to die; they were tired out from living a long time and even though it was sad, everyone had to go sometime. Lots of young guys were dying every day in the War of course, but Artie hadn't known any of them personally, so he hadn't really thought a lot about it till Wings Watson was killed.

The scariest part was that now Artie understood that Roy could really get killed. He knew it in his mind all the time, of course; thousands of American guys had been killed on Guadalcanal when Roy was there with them fighting the Japs, and more were getting killed right now in the Solomons where Roy was right this very minute. But he had always before just thought of those guys as "casualties," part of the score against us, and he didn't believe in his guts that Roy would really die way out in those weird little islands with palm trees and coconuts. But if his own buddy and teammate was killed in Italy, it suddenly seemed possible that Roy could really get killed in some crazy place like Vella Lavella.

On a clear afternoon at the end of September when Mom was hanging the wash on the backyard clothesline, Artie went out and offered her some of the Coke from a bottle he'd opened when he came home from school.

She took two clothespins out of her mouth and had a swallow of the Coke.

"Thanks," she said. "You're a pal."

"Mom? I was just wondering."

"What?"

"Do you believe in Heaven? I mean, like it's really a place people go when they die, unless they're so terrible they have to go the other way?"

"A place? You mean like Birney is a place?"

"Aw, c'mon. Birney's just a town."

"Oh—you mean a bigger place? Like Chicago?"

"Stop pulling my leg, Mom."

"Well, lots of people seem to think Heaven is a 'place.' Clouds instead of houses, and angels playing harps."

"But you don't think that way."

"Not really, no."

"So what do you think it is? If it is?"

"Oh, I think it's there, all right."

"Where? Out in the universe, you mean?"

"No. I think it's all around us. In the grass, trees, sky. Even clean laundry."

"So you think if a person dies they come back as a tree —or a sheet?"

"Not exactly. I think they become a higher part of things. In a way we can't see or understand."

"But how do you *know*?"

"I don't 'know' like in a book. I have Faith."

She unfurled a sheet and it billowed out in the wind.

"Just like I have Faith that Roy will come home from the War," she said.

"But what about Wings Watson?"

"Is that what you've been brooding about?"

"I've just been thinking is all."

"Thinking is fine. Sometimes praying is better."

"I do that too."

"I know," she said.

She pinned up one end of the sheet, standing on the toes of her old blue Keds. Artie grabbed the other end, and took a clothespin out of the basket to hitch it in place.

"I get scared too," Mom said. "So does Dad. So does everyone. There's lots to be scared about."

"So what do you do? Besides pray?"

"Think about what's next."

"You mean, like when the War's over?"

"No. That's too far away."

"Like what, then?"

"Supper," she said. "I think about what we're going to have for supper."

"What are we?"

"Tuna fish with noodles."

"Dessert?"

"Tapioca."

"That's neat."

"See? It's even nice to think about."

"I get it."

Artie tried to concentrate on saying his prayers for Roy and America, and thinking about good stuff, like tuna fish with noodles and tapioca for dessert, and keeping his mind off sex.

Since his pow-wow on the subject last summer with Chief "Pops" Hagedorn, Artie had kept his hands off his thing at night except to just check and make sure it was still there. As Pops had predicted, the Lord in his wisdom had provided "release of excess" around every week or so in a wet dream. The trouble was, the Lord didn't make up the dreams the way Artie would have most enjoyed them. They were all tangled up and crazy, like the one where Artie was an escaped prisoner from a Florida chain gang, hiding out in the swamps, when he came upon this woman who had the body of Dorothy Lamour, sarong and all, and the head of Shirley Colby. She licked her lips playfully and started taking off her sarong just as a giant alligator came into the picture and started chasing Artie up a tree, and then everyone including the alligator and the Lamour-Shirley woman turned into monkeys. Artie would have imagined the whole thing differently and left out the part where they all turned into monkeys, but at least he woke up wet and "relieved of excess" so he figured he just had to relax and accept the fact that the Lord worked in mysterious ways, his wonders to perform.

For a week or so after Wings Watson got killed, Artie turned kind of sour on the War. He took thirty-five cents that he could have used to buy a quarter and a dime War Stamp and spent it all on a cherry Coke and banana split at Damon's Drugs, and afterward read through the College Football issue of *Sport* magazine instead of trying to find out the latest stuff about the invasion of Italy. He went out to Roy's rock at Skinner Creek by himself and prayed to

God to keep Roy safe, and after praying he tried to concentrate his mind on sending messages to Roy by mental
telepathy. Last winter he had read this article about how
Beatrice Houdini, the wife of the great escape-artist ma-
gician, had given up trying to contact her husband from the
dead. Mrs. Houdini explained to the press that "Harry
could escape from anything on earth. If he can't slip
through a message for me from Heaven then the deal is
off."

What stuck in Artie's mind was that Mrs. Houdini evidently believed in Heaven, and he figured he had a better
chance of contacting Roy if he ever died since Houdini and
his wife were only related by marriage but Roy was Artie's
own brother. As everybody knew and said all the time,
"Blood is thicker than water." Artie thought if he could
contact Roy by mental telepathy while he was still alive,
then maybe he'd have an easier time of doing it if Roy got
killed and his spirit merged into the trees and clean laundry
of the earth that made up the mystical realm of Heaven.
Artie just tried to concentrate on sending Roy simple messages like "Hello, it's me, Artie—come in if you hear me."
Sometimes the wind would stir in the trees and Artie
thought maybe that was Roy signaling back, but there
wasn't any real proof and he concentrated so hard on sending and trying to receive the messages that he got these
fierce headaches, so after a while he gave up and wrote Roy
a long V-mail letter.

When he told about Wings Watson getting killed he got
real mad at the evil, power-mad Nazis, and suddenly his
old patriotism revived again. He realized that Wings Watson's death had demoralized him, making him wonder
about the sense of the War, questioning the weird events
of the world that made a guy from Illinois have to go and
get killed by a bunch of Germans way over in Italy, but
now he saw that such brooding and questioning of the right-

ness of things was just the effect that the Nazis *wanted* to have on you when they murdered one of your own neighbors in cold blood. Artie vowed that he'd never be demoralized like that again, falling into the trap of doubt and despair. He pledged to himself as the brother of a fighting Marine that he'd renew his Home Front efforts with even greater zeal.

Artie wanted to find a more serious, grown-up way of helping the War Effort now. Buying War Stamps was still okay, and he certainly wasn't going to waste his money anymore on binges of banana splits, but filling up the Stamp book was really just a duty that didn't give him much of a charge anymore. Collecting scrap paper seemed like kid stuff now, and in fact it was the younger boys who had taken up that campaign, little kids in the fifth and sixth grades who were rolling their own red wagons down the street and knocking on doors for papers and magazines the way Artie and Tutlow had done the year before.

Collecting scrap metal seemed more serious because it was harder, heavier work and what you collected went directly into making armaments, but the trouble was most of the good stuff had already been rounded up in the big drive of the Cho-Ko-Mo-Ko Scouts last summer. Artie knew darn well that every farmer in fifty miles had been cleaned out of his last rusty shovel and broken tractor chain. When he tried to take two beat-up old pots from his own kitchen to start a new drive, Mom caught him and told him in no uncertain terms she needed those pots more than the Armed Forces did.

"But the thing is," Artie said, still holding on to the pots, "only 7,698 more of these will make a whole pursuit plane."

"The Air Corps can make its own planes," she said, "but I've got to make our suppers."

Artie surrendered the pots.

He went down to his Dad's filling station and rummaged around in the garage till he found an old tire iron he figured could be made into a machine gun barrel, but Dad said it was essential to his own effort and he couldn't give it up to the War Effort.

"Cripes," Artie said, "there's nothing any good a guy can do anymore on the Home Front."

Dad took one of the rags from his pocket and swiped it across his big forehead.

"There's plenty," he said.

"Like what?"

"A guy can brush his teeth after meals, he can clean his plate even if it's Spam or liver, pick up his clothes, and study his lessons."

"Heck, that's just regular stuff."

Dad put an arm on Artie's shoulder and spoke some philosophy.

"Keep your eye upon the doughnut, and not upon the hole," he said.

Artie sighed and stuffed his hands in his pockets. He figured that meant you should take care of the little things and the big things would work out for the best. That's the way adults always talked, telling you the best way a kid could help win the War was to obey his parents and teachers, which was okay for keeping the nation's mighty War Machine running smoothly, but it wasn't very inspirational.

Artie realized he'd better talk things over with another patriotic kid.

3

"WE got to figure out something *real* to do," Artie said.

Warren Tutlow nodded, knowing exactly what his buddy meant.

They were chowing down on nickel hamburgers and bottle Cokes at Bob's Eats on Main Street, trying to figure out a new, glorious, and (hopefully) dangerous way to serve the Home Front.

"You listen to 'Captain Midnight' last night?" Tutlow asked.

"Sure," said Artie. "They had the 'Secret Squadron Signal Session' on the air. Couldn't you get the message?"

"Heck, yes," Tutlow said. "I know how to use my Decodograph. All I meant was, Captain Midnight and his guys get to go to the South Pacific and outwit the Japs, and we're still stuck right here in Birney."

"Well, somebody's got to be on the Home Front, I guess."

"We're *veterans* of the Home Front," Tutlow said. "The little kids could do that stuff now."

"That's the whole thing. We got to think up something the little kids would be too little to do, something really big."

Tutlow pushed his glasses back hard against his nose, which probably created pressure on his brain and made him think better.

"How about inventing a secret weapon?" he asked.

"That's not as easy as rolling off a log," Artie said.

"You got that from 'Red Ryder,' " said Tutlow.

"Got what?"

" 'As easy as rolling off a log.' That's what they say when they tell you to send in your coupons for a Red Ryder BB gun. 'It's as easy as rolling off a log.' "

"Well, anyway," Artie said, "you can't just go around inventing secret weapons. You got to have factories and stuff."

"I got a chemistry set."

"I'm no good at chemistry."

"You could be the guy who tests the weapons to see if they work."

"Like fun," Artie said. "I'm not gonna get blown to kingdom come."

"You got a yellow stripe down your back or something?"

"Boy, are you in a crummy mood today."

"I'm sorry. I guess my morale is low."

"Well, that's why we got to think of something."

Artie took the top bun off the rest of his burger and splashed some more catsup on it.

Tutlow started to take a bite of his own burger when he stopped with his mouth open, looking like he'd been

conked on the bean. He was staring at something on the wall.

"That's it," he said, putting his hamburger down without even taking the bite.

"What is?" Artie asked.

"Lookit, on the wall, the new poster," Tutlow said.

Artie turned and looked at the new patriotic poster Bob had put up. It was a picture of Uncle Sam with a finger to his lips, and it said: Even In This Friendly Diner There May Be Enemy Ears—Stop Loose Talk and Rumors.

Artie read the poster and then glanced quickly around Bob's Eats, seeing only a couple of kids from the School Traffic Squad, and an old guy who looked like a truck driver.

Artie leaned across the table and whispered.

"Where's the 'Enemy Ears'?" he asked.

"I don't know. But they might be anywhere. Right here in Town."

"You saying there's enemy agents in Birney?"

"They caught a German spy in Chicago, didn't they?"

"The FBI did, yeah."

"Well, the FBI needs help. They haven't got enough guys to go to every town in America."

"You think we should call them and ask? The FBI?"

"Not till we got evidence," Tutlow said.

"Of spies?"

Tutlow nodded slowly.

"Wow," said Artie. "That makes us *counter*spies."

Tutlow put a finger to his lips, and spoke out of the corner of his mouth.

"Quiet," he said. "There may be 'enemy ears.' "

Artie clammed up, making his face look expressionless, so no one could read it. He was almost too excited to finish his hamburger. They had finally found something *real* to do.

Just then Fishy Mitchelman burst in the door, his long arms flapping.

"Comin' in on a Wing and a Prayer," he sang in his cracked, off-key voice as he pulled out a chair from the table where Artie and Warren were sitting, plunked himself down in it, leaned over Artie and pressed his mouth onto the straw sticking out of Artie's Coke bottle, and took a big slurp.

"You dooh-dahs getting much?" Fishy asked.

"Is that all you still can think about?" Artie said disgustedly, using his thumb and forefinger like tweezers to pluck the straw Fishy had slurped on out of the Coke bottle and drop it on the table. By now, Fishy might have some sex disease he was conveying around.

"There's a War on, you know," Tutlow said.

"Gotta have music," Fishy said. "Listen to this, and guess me."

Fishy put his big hands on the table and started beating out a staccato rhythm, closing his eyes and bobbing his head back and forth, then he suddenly stopped and looked at Artie and Warren with hopeful eagerness.

"Who am I?" he asked.

"Samuel F. B. Morse?" asked Tutlow.

"Foog," said Fishy, squinching his face like he smelled something bad.

"I give up," said Artie.

"Gene Krupa!" Fishy exclaimed.

"Well, that's good," Artie said. Actually, he was glad to see Fishy get interested in something besides sex; he figured maybe there was hope for the guy after all, and imagined what a swell counterspy he would make, if he just got serious.

"Would you like to put your talent to work for the War Effort?" Artie asked, wanting to give Fishy the benefit of the doubt.

"Banzai!" Fishy shouted, and Warren Tutlow, shaking

his head, gave Artie a kick in the shins under the table.

"Never mind, we got to be going now, Fish," Artie said and stood up.

Warren stood up too, and they went to pay Bob for their Cokes and burgers.

"Where you guys goin'?" Fishy asked.

"Secret," Warren Tutlow said.

"Fish-*ee!*" said Mitchelman, googling his eyes around and flapping his arms. He was one guy the War hadn't changed at all.

They sat cross-legged on the floor of Tutlow's room with the curtains drawn, and Artie lit the stub of a candle that his patriotic pal had stuck in the top of a Coke bottle. The secrecy was necessary because of the great new mission they were going to undertake.

They were going to be counterspies.

After Artie lit the candle he was kind of stumped.

"Okay," he whispered. "What do we do next?"

"Well, if you look for enemy agents, what kind of people do you look for first?"

"Pre-verts?" Artie guessed.

"Well, maybe, but that's not the first thing."

"What is, then?"

"*Foreigners,*" Tutlow said in a hissing whisper.

Artie slapped his hand on the side of his head for being such a dope he hadn't thought of that right off.

"So the first thing we do," Tutlow continued, "is check on the movements and activities of foreigners right here in Town."

"Have we got any?" Artie asked.

"I could name you three, and there may be even more. For all we know, there may be foreign spies among us *posing* as Americans. But anyway, there's three real ones I can think of, using their own foreign names."

"You don't mean old man Weiskopf at the dry goods store?"

"He's German, isn't he?"

"Yeah, but he's Jewish, so he doesn't count."

"I know Jews are real strange and they have these weird customs and all, but they still count."

"I mean they don't count as *Germans*. The Germans go around killing Jewish people, it's part of what they do in the War, so the Jewish people hate Germans as much as we do."

"Well, if you ask me, he's still *foreign*, so you never can tell."

"If you ask me, he's a nice guy. Besides, he's too old for spying and sabotage."

"Okay, that still leaves two more foreigners right here in Town."

"Are you thinking of Mr. LaPettier, at the bank?"

"He's French. That's Allies."

"I know that. I was just naming foreign guys."

"They got to be Axis guys."

Artie scratched his head real hard, then shrugged.

"I give," he said.

"You forget about the LaBiancos?"

"The LaBiancos! You crazy? Raymond LaBianco's in the Navy. Besides, his folks were *born* here."

"Their ancestors still come from Italy, which is an Axis power. They still got relatives there, and in Wartime, you never know."

"The good Italians are on our side now anyway. It was just Mussolini that got them in with Hitler."

"For all we know, the LaBiancos over in Italy may be on Mussolini's side."

"You don't even know that. Anyway, I'm not spying on any LaBiancos."

"I didn't mean we should. I just meant we got to count

them as foreigners. Anyway, you haven't even got to the prime suspect."

"I can't think of any. Who?"

Tutlow put his fingers at the outer corners of his eyes and pulled them upward, slanting.

"So solly you forgot about Wu Sing Lee," he said.

"The Chinese Laundryman?"

"Ah so."

"But the Chinese are on *our* side. They're fighting the Japs!"

Tutlow, still stretching his eyes into slants, leaned forward and raised his upper lip over his teeth, looking sort of like a gopher, but speaking in a sinister, Oriental accent.

"How you know for sure Wu Sing Lee not actu-ry *Japanese*?"

"'Cause they don't have laundries. Chinese have laundries."

"How you know Wu Sing Lee not Japanese spy posing as Chinaman, using laundry to throw Amelicans off scent?"

"What makes you think he *is*?"

Tutlow took his hands from his eyes and let his upper lip down to normal, getting real serious now.

"I don't know for sure, but I know how we can find out. Lookit here."

Tutlow reached under his bed and pulled out his terrific War Scrapbook. Artie scooted over next to him, and tried to see the article he turned to by the secret light of the flickering candle. It was a clipping from *Time* magazine that was underlined in parts with a yellow crayon. The headline said, "How to Tell Your Friends From the Japs."

Tutlow pulled the scrapbook away from Artie and cleared his throat so he could read the important parts out loud. He made his voice real deep and serious, so it almost sounded something like H. V. Kaltenborn.

"'Those who know them best often rely on their facial

characteristics to tell them apart: the Chinese expression is likely to be more placid, kindly, open; the Japanese more positive, dogmatic, arrogant. Japanese are nervous in conversation, laugh loudly at the wrong time. . . . Most Chinese avoid horn-rimmed spectacles. . . . Japs are likely to be stockier and broader-hipped."

Tutlow slammed the scrapbook decisively and looked up at Artie.

"Well?" he asked, like he'd made his case.

"I dunno," Artie said. "I never paid much attention to Wu Sing Lee."

"In that case," said Tutlow, "I guess we got our work cut out for us."

He blew out the candle and Artie felt a shiver go through him as he sat there in the darkened room, about to take on the mission of a Home Front counterspy.

A high-pitched, tinkly bell sounded (like the kind that might be in a Japanese shrine!) as the two boys walked in the door of Wu Sing Lee's Hand Laundry in a little alley off Main Street. Foreign odors, like tea and old seaweed, wafted in from the long, plain curtains that separated the back of the shop from the little counter and the shelves behind it with packages of laundry in the front, the only part of the place that customers could actually *see*. God only knew what mysterious rites were performed behind the curtains, where it was rumored that the lone Chinaman (if that was in fact his true nationality) not only washed and ironed the clothes but also slept, ate, and cooked his inscrutable Oriental meals.

Wu Sing Lee came out from the back of the shop with such a swift, delicate movement that the curtains barely seemed to part, and it was impossible to even catch a glimpse of what lay behind them.

"Help you please?" asked Wu Sing Lee with a kindly, open smile that was deceptively Chinese in nature.

"Uh, yeah, I got this laundry here to be washed," said Artie, placing a pillowcase full of dirty socks and underwear on the counter. His mother always did all their laundry, but Artie had scrounged around in the closet and found some old stuff left over from Camp Cho-Ko-Mo-Ko that she hadn't discovered yet. While Wu Sing Lee took the bundle and handed a ticket to Artie, the crafty Tutlow, whistling "I'd Like to Get You on a Slow Boat to China," slithered clear over the counter so his head and shoulders were hanging down on the other side of it, so he kind of reminded Artie of a horse caught on a fence. Actually, what he was doing was checking out the laundryman's size to see if he was "stockier and broader-hipped" than Chinese people are supposed to be.

"So when exactly will these be all done?" Artie said in a voice louder than normal, intended to keep Wu Sing's attention away from Tutlow's spying.

"Today Monday, be wash Friday."

"Well, are you really *positive* about that?" Artie asked, testing him for one of the Japanese qualities.

"Oh, sure, sure," the man said.

"Well, I have to be really positive, 'cause I'm going on this camping trip, with Boy Scout Troop Seventy-three, and we're going up to Devil's Toothpick, so I got to have all my socks and stuff."

"You have Friday," Wu Sing said, still smiling.

Tutlow crawled back from over the counter, and, pushing back his glasses that were falling from his nose, said suddenly to the laundryman: "You hear the one about why the chicken crossed the road?"

"One about chicken?" Wu Sing asked.

"To get to the other side!" Artie piped up, and he

and Tutlow whooped and laughed, slapping their legs.

Wu Sing stared at them, still smiling but looking definitely *nervous*.

"Well, I'll be back for the laundry Friday if you're absolutely *positive* it'll be done."

"Be wash, be wash," Wu Sing said, sounding *nervous*, *positive*, and even *dogmatic* all at the same time.

Artie was anxious to get out of there, but Warren stopped him at the door, to ask one final key question.

"If you don't mind my asking, sir," he said to Wu Sing, "which do Chinese people really like better—chow mein or chop suey?"

Wu Sing suddenly began to laugh. He was laughing so hard his eyes were squinting.

"What's so funny?" Tutlow asked.

Wu Sing continued to laugh, like this serious question was some kind of great joke. Tutlow shot a glance at Artie, who nodded, realizing Wu Sing Lee was *laughing loudly at the wrong time.*

The boys hurried out of the little shop, breaking into a run as they got to the sidewalk, knowing now the awful truth:

Wu Sing Lee was a Jap.

Artie was standing on top of the Odd Fellows Building, whose three stories made it the tallest structure on Main Street. He was wildly waving his semaphore flags above his head. The reason he was only flapping them back and forth instead of actually forming letters of the alphabet in semaphore code was that Warren Tutlow didn't know semaphore, and he said they would lose precious spying time if he had to go to the trouble of learning, so when Artie spotted Wu Sing Lee coming out of his laundry he should just wave the flags back and forth above his head. Tutlow was up in a maple tree back of Main Street, watching Artie through a pair of Boy Scout binoculars.

"Artie, what are you doing up there?"

Darn it all, Caroline Spingarn's telescopic eyes had picked out Artie from clear across Main Street where she was coming out of Damon's Drugs.

He shook his head back and forth as hard as he could, trying to signal her to keep her trap shut, but it didn't work.

Caroline cupped her hands to her mouth and called out louder.

"Is there going be an Air Raid?" she shouted.

Now several other people stopped on the street and looked up at Artie. Luckily, Wu Sing Lee had already walked into the bank, so he didn't see Artie himself, though that was just luck after Caroline had drawn the whole world's attention to him.

"I'm just practicing!" Artie shouted back.

"Just for Boy Scouts, or a real Air Raid?" Caroline called up at him.

Artie could have croaked her. In the first place, everyone in Birney had pretty much forgot about Air Raids anymore. In the first summer of the War their whole part of the state had a blackout once to practice up in case of Air Raids, but it was called for 10:30 at night when all the farmers and most everyone else in towns like Birney had already turned off their lights and gone to sleep, so you really couldn't tell if the blackout had even worked, except in bigger places like Moline. In the meantime, the Nazis had never tried to fly on the polar route from Norway to bomb Chicago and now the whole Luftwaffe was busy defending its own cities against the American Air Corps and the British who were striking back at them from bases in England.

That just showed how much Caroline knew about what was going on in the War. Even if it had been a real Air Raid practice, the last thing a person should do was stand in Main Street and yell up at a Boy Scout carrying out Civil Defense duties on top of the Odd Fellows Building.

Now a whole bunch of people had come out of shops and stores on Main Street to look up and see what was happening.

"Better get down from there, boy," some old guy in overalls yelled. "You ain't got any net below."

Artie brought his arms down, put both semaphore flags in one hand, and headed for the fire escape. He didn't want to get bawled out by anyone from the Odd Fellows Building about using their roof without permission, especially since his Dad wasn't even a member of the Odd Fellows Lodge but belonged to the Moose. Besides, Artie would have had to make up a real whopper to cover up the secret truth that he was counterspying on a suspected Jap.

By the time he climbed down from the top of the building to the street the crowd had broken up and everyone had gone on about their business, except for Caroline Spingarn.

She was standing there balancing on one foot while she picked at a scab on her right knee. Artie thought she looked like the picture of a whooping crane in the seventh grade Science Studies book. Since the time she'd come out to visit him at Cho-Ko-Mo-Ko in the middle of the summer, Caroline had grown a couple of inches and her arms and legs stuck out like skinny poles from the little dresses she always wore that looked like they'd shrunk now. She was always falling down in the schoolyard or tripping over herself in the halls and the little bows and ribbons she wore in her hair looked silly now instead of cute. The worst part was that she kept following Artie around all the time and asking him stupid questions.

"So what were you doing on top of the Odd Fellows Building?" she asked him, picking off a tiny piece of scab and holding it between her fingers like it was some kind of scientific specimen.

"None of your beeswax," Artie said, and started walking off down Main with a swift, military step.

Caroline scrambled to catch up with him.

"You're not even nice anymore," she whined. "Do you know that?"

"I'm busy," he said. "Don't you know there's a War on?"

"That's no excuse," she said, "Why don't we go have a Coke at Damon's?"

"Why don't you go home and play with your paper dolls, Little Imogene?"

That's who Caroline really reminded him of these days —Little Imogene, the bratty kid in the funny papers.

"Did I hear you right, Artie Garber?"

"If you didn't, I'll make it as plain as the nose on your face. You're getting to be a real pest, Caroline Spingarn."

Blotches of red came out on Caroline's pale, squinting face.

"You'll be sorry you ever said that, Artie Garber."

"Oh, go fly a kite."

Caroline burst out crying and ran, her knees knocking together and arms flying crazily.

For a moment, Artie had a panicky feeling that she might really try to do something to make him sorry. But he realized that was crazy. What could she do? She was only a girl.

Back up in Tutlow's bedroom with the curtains drawn and the candle flickering from the Coke bottle, Artie complained that Caroline was worse than a "counter-counterspy."

"She can't help it," Tutlow said. "She's just a girl."

"Well, I'm through with girls for the Duration. I swear on my oath as a counterspy."

"Never mind," Tutlow said. "We got the info we need anyway. Wu Sing leaves his laundry every day at noon to go to the bank, which takes about ten minutes, and again he closes up at six and walks around and around the Bandstand in the Town Square."

"That sure is suspicious," Artie said. "You think we ought to check underneath the Bandstand for hidden explosives?"

"Maybe he's only taking his constitutional," Tutlow said. "Anyway, the first thing we got to do is, while Wu Sing is out going around the Bandstand, we ought to get into that hidden back room of his and search for evidence."

"You mean break into the laundry?"

"It's not 'breaking in' if it's counterspy work."

"How do we get inside, though?"

"There's got to be something for opening doors on the Official Scout jackknife."

There was. It might not have been intended on purpose for jimmying doors open, but one of the terrific metal gougers that pulled out of the belly of the jackknife slipped right under the simple latch on the back door of the laundry and flipped it up and open.

The boys quickly slipped inside, pulling the door shut behind them. It was dark, and smelled heavily of starch and foreign stuff. Tutlow struck a match, and in the eerie, wavering glow, Artie could make out a table, some shelves with little bowls and glasses and tiny teacups without handles. There was also, to his amazement, a Betty Grable pinup calendar. Did it mean Wu Sing was trying to pretend to be American, or did he look at Betty Grable while lying at night on his narrow little cot and beat off, Oriental style? Or did Orientals even beat off? Maybe the Chinese did and the Japanese didn't, or vice versa, and it was one way of telling them apart, but the article about telling them apart didn't go into stuff about sex.

"Eureka!" Tutlow said in a loud whisper.

He had gone to the table and pulled out the one drawer in it. Artie hurried over to look, expecting to see some kind of bullets or homemade bomb parts. Instead, there were stacks of little papers with Chinese (or Japanese) writing on them. Tutlow started stuffing them into his pockets.

"Hurry," he said, "get all you can."

Artie picked up one of the little papers and looked at it by the light of the match.

"I think it's just laundry tickets," he said.

"That's what he *wants* you to think, dumbo. It might be Japanese code about troop movements, or Home Front morale or something."

Artie dutifully grabbed a bunch of the papers and shoved them in his pockets.

"Okay, we better scram," he said.

He was getting the heebie-jeebies thinking about the treacherous Wu Sing bursting in on them, shooting out his arms and legs in some complicated jujitsu movement, and knocking out Artie and Tutlow at the same time. When they woke, they'd be bound and gagged and have little slivers of bamboo under their fingernails, all ready to be lit by the fiendish Jap agent.

"First, I got a surprise for this yellow-bellied Son of the Rising Sun," said Tutlow.

He waved out the match just as it was about to burn down to his fingers, quickly lit another one, and pulled from his coat pocket something that looked like a home-made firecracker.

"What the heck is that?" Artie asked.

"Stink bomb," Tutlow said. "Made it with my chemistry set."

Tutlow started to light the thing and Artie grabbed his arm.

"That's not fair," he said.

"Huh?"

"I mean, this is America. You can't punish a guy before he's proved guilty."

Tutlow pointed around the room.

"How guilty can you get?" he asked.

"He still deserves his day in court," said Artie.

"Don't worry, he'll get one all right. Then they'll hang him from the highest cottonwood."

"You're thinking of cowboy stuff, not spies."

"Have you got a yellow streak down your back or something?"

"You dope!"

Artie shoved Tutlow backward and he fell against the shelves, knocking over teacups, glasses, and bowls, some of them shattering as they fell to the floor.

"Now you've gone and done it," said Tutlow.

"Now we really gotta scram," Artie said.

"Not till I light this."

"Then he'll know somebody was here on purpose," Artie argued. "He might just think the broken stuff was an accident."

"We want him to know, dopey. Then we can watch his behavior. If he goes to the cops or the FBI, he might be okay, but if he just vamooses that'll prove he's a dirty spy."

In the face of Tutlow's relentless logic, and his own fear of being caught in the act, Artie gave up.

"Okay, hurry up and light the stupid thing," he said, moving from one foot to another like he had St. Vitus's Dance.

Tutlow lit the stink bomb, tossed it into a corner, and he and Artie charged out of there like a couple of madmen.

The next day, Wu Sing's laundry was closed, and the day

after that, there was a sign on the door that said "Gone to
Clean the Axis." The rumor was that he volunteered to be
a spy for the U.S. Army. Tutlow thought the truth was Wu
Sing had realized someone was on to his dirty game, and he
had probably fled across the country to some secret spot off
the coast of California where he was picked up at night by
a Jap submarine and taken home to Tokyo to report on the
War Effort in Birney, Illinois. Artie hoped that was true.
He worried about Wu Sing never having his day in court,
so he'd at least have learned all about the American Way.

4

Dear Roy,

Everything is fine here on the Home Front. In fact this Front has been real busy lately, and me and this guy Warren Tutlow have done some secret kind of work that I'm afraid to even write down on V-mail, but I'll tell you all about it when the War is over. Right now I'll just give you a hint: someone posing as another kind of person right here in Birney was discovered by me and Tutlow and has flown the coop. Due to this, Birney is more purely red, white and blue, and alot less yellow, if you get what I mean.

Shirley Colby is pining away for you but keeping a stiff upper lip, even though she misses you like crazy. I try to help keep her morale up, and she's coming to supper with us on Sunday for her eighteenth birthday.

Mom baked a pineapple upside-down cake, and Dad used up all the rest of the Red Stamps in our ration book just so we could have steak. I got Shirley this really neat present, a record that is real great by the Andrews Sisters called "Don't Sit Under the Apple Tree." Maybe you've already heard it a million times, but I never know what hits you guys get to hear out there. Do you get "The Hit Parade"? If you want, I could send you a list of the Top Ten Hits every week, but maybe you'd rather not if you can't get to hear them. Just let me know.

Notre Dame has a great team this year with a real tall skinny guy named Angelo Bertelli at quarterback, passing like crazy from this new formation which is called the "T Formation" which has so far baffled the opponents of the Fighting Irish. To tell you the truth, i don't like it as well as the old "Shifting Box" formation invented by Knute Rockne. In the "T" the backfield doesn't get to dance around before the play, so I hope it just turns out to be a flash in the pan. I figure when the other teams get used to it they will learn how to stop it cold and the Irish will go back to the good old "Shifting Box."

Well, that's all the important stuff for now and I see I am running out of V-mail so I'll just say "Keep 'em flying," and "Don't let the bedbugs bite!"

*Your brother,
Artie Garber*

Artie looked over the letter again, making sure there wasn't any stuff he should censor, then folded the lightweight paper, licked the flaps, and sealed up the neat, single piece of paper that served as its own envelope in a V-mail letter.

Actually, he had already "censored" some of the news

by not putting into the letter that Shirley had refused to go
to college in the fall after graduating from high school in
June, but instead got a job after Labor Day as ticket girl at
the Strand. Artie was pretty sure Roy wouldn't mind about
Shirley staying home and keeping the fires burning for him
instead of running off to college (she probably wrote him
that anyway), but he didn't know if Roy would like the
idea of her having a job, especially one where she sat in the
lighted cubicle of the Strand Theatre ticket booth right on
Main Street where everyone could pass by and look at how
pretty she was every night except Sunday. Artie would
never keep a secret from Roy, except when he was out
there fighting and it might be bad for his morale. Artie had
to be real careful about that, because sometimes the very
thing he thought would boost a person's morale just boo-
meranged. Like when Shirley came over for her birthday.

After supper Artie cranked up the big Victrola in the
living room and put on the birthday present he'd got for
Shirley. The Andrews Sisters were really neat, and Artie
loved how they belted out the good part:

> Don't sit under the apple tree
> With anyone else but me,
> Anyone else but me,
> Anyone else but me—
> *No No No!*
> Don't sit under the apple tree
> With anyone else but me,
> Till I come mar-ching home.

Artie was glad he had already mailed the letter to Roy
reporting on Shirley's stiff upper lip, because by the time
the song was over both of her lips were quivering, and tears
were rolling down her cheeks.

"It's not supposed to make you feel bad," Artie said,

feeling discombobulated. "It's supposed to *boost* your morale."

"I guess I'm not a very good patriot," Shirley said.

"No, don't say that!" Artie shouted.

"What's going on in there?" his mother called from the kitchen. She and his Dad were doing the dishes and wouldn't let Shirley help because it was her birthday, and Artie knew anyway they liked to do it by themselves so they could horse around and nuzzle each other.

"Nothing!" Artie yelled toward the kitchen, and then he sat down on the davenport next to Shirley. She had taken out one of her dainty little hankies with rosebuds stitched around the edge and she turned her face away from Artie as she pressed it to her nose and made a delicate, ladylike little honk.

"Listen, Shirley, I got something to show you that really *will* boost your morale; just sit tight and I'll be right back, okay?"

Shirley nodded and Artie rushed up the stairs to his room. He could hear his Mom and Dad singing "Don't Sit Under the Apple Tree," using the same fast rhythm as the Andrews Sisters and belting out the "No—No—No!" like sixty. He hoped it didn't make Shirley feel worse.

Except for her nose being kind of pink she looked just fine when Artie charged back downstairs, carrying his own newly begun War Scrapbook. He sat down next to Shirley and started flipping madly through the scrapbook to one of the last pages that had things in it. There was a clipping he had torn out from a *Newsweek* magazine in Damon's Drugs, which he figured was not too terrible to do because if he had bought the thing he wouldn't have been able to buy a new Defense Stamp that week, and anyway he figured this story wouldn't matter much to most people, if they didn't have brothers in the South Pacific who had girl friends back home in Birney. Artie pointed his finger at the clipping he meant and shoved the scrapbook over on Shirley's lap. He read it again as she was reading it herself. It was written by a war correspondent out there who reported: "Maybe there are some beautiful natives somewhere in the South Pacific, but if so the Japs have occupied them. The only ones I have seen have been blacker than black. The first white girl I see back in the States who smiles at me, I am strictly going to crumple from hunger."

Shirley's cheeks got as pink as her nose.

"Well," she said, "I hope he doesn't crumple when he sees me."

"Not old Roy," Artie said. "Anyway, you don't have to worry about him sitting under the apple tree out in Eniwetok or any of them."

"Coconut tree," said Shirley.

"Huh?"

"I don't think they have any apple trees out there."

"Oh. Well, then he won't be sitting under the coconut tree. With anyone else."

"It's a shame, really," Shirley said, looking as far away as the Solomon Islands.

"What is?"

"Roy, and all those boys, in their prime. Without any girls."

"But they got the War," Artie said.

"Yes. That's what we've all got."

"You make it sound like the measles or something," Artie said.

Shirley turned toward him and smiled.

"You're sweet," she said. "You really *do* keep my morale up."

"Shoot," said Artie, looking down at his shoes and burning with pride.

Just then his Mom and Dad came in, holding hands, and Artie grabbed the scrapbook off Shirley's lap and slammed it shut. He didn't want his folks to know he'd been showing Shirley the article about the guys not having any white girls to sit under trees with in the South Pacific. They might think he was being too sexy.

"Are we interrupting anything?" his Mom asked.

Artie scooted away from Shirley to the other side of the davenport, feeling his cheeks get hot.

"Heck, no," he said. "I was just showing Shirley some stuff about the War."

Mom winked at Shirley.

"He never shows *us* anything," she said.

"It's the age," Dad said, sinking into his easy chair and looking philosophical. Mom sat in the rocker, and gently started swaying back and forth.

"Artie was keeping my morale up," Shirley said. "He always does."

"So you like being a wage slave?" Dad asked Shirley.

"She's a ticket girl, Joe," Mom corrected.

"It's wonderful for taking my mind off," Shirley said. "And I'm going to save money. I opened a savings at the Federal."

"Shouldn't you just Buy Bonds?" Artie asked.

"A savings is a fine thing," Dad said. "The rainy day always comes."

"Or a sunny one," Shirley said. "Like when Roy gets home."

"What about college?" Mom asked.

"I'll wait till Roy gets back. So we can both go together."

Dad looked real surprised.

"Roy wants to go to college now?"

"Oh, yes!" Shirley said.

"I always knew he would," Mom said.

Dad sighed.

"It took a war," he said.

Mom smiled at Shirley.

"And the right girl," she said.

Shirley looked down at her lap, modestly.

"How do your folks feel about it?" Dad asked her.

"I'm afraid they don't understand. They think I should go right now. But they can't make me. You can't make someone study and learn if their heart isn't in it. It's not like washing dishes."

"Hats off!" Mom said.

"Now, Dottie, we mustn't take sides," Dad said. "Against Shirley's folks."

"It's a free country," Mom said.

"Sure," Artie put his two cents in. "That's what Roy and the boys are fighting for."

"We didn't like it when the Colbys told Roy he couldn't give Shirley an engagement ring," said Dad. "It works both ways."

" 'The truth shall make you free,' " Mom quoted.

"The Colbys have rights, too," Dad said.

"I think I better be going now," Shirley said, and stood up. "Thank you for the scrumptious meal."

Artie hurried to get Shirley's record off the Victrola and put it back in the jacket. Dad beat him to getting Shirley's coat, and got to be the one to help her on with it.

"Thanks for the wonderful record, Artie," she said. "Will I see you at the Strand sometime soon? Or don't you go to the movies anymore?"

"I was wondering that myself," Mom said.

"I been too busy," Artie said, looking down at the rug.

"Never knew you to be too busy for the movies," his Dad said.

Artie felt like scramming up the stairs, but he knew he should just act natural about this so he didn't give away his secret strategy.

"*Sweet Rosie O'Grady* is on till Wednesday," Shirley said. "It's beautiful, in color and everything."

"Wouldn't mind taking that in myself," Dad said.

Mom poked him.

"I bet you wouldn't."

Dad put his arm around Mom and squeezed.

"We'll all go," he said. "How about it, son?"

"I'm pretty tied up till Wednesday," he said.

"You don't like Betty Grable anymore?" Dad asked. "Better take the boy's temperature, see if he's normal."

"Come on, Dad," Artie said, feeling his ears get red.

Shirley started to say something and then she looked at Artie and her expression changed, like she'd just thought of something else.

"Well, I didn't mean to be drumming up business for the Strand," she said, smiling. "After all, there's more to life than movies, especially nowadays. Personally, I want to start practicing up on some of your recipes, Mrs. Garber, like that wonderful kidney bean casserole we had tonight."

"You can do that one blindfolded," Mom said, "and I'll show you how any afternoon in a jiffy if you promise to call me 'Dot' from now on."

"Why, thank you—Dot."

Mom suddenly reached out and hugged Shirley and then everyone said good night and Dad drove her home. Just before going, Shirley gave Artie a special smile.

He knew darn well she could tell he'd been embarrassed about the Betty Grable stuff and she'd changed the subject to the kidney bean casserole just to help him out of his fix.

That's what he called a real friend, and a girl his own big brother would be lucky to come home to.

Part of Artie's plan to stay pure and not spill his seed anymore until he was married and was doing it to have kids was to stay clear of any sexy movies like the one about Princess Tahia that got him in so much trouble at Cho-Ko-

"And the right girl," she said.

Shirley looked down at her lap, modestly.

"How do your folks feel about it?" Dad asked her.

"I'm afraid they don't understand. They think I should go right now. But they can't make me. You can't make someone study and learn if their heart isn't in it. It's not like washing dishes."

"Hats off!" Mom said.

"Now, Dottie, we mustn't take sides," Dad said. "Against Shirley's folks."

"It's a free country," Mom said.

"Sure," Artie put his two cents in. "That's what Roy and the boys are fighting for."

"We didn't like it when the Colbys told Roy he couldn't give Shirley an engagement ring," said Dad. "It works both ways."

" 'The truth shall make you free,' " Mom quoted.

"The Colbys have rights, too," Dad said.

"I think I better be going now," Shirley said, and stood up. "Thank you for the scrumptious meal."

Artie hurried to get Shirley's record off the Victrola and put it back in the jacket. Dad beat him to getting Shirley's coat, and got to be the one to help her on with it.

"Thanks for the wonderful record, Artie," she said. "Will I see you at the Strand sometime soon? Or don't you go to the movies anymore?"

"I was wondering that myself," Mom said.

"I been too busy," Artie said, looking down at the rug.

"Never knew you to be too busy for the movies," his Dad said.

Artie felt like scramming up the stairs, but he knew he should just act natural about this so he didn't give away his secret strategy.

"*Sweet Rosie O'Grady* is on till Wednesday," Shirley said. "It's beautiful, in color and everything."

"Wouldn't mind taking that in myself," Dad said.

Mom poked him.

"I bet you wouldn't."

Dad put his arm around Mom and squeezed.

"We'll all go," he said. "How about it, son?"

"I'm pretty tied up till Wednesday," he said.

"You don't like Betty Grable anymore?" Dad asked. "Better take the boy's temperature, see if he's normal."

"Come on, Dad," Artie said, feeling his ears get red.

Shirley started to say something and then she looked at Artie and her expression changed, like she'd just thought of something else.

"Well, I didn't mean to be drumming up business for the Strand," she said, smiling. "After all, there's more to life than movies, especially nowadays. Personally, I want to start practicing up on some of your recipes, Mrs. Garber, like that wonderful kidney bean casserole we had tonight."

"You can do that one blindfolded," Mom said, "and I'll show you how any afternoon in a jiffy if you promise to call me 'Dot' from now on."

"Why, thank you—Dot."

Mom suddenly reached out and hugged Shirley and then everyone said good night and Dad drove her home. Just before going, Shirley gave Artie a special smile.

He knew darn well she could tell he'd been embarrassed about the Betty Grable stuff and she'd changed the subject to the kidney bean casserole just to help him out of his fix.

That's what he called a real friend, and a girl his own big brother would be lucky to come home to.

Part of Artie's plan to stay pure and not spill his seed anymore until he was married and was doing it to have kids was to stay clear of any sexy movies like the one about Princess Tahia that got him in so much trouble at Cho-Ko-

Mo-Ko. The only movies he had seen since his talk with Chief Pops Hagedorn were *Frankenstein Meets the Wolfman* and *My Friend Flicka.* He figured he was pretty safe from getting sexed up by a couple of ugly monsters, or Roddy McDowall and a horse. By the same reasoning, he knew he would just be asking for it if he went to see Betty Grable in *Sweet Rosie O'Grady.* He had seen a picture of Betty Grable dressed up as Sweet Rosie in an article about the movie in one of the magazines at Damon's Drugs, and that was enough warning. Sweet Rosie looked like some kind of chorus girl with this terrific sexy costume, and he knew the movie would show her dancing and shaking her boobs and her behind around and twinkling her long, shapely legs in arousing rhythms.

Artie told his parents he couldn't go with them to see Betty Grable on account of he had extra homework in Science and had to stay home to do it. He figured that was true in a way, since his effort to keep from spilling his seed until he got married in ten or so years was, he felt, a true "scientific experiment."

"I thought you didn't like Science," his mother said suspiciously.

"I don't, and I'm not any good in it, which is why I have to work extra hard at it," Artie explained.

His mother reached over and pulled down the lower lid of his right eye, squinting at it.

"What the heck are you doing?" Artie asked, pulling away from her.

"Are your eyes bothering you? Sometimes going to the movies hurts your eyes, and it may mean you need glasses."

"I don't need any glasses!" Artie shouted.

"Simmer down, son," his father said, and then smiled and took Mom's arm. "Boy just doesn't appreciate the finer things of life yet, like Betty Grable's gams."

Mom poked Dad with her finger right in the midsection. "I'll gam *you*," she said, and they both nuzzled each other and giggled.

"Mush," Artie said beneath his breath, and hightailed it up to his room before they got going on him again about the movies.

Mrs. Colby stood there looking down at him with an expression on her mug like she'd just eaten a lemon.

"Yes, what is it?" she asked.

Artie whipped off the old felt cap he was wearing with funny buttons on it, wadded it into a ball and stuck it in his pocket.

"Is Shirley home, please?"

"Shirley is indisposed."

"You mean she's sick?"

Mrs. Colby looked like she'd taken another bite of the lemon.

"She is not *ill*. She is indis*posed*."

Artie wasn't quite sure what this meant unless it was a fancy way of saying Shirley was in the bathroom, or maybe it was just some kind of upper-crust language for giving you the bum's rush. He started to turn and take off when he heard this amazing shriek from inside the house.

"*Mother! How dare you!*"

The voice didn't even sound human, but more like some deranged monster on the scariest radio program of all, "The Inner Sanctum."

Mrs. Colby's body jerked in a funny way, like someone had poked a broomstick in her behind.

Artie wanted to disappear, and at the same time he wanted to know what in blazes was happening.

Shirley exploded into the doorway.

She was wearing an old Bearcat sweat shirt, faded dungarees, and men's black socks. She didn't have on any makeup and her hair wasn't combed, but Artie thought she was weirdly beautiful, like some kind of Illinois Joan of Arc who had just burst out of her chains.

"How nice of you to come by and see me!" she shouted at Artie. "Please come right in, and forgive some people's poor hospitality!"

Mrs. Colby looked like she might spit, but instead she just spoke at Shirley through gritted teeth.

"You keep a civil tongue in your head, young lady."

"I was just stopping by to say hello," Artie said. "Hello. I guess I better be going now."

He turned and started off but Shirley yelled after him, "You come right in and make yourself at home!"

Artie doubted he could "make himself at home" but he knew if he didn't go in he was no friend of Shirley's. For all he knew she *had* been locked away in her bedroom or something and maybe Artie was her only chance to get a message out to the forces of freedom.

In the living room, Shirley sat down on the davenport and patted the cushion next to her, so Artie sat down there.

Mrs. Colby didn't sit down but she didn't leave either. She stood in the middle of the room with her arms folded, tapping her left foot noiselessly on the rug.

"Nice of you to come by, Artie," Shirley said. "How have you been?"

"Oh, I can't complain," he said.

He felt like he was in a play, where you and the other person were pretending to be other people in some other place than you really were. Mrs. Colby was like the audience that you had to pretend wasn't there. But then she spoke up.

"You really ought to go and lie down, Shirley. You're not yourself today."

As if on cue, Shirley became like the Illinois Joan of Arc again, with the avenging shriek.

"You don't know *who* I am!"

"I know I didn't raise you to be a tramp!"

Shirley jumped up and squeezed her arms across her chest like her mother was doing. It looked like they were about to start some kind of Japanese jujitsu match where you had to begin in the arms-folded position before you struck out with a deadly blow.

"How dare you insult patriotic American women!" Shirley yelled.

"Tramps in uniform, using the War as an excuse to mingle with men!"

"They don't *mingle* with them, they *serve* with them!"

"Brazen hussies!"

"Patriots!"

Artie cleared his throat.

"You talking about the WACs," he asked, "or the WAVEs?"

Mrs. Colby looked at him blankly.

"*Waves?*"

"That's the WACs, only for the Navy," Artie explained.

Mrs. Colby rolled her eyes toward the ceiling.

"Spare me," she said.

"You see!" Shirley yelled. "*Artie* understands!"

"Don't drag that child into this!"

Artie felt his ears get hot. He stood up and folded his arms on his chest like the other combatants.

"I'll be twelve and a half the eighteenth of this month," he said.

"He's old enough to love his country," Shirley said, "which is more than I can say for *some* people."

"*My* ancestors settled in Massachusetts two years after the *Mayflower*."

"They're my ancestors, too!" Shirley shouted.

"They must be turning over in their graves," Mrs. Colby said, "to think a young lady of their own lineage wants to join the *Army*."

"WACs!"

Artie was dumbfounded.

"*You* want to join?" he asked Shirley.

"You see?" Mrs. Colby said smugly. "Even the child is shocked."

"I am not," Artie lied. "I was just surprised."

Shirley burst out crying.

"Everyone thinks I'm a useless little fluff," she wailed.

"I think you're great!" Artie said.

Mrs. Colby went over and tried to stroke Shirley's head but she jerked away.

"You should go to your room and lie down," Mrs. Colby said.

"I want to go to Fort Des Moines!" Shirley sobbed.

That was where you went to become a WAC.

"The only place you're going if you leave this house is Sweetlawn Manor," Mrs. Colby said.

Shirley got an old hanky out of her pocket and blew her nose.

"When the War is over I'm going to a *real* college," she said.

Mrs. Colby shook her head, like Shirley had given a wrong answer.

"That comes *after* finishing school."

"I don't want to get 'finished'—I want to get educated!"

"If that's what you want you know very well you could have talked your father into Urbana this fall."

"I told you I'm waiting till Roy comes home."

"You have no obligation to that boy; you're not even engaged to him."

"I'm in love with him."

"You're in love with his uniform."

"You act like I'm stupid."

"You are if you're so in love with uniforms you want to wear one *yourself*."

"Why shouldn't I, if the man I love is wearing one? Why shouldn't I do a job that will free a boy to go fight?"

"Because you're a girl, and you will someday, hopefully, be a *lady*."

Shirley stood up.

"Come on, Artie," she said. "Let's get out of here."

"Where do you think you're going?"

"For a walk. To get some fresh air so I can breathe."

"If you're going out, you'd better get dressed."

Shirley looked down at her sweat shirt and dungarees.

"I *am* dressed."

"You look a sight."

"I'm not going to a tea party. We'll probably go for a walk in the woods."

"You'll have to cross Route One. Passing motorists will think you're some kind of a tramp."

Shirley took a deep breath.

"I'll just be a second, Artie. I have to go put on my hoopskirt, I guess."

Artie stood up and Mrs. Colby sat down as Shirley minced out of the room, imitating a prissy society lady.

"What am I going to do with her?" Mrs. Colby sighed.

"Maybe you should let her join the WACs," Artie said, trying to be helpful.

Mrs. Colby looked daggers at him.

"I didn't ask your advice, young man."

"You asked what you should do with Shirley."

"The question was rhetorical."

"Pardon me."

Artie sat down again and Mrs. Colby stood up and started pacing around the room.

"Who do you like best," Artie asked, trying to make conversation, "General Eisenhower or General MacArthur?"

Mrs. Colby closed her eyes. There were tears running down her cheeks. Suddenly Artie felt sorry for the old bat.

"Don't feel bad," he said.

"I allowed her to work at that horrible movie house. Taking tickets. Isn't that bad enough? What more does she want?"

"I guess she wants to join the WACs."

"My only child. My own daughter."

Shirley came down the stairs then, wearing a dark blue skirt and a yellow cashmere.

"Let's go," she said. " 'Bye, Mother."

"Nice talking to you, Mrs. Colby," Artie said.

Mrs. Colby turned her back, and Artie took off with Shirley.

They didn't say a word all the way out to Skinner Creek. When they got there, Shirley sat down on the rock and pulled her legs up to her chin, smoothing her skirt down over her legs. Artie decided to build a fire. It wasn't real cold yet, but there was an early October zip in the air, and anyway, Artie thought fires were good for helping people talk.

When Artie got the fire going, Shirley reached in her purse and took out a pack of Luckies.

Shirley was sure full of surprises today, but Artie knew enough to keep his trap shut. He watched as she lit the cigarette with a trembling hand, and blew a long stream of smoke. She started talking then without even looking at Artie, just staring off into the trees, the distance.

"I'm taking you into my trust. I hope you won't tell your folks about this."

"That you want to join the WACs?"

"That I *smoke.*"

"Scout's Honor I won't."

"Artie? You don't mean to say you think *your* folks would have a conniption because I want to join the WACs?"

"Huh? Well, no. *Shoot,* no. I mean, they'd just be sad you were leaving Town is all, probably."

"Don't you think Roy would be proud of me?"

"Roy? Well, sure. But I mean, he already *is*. Proud of you."

"For what? Sitting around and twiddling my thumbs while the world is on fire?"

"But you're keeping the *home* fires burning for him."

"If I joined the WACs, I'd be freeing a man to go help him fight and get the job done sooner."

"Yeah, but maybe he fights better because he knows you're at home, so he has someone to come home to."

Shirley blew some smoke through her nose and looked Artie right in the eyes for the first time since they'd left her house.

"That's how *you'd* feel too, isn't it? You'd want your girl to stay home when you went off to War. You'd think she was weird if she joined the WACs."

"Heck, no! I'd think it was neat!"

Artie could feel his cheeks getting red, not because he had lied, but because he would never have thought it was neat for a nice girl to join the WACs until he found out Shirley wanted to do it. He figured the girls who joined the WACs must be kind of mannish and homely or they wouldn't want to dress up like men and march around in uniforms. But then when he found out that Shirley wanted to do it, he saw how a pretty girl might want to sacrifice her looks and even her reputation (lots of people thought girls joined the WACs just to find a man) in order to serve her country and get the War over faster so her man could come marching home.

He wasn't sure Roy would see it that way, but you never could tell. Maybe now he'd been fighting so long he'd be glad about anything that freed another man to help him get the job done.

Shirley was still staring at him, and he worried that he hadn't been enthusiastic enough.

"If you join the WACs," he said, "I'll come over to Fort Des Moines and visit you."

Shirley smiled for the first time all day.

"You would, wouldn't you."

"Darn tootin' I would!"

"Well, it's a nice pipe dream, anyway. But I guess that's all it is."

"How come?"

"I couldn't hurt Mother that way. She'd think the world had come to an end if I really joined the WACs."

"What do you care what the old battle-ax thinks?"

"Artie Garber!"

"Huh?"

"How dare you call my mother a terrible name!"

"But that's how she was acting like to you!"

"She's only doing what she thinks is best for me."

"But *you* don't think it's best for you."

"I don't agree with her, but I still love her. She's my *mother*."

Artie's head was spinning, but then he realized the old saying was right: *Blood is thicker than water.*

It was okay for someone to criticize their own folks and even yell at them, but catch an outsider doing it and they would come to their own folks' rescue every time. Shoot, that was how Artie felt when people said anything bad about Roy, or Mom and Dad either.

"I'm sorry," he said.

Shirley stubbed out her cigarette on the rock, and stood up. For a second Artie was scared she was going to go off mad and never speak to him again, but all she did was put her hands behind her back and walk around the fire, kicking little rocks and twigs toward it.

"Mother and Dad were hurt real bad once," she said. "They *still* hurt. Maybe they always will."

"You mean 'cause they lost all their money in the Crash?"

Shirley's cheeks colored, and Artie was afraid she'd get mad again but all she did was pick up a rock and throw it in the creek.

"It wasn't just losing the money," she said. "It was losing their friends. Or people they *thought* were their friends."

"That sure is crummy all right."

"Now they don't trust anyone. They say when it comes right down to it you can only depend on your own family."

"Is that how you think, too?"

Shirley picked up another rock, tossed it up and caught it, and then instead of throwing it into the creek she just dropped it.

"I hate to think that way. But maybe I do, in my heart."

Artie felt real sad.

"You don't trust *me*, even?"

Shirley smiled, and came back and sat on the rock.

"Sure I do. But you're almost my own family, or will be anyway, when Roy and I get married."

"I sure am glad."

"I must trust you a lot, the way I go on babbling to you."

"You don't 'babble.' You talk swell."

"I never could talk to girl friends. I never even *had* any."

"But you're popular! You're a cheerleader!"

"*Was*. Anyway, I think the whole thing was a fluke. I think they were just scared of me because I was different, so when I tried out they chose me. I was different, so they thought I was special."

"You *are* special."

" 'Special' isn't always good. I wish I was more like other people, really. Had girl friends and all that."

Suddenly she laughed, like she'd thought of some terrific joke.

"Maybe that's why I want to join the WACs," she said.

"What is?"

"To be like other people. Regular people. Nobody could think I was snooty if I was a WAC. And I'd have lots of girl friends, without even trying. I'd *have* to. I'd be one of them."

"I thought you wanted to join so you'd help the War get over."

"I do. I honestly do. But a person can have more than one reason for doing something. Reasons they didn't even know about. Or just suspected. I've probably got a whole barrel of reasons for wanting to be a WAC."

"What else?"

Shirley got the pack of Luckies out of her purse again and lit up another one.

"Not the ones people think. I mean, it's not because of sex or anything. Not the way *they* think, anyway."

"What way is it, then?"

"Well, the truth is, a person thinks about sex when they don't have anything to do but twiddle their thumbs. If I was in the WACs I'd be too busy and tired to think about it all the time."

"Do you? Think about it all the time?"

"I think about Roy—and—well, about *it*. With him, of course."

"Well, that's normal, I guess."

"Sometimes I wonder. Sometimes I wonder if something's wrong with me."

"What?"

"It's terrible."

Shirley looked small and frightened and beautiful, and Artie wished he could go and put his arm around her. He wished he was her actual boyfriend coming home from the War, and he could do it with her. Then he felt guilty as hell for even having such a thought, which was not only sinful but unpatriotic, thinking that way about the girl of a Marine who was also your own brother!

"Sometimes," Shirley said in a painful whisper, "I think I'm oversexed."

Artie knew lots of girls worried about being oversexed, especially when their guys were off in the War. It was like a disease that could strike anyone, just like polio, and ruin your life.

Artie took a deep breath, and got up the courage to speak.

"I think I am too," he said.

Shirley didn't say anything, but just stared into the fire. Maybe she didn't even hear what Artie said, absorbed as she was with her own burden.

Artie didn't bring it up again. He just sat staring into the fire, like Shirley.

The two of them sat transfixed, like witches hexed, watching the licking flames and the hot red glow of the popping embers.

In the crisp clear days of October, America was beautiful, just like in the song. Artie had never been "from sea to shining sea," nor had he seen "the purple mountain's majesty" but he knew they were out there, believed in them, and saw every day with his own eyes the beauty of the gentle hills, the creeks and cornfields, the solid old white frame houses and the ancient oaks of Town. He believed, in fact, that God had "shed his grace" on this land, that this grace was tangible, visible, in the arch of rainbows over wet fields, the slant of shed sunlight on the sides of old barns. His pride in his country was sustained by the signs of nature and the symbols of men, not only the bright stars and stripes that flew from public buildings and hung from private porches but the comforting, everyday emblems of home: Bob's Eats, Joe's Premium, Mail Pouch Tobacco.

This was what Roy and all the other boys were fighting to save, preserve, and protect, along with the people who were lucky enough to live in and of it, and all this was sacred, worthy of any sacrifice, including life itself, for without it, life would be hollow and dumb.

Sometimes home seemed so beautiful and right it was hard to believe the War was really going on out there in the fringes of the world, the bleak foreign battlefields and alien oceans. When Birney beat Geneseo 13–6 Artie felt so good about everything he went to Damon's after the game to see if the latest magazines had any hopeful news about the War. Leafing through them, though, he found only gloom and frustration. The whole situation was summed up in one blunt headline:

NATION WARNED OF GRIM TRIALS, WITH WORST OF WAR YET TO COME

Yet to come!

If that wasn't bad enough, some General said in the same article that "our losses may well be so heavy they will be felt in every town and village in the U.S."

Birney had already lost Wings Watson, and his teammates were strewn around the world now, from Bo Bannerman with the Air Corps in England to Roy with the Marines in the South Pacific.

If the worst was yet to come, Roy himself might be stabbed by some Jap leaping down from a coconut tree in the dead of night, or blown to smithereens by a mortar shell, with only his "remains" shipped home in a box.

Artie felt his knees go watery, and he stuck the magazine back in the rack.

IV

1

SLINGIN' Sammy Baugh was crying.

That's how crummy things were at the start of the New Year of 1944.

The most shocking thing to Artie about the full-page picture in *Life* of Slingin' Sammy bawling like a baby was that he wasn't even crying about the War. The star passing quarterback of the Washington Redskins was crying because his team was getting beat 41–21 by the Monsters of the Midway, the champion Chicago Bears. Artie had seen lots of pictures of grown men crying because their loved ones were going off to battle, or their comrades were getting killed all around them, but this was the first one he'd seen of a he-man crying in the midst of Wartime because his team was losing a football game.

It figured, though. The War had gone on for more than

two years now, and people were tired of it. They wanted
something else to get worked up about, even if it was losing
a football game.

The worst part was that after all the fighting and dying
there still wasn't any end in sight. The new issue of *Life*
predicted for the New Year, "The Most Sobering Fact
About It Will Be Death," and went on to say that even
though lots of people had thought Hitler would collapse in
'43 and the War would be over that Christmas, the truth
was, "We are still far from Victory." After the great invasion of Italy, where Wings Watson got killed, the valiant
American and British armies were all bogged down. The
depressing story about it in the magazine said, "In the Mud
and Mountains the Allied Advance Has Been Virtually
Stopped." Over in the South Pacific where poor old Roy
was still fighting his heart out, it seemed like there wasn't
any end to the number of rinky-dink little islands the
Marines had to capture just to inch a little bit closer to the
Japanese homeland. Last year it was Guadalcanal and
Midway, now it was Tarawa and Kwajalein, and the same
old stuff all over again.

Artie flipped through the *Life* in Damon's Drugs, it
seemed like he'd seen the same pictures a zillion times:
muddy soldiers crawling out of foxholes, or bloody soldiers
lying on beaches, ships and planes being blown up; bodies
of dead Japs rotting in caves; all the same old stuff. Artie
felt guilty that the War really bored him now, but at least
he wasn't the only one. In fact, he was part of a whole new
problem that was sweeping the nation.

He was "slacking off."

That was the newest Wartime term, and it didn't have
anything to do with sex, even though it sounded a lot like
"whacking off," and was almost as bad. It meant you had
got lazy and bored with helping out on the Home Front,
and weren't doing your part in the War Effort anymore.

After looking at the new *Life* with all the depressing War news, instead of getting inspired to go out and start a new scrap drive or something, Artie just wanted to put off his homework and squander what money he had on him for a dime giant hamburger and a chocolate malt at Bob's Eats.

He was "slacking off."

As he moseyed down Main Street from Damon's to Bob's, Artie started singing the new hit song to himself. It wasn't one of those rousing ballads about our Brave Boys and the evil enemy; it wasn't about the War at all. In fact, it wasn't about anything; it was only these rhyming words that went:

> Mairzy doats and doazy doats
> And little lamsy divey . . .

It was just a fast way of saying "mares eat oats and does eat oats and little lambs eat ivy," which didn't mean anything at all. Maybe that's why people liked it so much. Since it didn't mean anything, you didn't have to think about anything when you sang it or listened to it.

Artie was about to bite into his dime giant hamburger when a bony hand clamped him on the back of the neck, and a deep, grainy voice began to sing in an imitation colored-person's accent:

"Is you is, or is you ain't my ba-by?"

Artie swung around and saw Fishy Mitchelman, all duded up in an outfit that surely was the first of its kind ever worn in Birney, Illinois. Fishy had on a bright yellow sport coat with padded lumps at the shoulders, a black shirt with a thin green tie, and brown peg pants that were clinched in high above his waist and hung down to a gathering drape around the ankles, where the material billowed down and over a pair of pointy shoes. If not the real thing, it was sure a good imitation of the weird type of getup that

Artie had seen the hoods in big cities wearing in magazine pictures since just after the War had started.

"You got a *zoot suit*?" Artie asked incredulously.

Fishy held up his right hand and snapped his long, thin fingers.

"What's buzzin', cousin?" he said in a kind of chant.

Artie put down his hamburger in wonderment as Fishy took off his flat-brimmed porkpie hat, lofted it in a high, graceful toss that landed it right on one of the coat hooks on the wall, vibrating for a moment like a horseshoe settling around the stake, and then hanging secure. Fishy pulled out a chair from Artie's table, turned it backward, and sat down straddling it.

"Where'd you ever *get* that stuff?" Artie asked, staring transfixed at the exotic outfit.

"Me and Trixie rolled up to Chi for Kringle Time," Fishy said, pronouncing the nickname of Chicago as "Shy," the way the hepcats said it. Fishy acted real casual, like it was a normal, American thing for a mother to take her son to a big city for Christmas, instead of staying home and having turkey with all the trimmin's and opening presents under the tree.

"Well, what did you and your Mom find to do up there at Christmas, anyway?" Artie asked.

Fishy stuck both his hands in the air and snapped the fingers on each one, making a little bob with his head at the same time.

"We swang," he said.

Artie just nodded, like that was normal, too, whatever weird stuff it actually meant. He turned back to his hamburger, but before he could pick it up again, Fishy had suddenly rubbed his hands in his sticky, slicked-down, Brylcreemed hair and then grabbed the burger, taking a monstrous bite.

"Hey!" Artie protested.

Fishy flopped the burger back on the plate and stood up, chewing.

"Thanks," he said. "It was reet."

That was hepcat language for "neat."

"Where you goin'?" Artie asked.

Fishy hiked his pants up higher on his chest, and lifted the long, gold, looping key chain out of his pocket and twirled it around and around his finger.

"Goin' to Spingarn's party tonight."

"Caroline? She's having a party?"

"Didn't she give you the nod?"

"Huh? Well, I haven't talked to her lately. I guess she forgot."

Fishy twirled the gold key chain off his finger now, and stuck the end back in his pocket.

"Gotta fade," he said.

And he did.

Artie looked down at his hamburger. There were fingerprints of grease on the bun. He picked it up gingerly, turning it around to the opposite side from where Fishy had taken his enormous bite. Artie took a small nibble in a place that was free of fingerprints. It was okay, but he didn't feel hungry anymore.

He felt rotten that Caroline hadn't invited him to her party, and he couldn't help wondering if maybe besides her getting back at him for calling her a pest last fall he was just being punished in general for slacking off so much. Here he had just wasted most of a dime hamburger when people all over the world were starving, not to speak of wasting good money that could have bought a whole dime War Stamp.

Artie realized shamefully it was this kind of selfish, wasteful attitude that had made the last big bond drive such a fizzle all over the country. The only thing that saved the drive from being a complete bust was when the government released some secret documents about the horrible atrocities the Japs had done to Our Boys back a couple of years ago when they captured all those soldiers on the Philippines and put them in prisons to torture them. Some of the secret documents even revealed that the Japs had done atrocities on Red Cross nurses, and people really got stirred up about it. Tutlow had cut out a neat story for his War Scrapbook about how outraged people were over the atrocity reports, and Artie's favorite part in the article was: "A blond stenographer in Seattle said: 'I'll tell you what the girls in Business say. They say kill the little yellow bastards, each and every one. Kill the big ones, kill the little ones, kill the medium-sized ones.'"

That was the good old patriotic spirit, and a lot of people caught it along with the blond Seattle stenographer. Bond sales really picked up for a while, but then even anger over the atrocities fizzled away and most people went back to slacking off again.

Artie himself hadn't bought a War Stamp for over a month. He had spent all his money from holiday tips on his paper route for Christmas presents, and the only one that had anything to do with the War Effort was the carton of Camels he had sent to Roy. At least he hadn't cashed in his Bond that would someday be worth twenty-five dollars, like lots of people were doing. So many Americans had lost their patriotism and cashed in their Bonds that there were ads now in magazines pleading with people not to "make a coward out of your cash!" There was even a magazine article on "Wartime Slackers" that told how lots of demoralized citizens had taken the money out of their Bonds and gone to Florida to spend it betting on horse races, drinking champagne, and lolling around swimming pools. Artie wasn't that bad—at least not yet—but if he kept on the way he was going, he might end up squandering his hard-earned money betting on horses and buying champagne while he lollygagged around swimming pools.

Just then he happened to look out the window of Bob's Eats to see none other than Caroline Spingarn ambling by.

That's what she did now when she walked.

She *ambled.*

It was part of the amazing change that had come over Caroline almost overnight. Artie barely even noticed around Thanksgiving that her knees stopped knocking together when she walked, and instead of hanging her head and scrunching her neck down into her little shrunk-looking dresses, she stood straight and acted like she didn't even mind that she was taller than most of the other kids. Instead of babbling and asking questions about everything she just got kind of quiet, not like she was scared, but more like she was waiting, biding her time. Then she went to her Grandmother's house in Rock Island for the holidays, and when she came back to school she not only had these terrific new dresses that fit her, she had her hair curled under real sleek and shiny without any bows and ribbons sticking out of it, and she walked in this ambling, movie star rhythm that made her behind sway like it was moving in time to some sultry music. She acted real calm and cool and took her time about everything, like she was waiting for everybody else to catch up.

Artie slammed down his money to pay for the food he hadn't finished at Bob's and rushed outside to catch up with her.

He ran as fast as he could and then when he got about five yards away from Caroline he started creeping up on tiptoe to surprise her. He got right behind her and reached around and clapped his hands over her eyes, at the same time making his voice as deep as he could and singing in a hoarse, colored kind of tone, "Is you is, or is you ain't my ba-by?"

Caroline sighed, like she was weary of the world.

"Really," was all she said.

"Guess you forgot to invite me to your party tonight," Artie said.

He figured there was no sense in beating around the bush.

"Really?"

This time her eyebrows arched when she said it, sort of like Bette Davis in *Watch on the Rhine*.

She stood there staring at him grandly, and he felt like some kind of worm. He remembered back to the time he'd called her a pest and she had cried and threatened to make him sorry for it and he hadn't believed she could ever do it. That just showed how you couldn't predict anything when it came to girls.

Now he was already sorry, in a way he had never imagined possible.

"Well," she said, "I suppose if you think you can act like a grown-up you might as well come."

He was going to say something smart-alec about her new hip-swinging walk, but instead he just kicked at the sidewalk and looked down humbly at his shoes.

"Gee, thanks," he said.

Caroline yawned and delicately tapped her fingers to her mouth.

"Don't mention it," she said, like she was Greer Garson in *Mrs. Miniver*.

Then she turned and walked off, swaying like mad.

They had eaten all the pretzels and potato chips and drunk all the Cokes. Caroline went over to her new plug-in Victrola that you didn't have to crank up to play; you just turned on the switch. She was wearing this shimmery blue dress and real stockings that glistened too, and shiny black shoes with heels that made her even taller. She turned to look at the kids and her bright reddish blond hair, which now fell clear to her shoulders and turned under, swung across part of her face, sort of like Veronica Lake.

"Requests?" she asked coolly.

" 'Pistol-Packin' Mama'!" Ben Vickman shouted.

" 'Winter Wonderland' again!" said Marilyn Pettigrew.

"Why don't you get out the milk bottle?" Warren Tutlow asked.

There was a sudden hush, a general intake of breath, and everyone stopped whatever they were doing, except for Fishy Mitchelman, who sat by himself in a corner of the basement, drumming his drumsticks on an old washpan he had turned upside down.

"Milk bottle?" Caroline asked, pushing the hair back from her eyes with a slow, delicious gesture. "What in the world do you want with a milk bottle?"

Ben Vickman let out a whoop and suddenly the girls were all shrieking and giggling and the guys were pounding each other on the shoulders with their fists and yelping. The reason for all the commotion was that just before Christmas at Edith Lynx's party they had played spin-the-bottle, and the guys and girls had really *kissed*, not just the little pecks on the cheeks like they'd done the year before playing Post Office, but real grown-up kisses where you put your arms around each other and mashed mouths together, just like in the movies, right in front of everyone else!

Suddenly the door at the top of the basement steps opened, and Mrs. Spingarn looked down from the kitchen.

"Is everything all right?" she asked.

All the kids quickly shut up and settled down, the boys straightening ties and coats, the girls smoothing their skirts.

"Everything's hunky-dory, Mother," Caroline said, and put on "Winter Wonderland" again.

Mrs. Spingarn went back in the kitchen and closed the door.

Caroline reached behind the record player and pulled out an empty milk bottle that she must have had there all along. In no time at all the girls were sitting on the cold cement floor of the basement, their skirts carefully spread over their legs. Warren Tutlow got to go first since he was the one who was brave enough to ask about the milk bottle. He looked at Caroline Spingarn like he was taking aim for her, gave the bottle a quick spin, and it ended up with the open mouth pointing directly to Betty Sue Beam. She was short and chubby and when Tutlow kissed her she kept her eyes squeezed shut and held her hands behind her back, so it wasn't much of a kiss at all.

Artie pushed in next ahead of Ben Vickman and they started to argue about whose turn was first when Caroline looked over in the corner and called, "Monroe? Aren't you going to play?"

Everyone looked at Fishy, who rattled off a few more beats on the washpan, then tossed his two drumsticks in the air, caught them, shoved them into his hip pocket and walked over to the circle of girls. Artie and Ben forgot their argument as everyone watched Fishy flop to his knees, rub his hands together, blow on the palms, and say, "Seven come eleven!"

Then he grasped the milk bottle right in the middle with his long, bony hands, gave it a terrific spin, and watched it end up pointing straight at Caroline Spingarn.

You could have heard a pin drop as Caroline stood up and walked to the center of the circle, very calm and composed, like it didn't mean a thing for a nice girl like her to be kissed by a sex maniac wearing a zoot suit.

Fishy got up and stood in front of her, looking slightly down at her eyes, she looking back up at him. Artie figured maybe she just liked the idea of Fishy being the only guy taller than her, and that's why she asked him to get in the game. So she wouldn't be embarrassed by having to bend down to kiss a guy.

Suddenly Fishy wrapped his arms around Caroline, mashing his mouth against hers at the same time, and instead of jumping away or screaming, Caroline mashed back, wrapping her arms around the padded shoulders, pressing herself against the zoot-clad body, as Fishy bent her back at the waist like he was doing a dip at a dance, but he didn't bob back, he just kept dipping and holding the kiss, like he thought he was Rhett Butler in *Gone With the Wind* or something, and the other kids were gasping and whistling through their teeth and Artie felt his stomach moving wildly and was scared he was going to heave his pretzels. He suddenly yelled out "Puget Sound!" and Tutlow called out the basketball hex words "Oogum Sloogum!" but Fishy and Caroline kept on kissing, till finally, out of breath and red in the face, Fishy pulled away, stood straight up again, blinking and swaying like he might fall over, and then he said "Fo-dee-do" in a hoarse whisper, and turned and walked wobbling up the basement stairs and out.

Everyone was talking all at once and Caroline went to the bathroom to fix her lipstick and Ben Vickman put "Pistol-Packin' Mama" on the record player. Artie couldn't tell if the game was over now, after the bombshell kiss of Fishy and Caroline, and he wasn't even sure if he wanted it to start again. He didn't like the idea of kissing Caroline right after Fishy had had his mouth all over hers and maybe had passed on some awful communicable sex disease he had picked up in the hotel bathrooms of Chicago; on the other hand, he wanted to kiss Caroline to show he could do it even better than Fishy, wanted to kiss her so great and so long and hard that even the memory of Fishy's kiss would be wiped out of her mind for the rest of Eternity.

Before he could even figure out how he had felt about it all, Caroline had ambled back from the bathroom, looking as cool and collected as if nothing at all had happened and the girls were back in the circle on the floor and it was Artie's turn to spin. He clutched the middle of the bottle and aimed the mouth toward Caroline, thinking maybe if he pointed it there first it would know it was supposed to end up there, and then he gave it all he had with his wrist. The bottle spun sluggishly, making only a couple of circles before it stopped dead in a perfect point toward Marilyn Pettigrew.

"Crum!" called Ben Vickman, who creamed for Marilyn Pettigrew, and must have thought Artie had spun for her on purpose. Fat chance. Marilyn was stuck on herself because she was a Science whiz and her Dad had a "C" card for gas rationing on account of being a Veterinarian and supposedly having to do "essential" driving to deliver calves and rescue stray pigs and stuff. Marilyn had a little pug nose and everything about her was pert and prissy, like the outfit she had on tonight, a plaid skirt and a white blouse with a matching plaid sash draped over the shoulder like she was ready to blow on a bagpipe.

Marilyn stood up with a coy smile, twined her fingers behind her back, and minced to the center of the circle. Artie stepped out in front of her, feeling as much like stomping on her patent leather foot as kissing her, but he tried to pretend she was really Maria Montez, a beautiful princess disguised as a bagpipe player.

Artie took a deep breath, grabbed her, and pressed his mouth on her prissy thin lips before she could even scream. Her arms flew out from behind her back and waved at her sides, like she was trying to fly, and Artie dipped her backward, just like Fishy had done with Caroline, but he went so far they both toppled over and fell to the floor and Artie was shook loose from her mouth and she yelled

"Heeeelp!" and Ben Vickman rushed over and yanked Artie up by the arm, saying at the same time "You win the Purple Heart, Garber!" and squeezing his hand on Artie's left tit in a terrible, painful hickey that would quickly turn black and blue. Artie yelled.

Mrs. Spingarn came storming down from the kitchen, turning on the ceiling light that flooded the basement with a harsh glare, and shouting, "I am very disappointed in all of you!"

Artie grabbed his coat and quickly went up to Caroline to apologize.

"I'm sorry," he said. "I guess I got carried away."

Caroline shrugged, like he didn't even count.

"You'll learn," she said.

Then she made the little brush of her hair back with her hand, and turned away. Now she reminded Artie of Lauren Bacall.

He bent forward, crouching, as he passed Mrs. Spingarn, hoping she didn't notice his hard-on.

At home in bed after Caroline's party, Artie did something he had never done before, something which probably ranked as a new kind of sin, no doubt a worse one, than those he had committed in the past.

He beat off thinking about a girl his own age, in his own class at school: the sleek new ambling Caroline Spingarn.

The sin itself was bad enough, but even worse was the realization that from now on he couldn't guard against lustful thoughts and deeds by avoiding sexy movies and magazines. Now that looking at Caroline Spingarn could get him just as hot as watching Princess Tahia or a Lana Turner pinup picture, it meant that if Artie was to keep himself pure in body and mind, *he would not even be able to go to school*! He would just have to sit around the house all day taking hip baths, and reading the Scout Manual and the Bible.

That was impossible, and Artie resigned himself to waging a lifelong battle with sin, which he was no doubt doomed to lose, along with his mind, his hair, and his childbearing seed, while acquiring in the process pimples, bad breath, and assorted forms of ravaging disease.

2

ARTIE really got down in the dumps. He caught two bad colds in a row, and had to stay home from school. It seemed like winter would never end. Like the War, it just kept dragging on. There weren't even any good snows to get your spirits up, just a few little flurries that quickly turned to slush, and then there was sleet, and long, cold rains that chilled you to the bone. For supper, they started having Spam a lot, which was some kind of Wartime imitation of meat that came in a can, and something called "Spanish rice," which Artie figured was invented to feed the growing numbers of refugees in the world. When he moaned about it, Dad got real hot under the collar and said how Roy was probably having nothing but C rations, and then Mom got sad about Roy still being halfway around the world and in danger every minute of the day. Artie felt awful, knowing he'd turned into a full-time slacker. He even let his homework slide, and started getting complaints from customers on his paper route, saying he'd missed the porch altogether and the paper had got all soggy from the rain.

He started staying home from school when he wasn't even sick. One morning he woke up full of remorse after jacking off the night before imagining him and Caroline Spingarn being trapped alone on a desert island.

He told Mom he had a terrible earache. At least that was something original.

As usual, he turned on the radio and listened to soap operas to keep his mind off sex. He listened to "Our Gal Sunday," "Young Widder Brown," "Ma Perkins," "The Romance of Helen Trent," "Stella Dallas," "Vic and Sade," "Lorenzo Jones," and "Just Plain Bill, Barber of Hartville." That got him safely through the day, but the sadness of the stories and the organ music that went along with them left him feeling even groggier than when he woke up in the morning. In the afternoon the sun had come out, and that made him feel even worse, being inside under the covers. He wondered if he'd ever feel like getting up and facing the world again, or whether he might spend the rest of his life in bed, becoming like one of those old cranks who sit in their house for years letting old newspapers pile up until they can't even get out the door and just die.

It was listening to "Jack Armstrong, the All-American Boy" that finally snapped him out of it. First it just made him feel worse, listening to Jack and his pals risking their lives just like Roy out in the South Pacific outwitting the Japs while he just lay in his bed like a wet noodle. Then it got him mad at himself, realizing he was wasting his own red-blooded All-American boyhood hiding under the covers and slacking off all day after jacking off the night before, and he decided right then and there that he was going to get himself fired up again and rejoin the fight for freedom.

Artie got dressed and went downstairs to get something to eat. Dad was still at work of course, and Mom hadn't come home yet from her day of wrapping bandages for the Red Cross with the Moose Ladies Auxiliary, but she'd left him a note saying there was a peanut butter and jelly sandwich for him in the icebox to have for lunch. It was way too late for lunch now, and anyway peanut butter and jelly struck him as too kidlike for his manly new mood of dedication. Instead, he made a big bowl of Wheaties, Breakfast of Champions, and ate it while he read the paper.

When he saw the ad for the new movie playing at the Strand he felt the thrill of knowing he was back on the right track, that God was looking down to help him regain his patriotism. The movie starting that very night was *Destination Tokyo*, a terrific War story about these guys on an American submarine who slip right through the entire Japanese Navy to strike at the Imperial stronghold. It came to Artie in a flash that he'd kill two birds with one stone in his exciting new effort to get back into action by going to watch the inspiring movie and then walking Shirley Colby home. He'd been neglecting her lately, but he'd make up for it by buying her a rainbow Coke at Damon's Drugs.

Artie crept up to the Strand ticket booth with his head bent low, and then popped up so he was staring right into Shirley's face. He raised his upper lip and stuck his teeth out so he looked like a Jap.

"*Destination Tokyo*, prease," he said in his best Oriental slur.

"Oh! Artie. You scared me."

"So solly, prease."

He slid his quarter under the little arc of an opening in the glass, and Shirley slipped his ticket through.

"How you doing?" she asked.

"Well, I been kind of under the weather, which is why I haven't been around for a while, but now I'm 1-A. In fact, how about I buy you a Coke when the show's over?"

"Oh, no, I can't," she said quickly.

"How come?"

Shirley's eyes flicked away, and her cheeks got brighter.

"I have to go right home."

"Well, I can walk with you."

"Not tonight," she said. "Maybe some other time."

She looked past him, over his shoulder, and Artie realized there were other people standing in line behind him.

"I can walk you real fast," he said.

"*Please*, Artie. Not now."

A guy behind him started whistling real loud.

"Okay," Artie said.

He took his ticket and headed for the door, feeling like he'd just got the brush-off. In the lobby, he looked around for Burt Spink, the fat, jolly Usher, who always had some kind of joke about the weather, like "Colder than a brass monkey's balls in December," or "Hotter than a witch's tit in Brazil." He figured old Burt would get his mood up again.

Burt wasn't there, though. Instead, there was some guy he'd never seen before standing at Attention by the ticket box, all decked out in a red jacket with gleaming gold buttons, a white shirt and little black leather bow tie and black pants with a red stripe down the side. All he needed was a little round black cap with a strap underneath the chin and he'd have looked like "Johnny," the midget mascot for Philip Morris cigarettes. Except this guy was tall and skinny, and he had a blond, flattop haircut and blotchy skin. Still, the outfit looked so much like the Philip Morris trademark Artie wouldn't have been surprised if the guy made the high-pitched "Johnny" yell: "Come in and call for Phil-ip Morr-ees!" Burt Spink always wore an old green soda jerk jacket and a wrinkled striped shirt.

The new Usher jerked his head toward Artie with military precision, like he was executing an "eyes left."

"Ticket, please," he snapped.

"Where's Burt Spink?" Artie asked as he handed over his ticket.

"If you mean my predecessor, I understand he has enlisted in the Armed Forces," the new guy said, tearing Artie's ticket exactly in half with a single *rip*, and handing him the stub.

"Oh, yeah. I forgot he was joining up when he turned eighteen."

"Follow me, please," the new Usher said sharply, and turned with a click of his heels to the door of the theater. The Movietone News was on, showing some Flying Fortress coming in on a wing and a prayer from a mission over Germany and Artie stopped a moment, staring at the screen, then heard a click and a solid beam of light shot forth from the heavy black flashlight the Usher carried and struck the tops of Artie's shoes.

"This way, please," the Usher instructed and Artie obeyed, even though the new guy was taking him farther down than he liked to go, right to the second row before the screen, where you had to crane your neck up to see the picture and the actors loomed over you like giants. The beam of the Usher's flash seemed to be pulling Artie forward like a magnet, and when it swung sharply to the left he sidled past a couple on the aisle and sat down in the empty third seat, even though he usually made a point of being on the right side of the theater. He was going to complain to the Usher that he had put him in the wrong place, but the beam snapped off and the Usher had turned and melted into the dark. Artie could excuse himself and go look for a place he liked better, but he felt stuck, like the darned Usher had nailed him into that seat and there was no use trying to shift.

He hated the Usher's guts.

Who did he think he was, anyway?

In fact—*who was he*?

Artie was sure he'd never seen the guy before, which meant he wasn't from Birney or Oakley Central or anywhere around there.

It was strange. Artie had a hard time concentrating on Cary Grant steering his submarine through the Japanese Imperial Navy, wondering who in the world the new Usher was and what he was doing there.

"Who is he, anyway?" Artie asked Shirley.

He had waited for ..er at the far corner of her block the next night after supper, not wanting to have to face Mrs. Colby but determined to have a word with Shirley on her way to work.

She was walking real fast, but as they rounded the corner away from her house she stopped and fished a pack of Luckies from her purse.

"Clarence Foltz?" she asked, as she pulled out a cigarette and looked up and down the block. It was bad enough for a girl to smoke, but a girl smoking "in the street" was even worse. It looked like the coast was clear, though.

"*That's* his name?" Artie asked.

"Why? What's funny about it?"

Shirley got the cigarette lit and took a big drag, blowing the smoke out of her nose.

"How do you spell it?"

"F-o-l-t-z, I guess," she said, and started walking again. "Never heard of it. Who is he?"

"The new *Usher*, for Heaven's sake."

"I know that. I mean, where does he live?"

"Miss Winger's Boardinghouse, I think."

"I mean where's he *from*? Like where do his folks live?"

"Michigan. Some little town."

"So what's he doing here in Birney?"

"Working. At the Strand."

"I know. But how come?"

"Men have to work. He's a man."

"Then how come he's not in the Army?"

"Artie, I swear. Are you practicing up for the FBI?"

"All I asked was a simple question, like any good citizen would."

They turned onto Main and Shirley stopped, threw down her cigarette on the sidewalk, and mashed it out with the toe of her loafer.

"For your information," she said, "it just so happens that Clarence Foltz was wounded in Guadalcanal."

Shirley started walking on, faster than ever now.

Artie had to take longer strides to even keep up with her.

"How come you didn't say so? Did he know Roy?"

"There were thousands of boys on Guadalcanal. They didn't all know each other."

"Well, where was he wounded?"

"Aren't you even listening? I told you, *Guadalcanal*."

"I mean where in the body? Did he get it in the leg? The stomach?"

"How do I know?"

"Sounds like you know just about everything else about him. You sure must have talked to the guy a lot."

"Of course I talk to him. We work together."

Shirley started going even faster, so she was almost running now.

"Hey!" Artie said. "Where's the fire?"

"I'm late!" Shirley said, and suddenly cut across the street.

Artie knew when he wasn't wanted. He stopped, took off his cap, and scratched his head, watching Shirley make tracks for the Strand.

"Fish-*ee*," he said to himself.

"Highly suspicious," said Warren Tutlow.

He was crawling out on the lower limb of the maple tree next to the Garbers' garage, holding the basketball cradled in his right arm.

"That's exactly what I thought myself," Artie said, figuring "highly suspicious" was really the same thing as "fish-*ee*."

Squinting through his glasses at the basketball hoop on the regulation white-painted wooden backboard nailed above the door of the Garbers' garage, Tutlow gently lowered his right arm with the ball balanced in his hand. He was going to try a one-handed underhand shot from the limb of the maple tree, just like the hot-shot show-off he was sometimes. They were playing HORSE, so if Tutlow made the crazy shot, Artie would have to climb out on the limb of the maple tree and try and duplicate it, or get another letter against him. He was already behind, HOR to H, as Tutlow had made one ordinary free throw that Artie had missed, as well as one of his stunt shots, an impossible two-handed backward fling while rolling down the driveway in Artie's old wagon. Just as Tutlow was about to shoot, Artie screamed "Puget Sound!"

According to their own rules, it was fair for one guy to yell some weird-sounding name he might have learned in Geography or History class to try to crack up the shooter and make him miss.

"Swishum!" Tutlow yelled quickly as the ball was in the

air, which was one of the words that was supposed to help make the shot go in and "swish" through the net.

But the ball hit the rim of the basket and bounced off harmlessly down the driveway.

"Tough luck, *Keemosabee*," Artie said as he ran to retrieve the ball.

Tutlow crawled backward on the limb of the maple and swung to the ground.

"If his name is Foltz—F-o-l-t-z—it's probably German," said Tutlow.

"That's what I figured, but I wasn't sure."

"Oh, sure. 'Foltz' is as German as horseradish."

Artie came dribbling the ball back up the driveway. "Horseradish is German?" he asked.

"Sure, they invented it," Tutlow explained. "They eat it to make themselves meaner."

"So maybe the Axis sent Foltz to infiltrate Birney when they lost their other agent," Artie said.

"It's exactly what they might do."

"They probably figured Wu Sing Lee was too detectable, being yellow and all, so they wanted to try a white man."

"I wouldn't put it past them."

Artie scratched his head, trying to figure out the sneaky strategy of the Axis at the same time as trying to figure out a new shot that he could make and Tutlow would find impossible to duplicate.

"The first thing to do," said Tutlow, "is try to search his room at the Boardinghouse. You know Miss Winger?"

Artie stood on one leg and tried to bend over backward, seeing if he might have a chance for a one-legged, two-handed backward shot, but he couldn't keep his balance.

"Heck, yes," he said, straightening up again. "Miss Winger used to baby-sit for me."

"Well, then, all you got to do is go over there and make up some excuse for going to Foltz's room while he's at work."

"What excuse?" Artie asked.

He set the basketball on top of his head, wondering if he could run to the basket, toss up the ball a few feet and then bounce it in off his head like the Harlem Globetrotters did.

"Say you're on a Treasure Hunt, and have to get something from the room of a new guy in town."

"Too fishy."

Artie gave up on the head shot and walked real casually across his front yard to the front porch steps, which were right on a straight line to the basket. He climbed to the top step and practiced aiming. Actually, he had practiced shooting from this position for the whole last week, but Tutlow would never know.

"You want me to sneak in and search his room while you attract Miss Winger's attention?" Tutlow asked.

"No! I don't want you setting any stink bombs in Miss Winger's place."

"Never said I would."

"You and your chemistry set."

"You going to take a shot, or can't you think one up?"

"I can think up a shot, and a better excuse than you can, too," Artie said. "This is one-handed, from the top step of the porch, without using the backboard."

Artie took his stance, and just as he released the ball Tutlow yelled, "Horseradish!"

"Swishum!" Artie retorted, and the ball sailed cleanly through the net. It was a good sign: "Swishum" had overcome the German "Horseradish" hex, and Artie knew he was destined to trap the conniving Nazi spy who was posing as an Usher while he tried to sabotage the town of Birney.

"Have another oatmeal cookie," Miss Winger said.

Artie nodded, and selected a big one.

"Don't mind if I do. Boy, I tell you, Miss Winger, your oatmeal cookies still beat anything."

Miss Winger gave him a pat on the knee, but it wasn't sexy or anything, coming from Miss Winger. She was sort of like a kindly grandmother in a kid's storybook, sparkly eyes behind rimless glasses, hair always up in a bun on top of her head, a high-collared gingham dress with a little velvet ribbon at the neck. She was plenty smart, though, and had actually been Artie's favorite baby-sitter because of the neat stories she read him, like *The Secret Garden*, and the Dr. Doolittle books.

"I haven't seen hide nor hair of you, Artie."

"Well, I been busy with Scouts, and school, and work for the War Effort."

"Isn't it the truth? I'm glad you found time for a visit. To what do I owe the pleasure?"

"Oh, just for old times' sake. I got to thinking about you. Somebody mentioned the new Usher at the Strand was staying with you, and I got to wondering how you were doing."

"Yes, Clarence Foltz took Mr. Veederman's old room. You know Mr. Veederman got into the Coast Guard, at his age? He was thirty-seven years old."

"Well, Henry Fonda was thirty-seven when he joined the Army. What's he like?"

"Mr. Veederman? Why, he seemed to be your ordinary, fast-talking Vacuum Cleaner Salesman, but I guess beneath that smile there was quite a bit of pluck."

"No, I meant Clarence Foltz, the new guy."

"Oh, Clarence is a real gentleman. Very quiet and reserved. Spends most of the day in his room. He was wounded, you know, but he doesn't like to talk about it."

"That's the second-floor room at the front, with the nice view of Hempstead's silo?"

"Yes, and I think he appreciates it. I think that boy has an eye for beauty."

"I bet. You still doing baby-sitting these days?"

"Oh, yes, I'm sitting the Buskerman boy tonight. Little Franklin? He's a real scamp. Can't sit still for a story. More like that brother of yours than you. How is Roy, anyway?"

"Oh, he's super, Miss Winger. Mowing down Japs over there on Eniwetok."

"To think of it. All those nice boys."

"Well, I got to shake a leg, Miss Winger, but thanks a lot for the oatmeal cookies."

"Take some with you. And don't be such a stranger!"

"Cross my heart and hope to die," said Artie, and hurried out with a handful of cookies.

He kept his promise to return much sooner than Miss Winger would have dreamed, but he hoped she would never find out. While she was over baby-sitting little Franklin Buskerman, and Clarence Foltz was busy ushering at the Strand, Artie slipped back to the Boardinghouse, saw there were no lights on except in the living room, where Miss Winger always kept a light going even when no one was there. Artie knew the door to the house was never locked and the roomers didn't have locks on the doors of their rooms.

He didn't turn on the light when he got inside Clarence Foltz's room, so no one would discover him, but used his trusty penlight. The first thing he noticed were the books. They were everywhere: on the desk, beside the bed, on the bed, under the bed, stacked in the corner. They were spread across the room in piles and pairs and alone, randomly, like a scattering of leaves: brown, yellow, black, green, red. Being a good counterspy, Artie avoided the obvious, and opened the main drawer of the desk. There too was a book. He picked it up, shining the penlight on it. Holy Toledo! Talk about a clue!

The book was *Guadalcanal Diary*. Artie flipped through it, noticing immediately how many parts were underlined in red pencil. It was obvious Foltz was a fraud; he had never even been to Guadalcanal, and he got all his info out of the book about it! Artie slipped it back in the drawer, and quickly scanned the books on the desk. Most of them were thin, and he didn't recognize the titles. He picked one up and read it. There were poems inside. He tried to read one, but he couldn't figure it out. He turned to another called "The Waste Land," which he figured must be about the War, like the way a country was after a battle. He turned to the end of it to see how it came out, and which side had won. There were strange, mysterious words he had never seen or heard:

Datta. Dayadhvam. Damyata.
Shantih shantih shantih.

Artie tried to mouth the sounds to himself, but none of it made sense. Then he slapped his hand to his head.

Of course! The book was *in code*. That was the only sensible explanation.

Artie crept back to the door, satisfied beyond the shadow of a doubt that Foltz was a German spy.

3

*T*UTLOW was wearing sunglasses.

March had "come in like a lamb" this year, and the days were kind of warmish and breezy, but it sure wasn't any weather for sunglasses yet.

"What you got those on for?" Artie asked. "It's not even summer."

"We're going to tail a man, aren't we?"

"I doubt he's going all the way to Florida."

"Don't be a sap," said Tutlow. "You tail a man, you don't want to be identified, do you?"

"Everyone in Town will identify a guy wearing sunglasses in March," Artie said. "They'll think you're cuckoo."

"Doesn't matter what other people think. The idea is not to get identified by the man you're *tailing*. Then he can't accurately identify *you* later."

"You're trying to be like in the movies is all you're doing."

Tutlow whipped off the sunglasses and glared at Artie.

"You want me to do this job alone?"

"It's *my* job!" Artie said. "I'm the one discovered the guy. I just *invited* you."

"Invited," said Tutlow scornfully. "This is no tea party, Garber."

Tutlow put the sunglasses back on. Artie thought they made him look blind, but he decided not to mention it.

They walked out to the Hempstead Farm in silence, to wait for Clarence Foltz to take his mysterious daily walk during which he disappeared for several hours every afternoon.

Foltz came out in an old leather jacket that reminded Artie of the kind German flyers wore. He headed for Main Street, and after he had gone about the length of a football field, Artie started to get up out of the weeds and start tailing, but Tutlow pulled him back down.

"You got to give him enough of a lead so he doesn't look back and see you," he explained.

"If he can't look back and see *us*, then how the heck can we see *him*?"

"I mean see us good enough to identify us."

"I thought he'd never identify you anyway cause of those corny sunglasses," Artie said.

Tutlow pretended he didn't hear that, and instead of saying anything he just got up, pulled the collar of his coat around his neck, shoved his hands deep in his pants pockets, and started trailing.

"Some guys think they're Humphrey Bogart or somebody," Artie said under his breath, but he just went along and followed Tutlow; there wasn't time now to mess around.

Artie's strategy was to try and just look natural, especially when they were walking down Main Street. People kept staring at Tutlow in his wacky sunglasses and his counterspy walk, so Artie made a point of being real casual, swinging his arms and whistling "Deep in the Heart of Texas," like there wasn't even a War on.

Just then the last person in the world Artie wanted to run into came ambling out of Damon's Drugs, right in front of him and Tutlow.

Caroline stopped and looked at them with a little smile, like she was highly amused.

"What do we have here?" she asked. "The Rover Boys?"

She was using this new kind of perfume that drowned out the smell of her Mild Camay Beauty Soap and reminded Artie of something Yvonne DeCarlo would wear in her harem.

"Sorry I can't shoot the breeze," Artie said. "We got business."

"What are you going to do," she asked, "hold up the First Federal?"

Tutlow shot her a corny comeback out of the side of his mouth.

"Take a powder," he said.

Caroline threw back her lovely head, the shining hair swinging in the sunlight, and laughed like Bette Davis in *Now, Voyager*.

Artie slunk on beside Tutlow, feeling like the worst kind of worm. He took deep breaths of air, trying to get Caroline's harem perfume out of his head, as they followed their man clear out of Town.

When they got to the edge of the woods by Skinner Creek, where Foltz had disappeared down the path into the trees, Artie stopped.

"Come on!" said Tutlow. "We're hot on his trail."

"I dunno," Artie said.

"Don't *know*!" Tutlow said in a hiss of rage. "You turning yellow on me?"

Artie supposed he was being really weird, but he had this funny feeling in the pit of his stomach. He knew he wasn't yellow, he knew he wasn't even afraid of risking his life for his country, but he still had this odd feeling, like something telling him not to go on any further. He couldn't explain it, though.

"There's nothing to sabotage at Skinner Creek," he said feebly. "Maybe he's just getting his exercise. They got to keep in shape, spies; it's not just all glory."

"You nit! He might be out to rendezvous with a paratrooper and help him hide the chute. You think the Nazis just parachute guys onto Main Street in broad daylight? Spies hide *out* in the woods, they make their *plans* in the woods, they keep their maps and ex*plo*sives in the woods."

Artie kicked his toe in the dirt.

"Okay," he said, "I guess we should go ahead and see."

Tutlow shook his head as he headed onto the path.

"For a minute there," he whispered, "I thought you'd gone yellow in the belly."

"Oh, go button your lip," said Artie, following along reluctantly but dutifully, wondering how come he had this funny feeling in the pit of his stomach.

They had lost sight of Foltz, but automatically figured he must still be following the trail, otherwise they'd have heard him if he suddenly dashed into the woods. The boys walked stealthily, keeping their eyes peeled for a glint of silver parachute silk.

The path was leading them straight to the clearing with the rock where Roy used to go to think about life, or lie on the ground beneath blankets with a beautiful girl and do the most wonderful thing in the world. Tutlow had bent to a crouch as he walked and Artie had done the same and now he felt a crick in his back and stopped a moment, straightened up, and looked around him. He blinked in the brightness, wishing he had a pair of sunglasses. The afternoon sun lit the trees and Artie felt caught and suspended in the eerie brightness, when suddenly the sound came, a song, from a tenor voice that was pure and high but not a girl's, a voice that was only a stone's toss away in the woods:

> So come ye back, when summer's in the mea-a-dow,
> Or when the vall-ey's hushed and white with snow—

Tutlow sprang erect, then crouched again and scuttled into the woods, throwing himself behind a large rock. Artie scooted after him, his breath coming hard, burrowing against the cold stone next to Tutlow.

> It's I'll be there, in sunshine or in sha-a-dow,
> Oh, Danny Boy, oh, Danny Boy, I love you sooooo.

Tutlow nudged his elbow into Artie's ribs.

"It's a signal!" he whispered. "He's calling his accomplice with code!"

"Shhhhhh!" Artie hissed.

Another voice spoke now, softly.

"Oh, Clarence. That was wonderful."

Artie froze.

Tutlow dug his fingers into Artie's shoulder and blasted a whisper into his ear.

"*It's a girl!*"

Artie lay there rigid and breathless, afraid to move or speak.

The spy's accomplice was not just "a girl."

It was Shirley Colby.

There had to be some mistake, or explanation.

Artie lifted his head, straining to hear what was said.

". . . for so long, I didn't know if I could do it any-more," came the voice of Foltz.

"Mmmmm, but you did, you did, so beautifully," Shirley said.

Her voice sounded far-off and dreamy, like it was lulled by some kind of dope.

That must be it. The crafty Nazi agent had doped up Shirley and lured her to the woods against her will.

"Beautifully for you, because you're so beautiful," Foltz said.

His voice was not clipped and military now like it was when he was ushering, it was soft and bleary. It almost sounded like *he* was doped! Maybe that was it. Maybe Shirley was playing a double agent's game, pretending to be taken in by the spy and all the time slipping some kind of dope into his Cokes and luring him into the woods to crack the secret of the whole Nazi network of sabotage in America.

"With your beautiful talent for it, you should do it all the time," said Shirley. "You were born to sing—and write, and paint, and all those beautiful things."

A bitter, choked kind of laugh came from Foltz.

"I was born to be miserable," he said.

"Stop saying that!"

Shirley's voice sounded sharp and clear now, untainted by any trace of dope.

"I'm sorry," said Foltz. "It's how I feel."

Just then Tutlow blasted another whisper right into Artie's eardrum.

"*I don't get it,*" he said. "*What's wrong with the guy?*"

"Shut up and listen!" Artie hissed back at him.

Shirley was speaking again—softly, gently.

"Clarence—if we did what you want to do—would it make you happy?"

stead of stockings. Not many women in Birney used it, but evidently lots of working girls in cities who had to wear stockings to offices every day had gone in for leg makeup for the Duration. So that's what Foltz had "dreamed of"— putting leg makeup on a girl's legs! And that's what Shirley was talking about when she asked him "what kind" he had got, and said she had heard of that kind—there were different brands of the stuff, like "Legstick" and "Stocking Fizz."

Artie tried to tell himself that what Shirley and Foltz were doing was helping the War Effort by conserving the vital material of nylon, but he knew darn well that didn't have beans to do with what was going on.

In his heart, Artie knew that he was watching something really pre-verted. In a way, this was even worse than doing It because this was so oddball. Shirley didn't seem to be doped, but Artie hated to think she would do such a thing —or let such a thing be done to her—of her own free will. Maybe the insidious Foltz had weakened her will by using some secret Nazi methods of mind control. Maybe this was just a technique for getting her all sexed up so she'd really do It when he finished with her legs.

Whatever the case was, Artie didn't want Tutlow or anyone else to find out that Shirley was the girl in the woods with the German saboteur. Nor did he want the demented Foltz to do anything else to the girl that Roy Garber was going to come home to before he even had a chance to come home. Without exactly planning what to do, just knowing he had to do something, Artie leaped up and screeched out the Cho-Ko-Mo-Ko tribal war cry:

"Eeeeeee-yaaaaaa-yooooo!"

Then he turned and took off like sixty, hurling his body forward, putting his whole throbbing heart and blanked-out mind into running.

Tutlow answered the cry with his own bloodcurdling

rendition of the Cho-Ko-Mo-Ko whoop, and at the same
time, Shirley Colby screamed. Clarence Foltz, his voice
undoped and militarily usherlike again, yelled, "Dirty bastards!"

The woods, so quiet and still only a moment ago, was
now thrashing with runners. Artie could see Tutlow charging ahead of him toward Town, not even looking back to
see if his counterspy comrade was okay or in trouble. Artie
not only heard the noise of his comrade fleeing ahead of
him, he heard the mad galloping steps of his pursuer
pounding behind him. Artie looked over his shoulder and
saw, only about a first-down's distance away, the wild eyes
and furious mouth of Clarence Foltz, charging for him like
a skinny Bronco Nagurski gone berserk.

In a desperate maneuver to shake the enemy, Artie cut
off the narrow path and plunged into the underbrush, flailing through tangles of bushes and branches that whipped
against his face and arms, lashing and cutting. His throat
and lungs were burning with the gasping sucks of breath as
he forced every muscle forward, fleeing, knowing no matter how much he hurt it was nothing compared to being
captured by a Nazi spy who would have no mercy, who
might punish a counterspy to death, or even worse, by
beating his privates to jelly. The pursuer was gaining
ground, the heave of his breath and the crash of his furious
steps coming closer. Artie bent forward as he ran, like he
was stretching for the tape at the finish line of a dash, but
then hands were on him, not around his ankles like a real
All-American tackler would do it, but on his back, grabbing, pulling him down.

"Eeeeeeyaaaaaa-yoooooo!" Artie screamed, but there
was no reply, only the faint, distant sound of dashing feet
as Tutlow fled to freedom. Hands were on him, jerking and
pulling him over onto his back, pinning his shoulders into
the hard ground. The enraged Foltz, gasping and trem-

bling, bent over Artie, the features of his Nazi-disciplined face contorted with hate.

"Bastard. Dirty little bastard," Foltz whispered with evil intensity.

"The other guy's name is Warren Tutlow!" Artie blurted out, at once feeling sick with shame, knowing he had not for even a second been able to carry on the mute tradition of courageous silence pioneered by the former Boy Scouts who refused as soldiers to give information to the enemy even though their privates were beaten to jelly. The next thing that came to his mind made Artie fear he was going crazy, for instead of thinking up a cunning plan of escape or at least a cutting remark like something Bogart would say from the side of his mouth if brought down by a Nazi pursuer, all he thought of was the dumb line of a silly song: *It must be jelly since jam don't shake like this.*

"Get up, ya little punk," ordered Foltz, yanking his arm and then twisting it behind him so hard it felt like his shoulder was being yanked from its socket.

"March!" came the clipped command of the Nazi agent and Artie stumbled ahead, coughing, the efficient Foltz twisting his arm as he pushed from behind.

The one thing almost as bad as having his privates beaten to jelly was being brought to face Shirley Colby as a captive counterspy. She was standing on the rock, wearing her sweater and coat and skirt just like a normal pretty All-American girl except one of her legs was tan and one was white. When she saw Artie, her mouth opened like she was hit on the head and then her whole face turned from shock to the sour look of hate, making her almost ugly.

"Artie Garber," she said. "You little sneak."

Anger flooded Artie so quickly and fully that instead of looking down at his shoes in shame and sorrow he stared right back at her, his jaw jutting out defiantly, and said, "Takes one to call one!"

Whap!

Foltz gave Artie a sharp cuff on the ear, and Shirley shouted, "No!"

She rushed to Artie, falling to her knees in front of him and throwing her arms around him. She was crying now and squeezing him, and he didn't know what to do, didn't know who was in the power of whom, which one was doped or mind-controlled by which, or what in the heck was going on here anyway, so he just stood there, stiff, silent, suspicious and totally confused.

"Oh, Artie," Shirley said, pulling back and looking at him through her tears, "I'm so sorry. I know you don't understand. But I want to explain. I want to explain everything."

"You traitor!" yelled Foltz.

Great Balls of Fire. Artie's worst fears were true.

Shirley put an arm around Artie and held him beside her, like they were both on the same side against the Nazi agent.

"Artie's my friend," she said bravely. "He'll understand."

"He's only a kid, for chrissake!"

"He happens to be the brother of Corporal Roy Garber, United States Marine Corps."

"Oh, so we're back to that," said Foltz in a pouting voice. "The big War Hero. I should have known."

"You should have known I'd be loyal to the man I intend to marry, since I told you all about it."

"Ha," Foltz said in that bitter, choked laugh of his.

"I think you'd better leave me and Artie alone for a while," she said to Foltz.

"Sure! I'll go, I'll go all right, I'll get my stuff and hit the road and go to the next lousy town in my lousy life."

"You'll do nothing of the sort, Clarence Foltz!"

Foltz put his hand over his face. He was sobbing. Shirley got up and went to comfort him.

"There, there," she said. "You just run along to your room and read some poems, and I'll see you tonight at the Strand. I have to explain this to Artie alone now, and then he'll understand everything."

"I don't want him to understand! I don't even want him to know. It's no kind of thing for a kid, anyway."

"Oh, yeah?" said Artie. Made bold again by Shirley's taking his side, and her obvious power over the Nazi agent, Artie spoke his mind.

"I may only be twelve years old, so I'm just a Boy Scout now instead of a soldier, but I'm still an American citizen, and I have a right to know about anything that threatens American freedom and democracy. Also, I have served as an Assistant Junior Air Raid Spotter."

Both Foltz and Shirley looked blankly at Artie, like he'd just spoken Chinese or something.

Foltz cleared his throat.

Shirley made a dainty little cough into her fist, then spoke to Foltz softly.

"You go on to your room, Clarence. Artie and I need to have a long talk."

Foltz sighed, and raised his hands about to his waist, turning the palms up, in a sign that meant *What the heck, anyway.* Then he shoved his hands in the pockets of his leather German aviator jacket and walked away, kicking at rocks as he went.

When Foltz was out of sight, Shirley sat down on the rock and lit a cigarette.

"Artie," she said, "you have to trust me. You have to promise you won't ever tell a soul about this."

"That you were fooling around with a German spy?"

"A *what*?"

"It's no use lying. I know darn well that guy is no veteran of Guadalcanal."

"All right, but he's no German spy, either, for Heaven's sake."

"Well, what the heck *is* he, then?"

"You mustn't ever tell. He's so ashamed."

"Is he some kind of criminal?"

Shirley shook her head, then she looked Artie right in the eyes.

"Clarence is Four-F," she said.

Artie knew she was telling the truth, or at least what Foltz had convinced her was the truth, but Artie smelled something fishy about it. He figured a guy who was classified 4-F in the Draft and couldn't go to War had to really have something terribly wrong, like be missing an arm or a leg or be so blind in both eyes he could only walk with a cane and a dog. The only 4-F guy he knew was Ribs O'Mahoney, and even though he could see all right and get around pretty good, at least he had a pretty bad limp.

"So what's wrong with the guy, anyway?" Artie asked suspiciously. "He sure can run fast, I'll tell you that."

"It's nothing you can see, that's what makes it so awful for him. People think a boy his age who's not in uniform is a slacker, a Draft-dodger. Unless of course they think he's already been in and discharged because of a wound. Which is why he pretends that's what happened."

"But what *did* happen? To make him Four-F?"

"Clarence has a punctured eardrum."

"He stole that!" Artie shouted, seeing through the phony story right away. "He copied it from Leo Durocher!"

"What in the world are you *talking* about?"

"Leo Durocher is Four-F because of a punctured eardrum. It was in all the magazines. Foltz must have read it and used it for his own excuse for not going in the Army!"

"Who's Leo Durocher?"

For a split second Artie thought Shirley was pulling his leg, but then he realized that smart as she was, she was still a girl, and so there were really important things she just didn't know about.

"Leo Durocher," Artie said patiently, "is the manager of the Brooklyn Dodgers."

"Well, that should show you that even real he-men can have punctured eardrums, and there's nothing they can do about it."

"But how do you know he isn't lying, just to dodge the Draft?"

"Because he *showed* me."

"His punctured eardrum?"

"No! You can't even see it. He showed me his letter from the Draft Board."

"Well, if it's true, what's he doing here? In Birney?"

"Running away. Everyone made fun of him. In his own hometown."

"Maybe his punctured eardrum's not the only thing wrong with him."

"What do you mean?"

"Maybe he's some kind of pre-vert."

"He's nothing of the kind. He's just very sensitive."

"You mean he's like a girl?"

"No! Lots of men are sensitive. Well, not lots of them, but the ones I care about. You are yourself. Sensitive. So is your brother, but he tries to cover it up, not to show it. When I saw that side of him, that's when I cared."

"You care about Foltz, then?"

"Yes. I worry about him. He's all bottled up inside."

"He must be pretty sad, I guess."

Shirley suddenly threw her cigarette away, only half-smoked. She got up and stamped her foot on it.

"He's lonely. I'm lonely too. Don't you see? We're *both* lonely."

She burst out crying and bent over, holding her face in her hands as she sobbed.

Artie stood up, feeling helpless, feeling like he was all thumbs. He squeezed his hands into fists and went to Shirley and placed a fist gently on her back, moving it a little ways up and down.

She sniffled and coughed, then straightened up and wiped at her eyes.

"I'm sorry," she said. "I just wish this horrible War was over. I don't know how long I can stand it."

"Don't worry," Artie said. "Everything will be fine."

He knew it would. It was up to him to see that it was, and he was going to do his duty.

4

THE first thing Artie had to do when he got back to
town was lie to Warren Tutlow. He was sorry he had
to do it, especially while he was sitting cross-legged
on the floor of Tutlow's room with the curtains drawn and
the candle in the Coke bottle lit, since they were supposed
to be exchanging true information as fellow counterspies,
but Artie knew the most important thing he had to do
was protect Shirley. He didn't want Tutlow snooping
around Foltz, for fear he'd find out the guy had anything
to do with Shirley.

"The poor guy is no kind of spy, German or otherwise,"
Artie said easily, since that part was true.

"So how come he pretends to be a wounded veteran of
Guadalcanal?"

Here came the hard part. Artie stared unblinking at the

flame of the candle so his eyes would get weird and not reveal he was lying.

"The funny thing is, he really *is*. He got shellshocked so bad they had to give him an honorable discharge, since he wasn't much good for anything anymore."

"Then how come he has the book about Guadalcanal with stuff underlined, if he really was there?"

"He got shellshocked so bad he can't remember what happened, so he reads the book over and over to try to remember stuff."

"Wow—a real amnesia victim!"

"That's not all. He got a case of the jungle rot, too."

"Ugh! You think you caught any off him?"

Tutlow scooted back on the floor away from Artie.

"I hope not, but I sure wouldn't want to hang around the guy much."

"Then who was the girl, anyway?"

"Remember Beverly Lattimore?"

"You mean Roy's old girl friend?"

"Yeah, well, I guess she's been about everybody's old girl friend."

"And now she's Foltz's?"

"I guess she feels sorry for the guy, him being shell-shocked and all."

"Holy Moly. If next year's football team never wins a game, it'll mean all the guys have got jungle rot!"

"I guess that's the kind of stuff that happens in Wartime."

Tutlow blew out the candle and pulled the curtains back, letting in the sunlight.

"I got the heebie-jeebies," he said. "Let's go play some HORSE."

"Good idea."

Taking care of Tutlow was one thing, but handling Foltz was another matter. Even though he was nothing but a

kinny guy with blotchy skin and a punctured eardrum, he
was bigger and older than Artie, and strong enough to
make a good tackle on him and just about twist his arm out
of the socket. Artie figured the best thing to use on him was
psychology, but he wasn't sure exactly what kind, and he
couldn't get anyone's advice without spilling the beans
about Foltz being too darn friendly with Shirley. Finally
he figured he would just go see the guy and lay his cards on
the table. His ace would be the threat of exposing Clarence
Foltz for what he was—a 4-F failure who was besmirching
the good name of the wounded veterans of Guadalcanal by
pretending he was one of them.

Artie put off his duty for more than a week, thinking
maybe if he waited a little while he'd come up with some
better psychological strategy to use on Foltz, or, better
still, that the impostor would just leave town on his own.

No such luck. When Artie went to the Strand one night
to slip Shirley a piece of Mom's angel food cake through
the ticket window, he poked his head in the door of the
lobby and there was Foltz in his spic and span uniform,
standing at rigid Attention by the ticket box like he was
some kind of Russian General in his Red Army outfit.

The next afternoon Artie got up his gumption, put on his
Boy Scout uniform to make his visit more official, and
marched right over to Miss Winger's Boardinghouse.

Miss Winger wasn't home, so he went right on up to the
room he knew Foltz was living in, and rapped sharply on
the door.

Foltz was wearing wrinkled pajamas and a moldy old
bathrobe, even though it was late in the afternoon. Artie
wondered if he'd been jacking off while he thought about
doing pre-verted stuff to Shirley Colby.

"Oh," said Foltz. "It's you."

He didn't ask Artie to come in but he held the door open
so he could.

Artie just nodded and went inside. Foltz started plucking books off the unmade bed so there'd be some place to sit down, but Artie just lowered himself to the floor and folded his legs into Indian pow-wow position.

Foltz shrugged and went over to a hotplate where something was cooking in a pot.

"Want some beans?" he asked.

"No, thank you."

Foltz picked up the pot, got a fork, and started eating the beans right out of the pot.

"Supper," he said. "What can I do for you?"

"Well, the best thing you could do, really, would be go somewhere else."

"You mean leave Town?"

"You hit the nail on the head."

Foltz ate some beans and then waved the fork toward Artie, like he was leading a band.

"And what will you do if I don't, officer?"

If Foltz was going to get smart, Artie was going to lay his cards right on the table with no ifs and buts.

"I'm afraid I'll have to expose you."

Foltz made his croaking little laugh.

"To who?"

"The United States Marines."

"For what?"

"Impersonating a veteran of Guadalcanal, and messing around with the girl friend of a Marine who really was there, and who is still out fighting for his country in the South Pacific."

"That's your privilege," Foltz said. "But it you ask me, the Marines have bigger fish to fry these days."

Foltz sounded as jaunty about it as Jimmy Cagney, and Artie decided to get him where it hurt.

"Too bad you're not man enough to be out there helping them," he said.

Then he was sorry.

Foltz started quivering, like he was going to go to pieces right then and there. He put the pot back down on the hotplate, turned, and went to the window. He just stood there, staring out, his back toward Artie.

"I should have known," he said. "Kids are the worst."

"Well, you asked for it," Artie said kind of feebly.

Foltz turned around suddenly and stared at him, the blotches on his face getting redder.

"I didn't ask for a punctured eardrum I never even knew I had till I went for my goddamn physical," he said.

"I guess not," Artie said.

"You think I wouldn't give my ass to be out there right now with your brother, doing my part? I tried to *join* the damn Marines. They turned me down. Semper Fidelis! Ha."

Before Artie could think what to say, Foltz started crying.

Artie didn't know what to do.

He just sat there, feeling crummy.

The crying started all at once and then, after Foltz had angrily clawed his hands at his face, the crying stopped. He brushed the moldy sleeve of the bathrobe over his eyes and then went back and picked up the pot of beans and started pacing the room and eating as he talked.

"You know what they did at the Draft Board when I asked if there was anything I could do, any kind of operation I could have to fix the damn thing? They laughed. I should get a medal, kid. I have given more laughs to more people in Wartime than Bob Hope with all his jokes. Me, I don't have to tell jokes. I *am* a joke."

He told how his whole hometown had laughed at him. The awful thing was they had laughed at him even before because he wasn't any good at sports and never went out for the teams and spent his time reading poems and painting pictures of trees and flowers and he wanted more than anything to join the Army and prove to the world once and for all he was a man and instead it was proved that in fact there was something really wrong with him all along; he must have been born being chicken.

"Chickie," they started calling him.

"Chickie Foltz."

Girls made fun of him. When he came along they sang the popular song:

> They're either too young or too old,
> They're either too gray or too grassy green . . .

But Foltz wasn't too young or too old, he was just too damaged to be of any use. That's what he felt like anyway, and he felt like it even more when the girls sang the part real loud at him that said:

> What's good is in the Ar-my
> What's left will never harm me!

Think what it must be like to be the kind of guy who couldn't even harm a girl! That meant you couldn't make them fall in love with you, much less make love to them. You were nothing, lower than a worm.

Foltz ran.

He dumped his books and paints in one suitcase and threw some clothes in another one and hitched out of town, carrying with him not only his damn damaged eardrum but the telltale Selective Service Card that every male (man or not) had to have on him at all times, the Card that bore the stamp of his official stigma: 4-F.

He hitched to Chicago, thinking he could be anonymous and left alone in a big city, that maybe he could even find a girl there who'd believe he'd been wounded on Guadal-canal when he told her the real-life stories he'd learned from reading *Guadalcanal Diary*, but the hitch was, he didn't have a uniform, and a twenty-year-old guy in Chicago without a uniform in 1943 might as well have been a leper fresh out of a leper colony. There were guys in uniform everywhere, pairs and bunches and gangs of them, sailors from the Great Lakes Naval Training Center, soldiers and Air Corps guys from camps and bases in Illinois, Iowa, and Michigan, Marines back home on leave from the East and West coasts to see their folks and girl friends, all of them wearing some uniform, seal of approval, safe and confident, clothed in the colors of war and service, surrounded wherever they went by the "V-girls" and "cuddle bunnies" who were ga-ga over any man in military dress, hot lips puckering and parting to please, please take me, I'm yours, for the night, the weekend, the forty-eight-hour pass, please! Even short guys were loved if they had on a uniform; they were thought to be cute and cuddly and extra brave for putting their little bodies on the line, going into battle along with everyone else, regular fellows who cocked their caps at a jaunty angle and walked with a strut and made everyone laugh and cheer when they got a real big luscious blonde on their lap, kicking her legs in hot delight and circling her long thin arms around the game little trooper.

Foltz got a job as a waiter in a fancy restaurant where the dinner was actually stuck on a sort of sword and soaked in oil and you had to set the food on fire before you served it to the customers. He had to wear a costume with silk knickers and knee socks, and he knew people stared at him not because of the outfit but because he was the only young guy wearing one. Poor excuse for a uniform. When he wasn't at work he stayed in his room reading poems, or went to movies where he sat in the safety of darkness watching the stories of other people's lives on the screen, but in Chicago there were always lots of servicemen at the movies, soldiers and sailors with their buddies having a good old time, or worse, with girls, holding hands and legs and boobs, necking and breathing in hard, heavy gasps, making it hard to concentrate on the cowboys chasing the Indians or the gangsters blasting the coppers up on the screen. Once at the fancy restaurant a drunken Air Corps Colonel with a girl who looked just like Lana Turner told Foltz he would make a good mascot for the French Foreign Legion in a getup like that and the girl laughed, her wet red lips spreading wide over gleaming white teeth, and after Foltz set their dinner on fire for them he turned around and went to the kitchen and shucked off his clothes and quit, knowing he had to run again.

This time he went to small towns where there weren't gangs of servicemen coming on passes and leaves to have a great time, towns with no attractions, off the beaten path, towns that rolled up the sidewalks at ten o'clock when the movie was over, towns where nobody knew Clarence Foltz and would believe, for a while, that he really was a wounded veteran of Guadalcanal. When they started to quiz him too closely about the actual nature of the wound, or what it was really like on Guadalcanal, he'd leave in the night and move on.

When he fled like that from a little town called Loogootee, in Indiana, a John Deere salesman gave him a ride to Birney, Illinois. He went straight to the only movie house, the Strand, where he saw *Five Graves to Cairo* and asked for a job. The regular Usher was leaving the next week for the Army and Foltz took his place.

Then he met the beautiful, lonely girl who worked in the ticket booth, the only girl who didn't make fun of him, who listened to him, who took long walks in the woods with him.

So here he was, and here he would stay.

Foltz had finished his pitiful supper, and he put the empty pot back on the hotplate.

"So go ahead and expose me," he said. "I'm tired of running."

Artie stood up from his pow-wow position, remembering the old Oriental saying, "He who laughs last, laughs best."

"There's one thing you're forgetting, Foltz," he said. "My brother."

"Don't worry, I know she loves him. I know she'll marry him when he comes home. I don't mind playing second fiddle."

"But Roy would mind. He'd kill you."

Foltz jerked the closet open and grabbed his Usher outfit off a hanger.

"If you'll excuse me now, I have to 'get into uniform.' "

He croaked his harsh laugh.

"Shirley just feels sorry for you," Artie said.

The blotches on Foltz's red face got brighter, but he didn't say anything. He just yanked his moldy bathrobe off and started unbuttoning the grubby pajamas.

Artie got the hell out of there, not wanting to see the nude body of the pre-vert.

The only thing left to do was call the guy's bluff. Expose him for what he was to the whole town, starting with Mr. Risley, the owner of the Strand.

First, though, it was only fair to warn Shirley.

Artie was determined that he wouldn't let her talk him out of it. As much as he liked her, he knew that right now she was under the influence of being a girl and couldn't help herself. Even though what he was going to do might make Shirley both sad and mad, he knew he was doing the best thing for her, as well as for Roy and America. He had thought the whole thing over for three days and nights, during which he tossed and turned and slept only fitfully, wakened by dreams of bombing raids and refugees. He was so tired in school he had to pinch himself to keep his eyes open. Before he went to Shirley's he took a cold shower and made himself a hot cup of Ovaltine for strength.

Shirley came to the door herself, looking all keyed up.

"Just the person I wanted to see!" she said, and grabbed his arm, leading him right to the living room where Mrs. Colby sat with her fingers pressed to her temples like she was trying to think of the answer to the $64 Question on "Dr. I.Q."

"You remember Donna Modjeski, don't you, Artie? Tell Mother about her."

"Donna Modjeski's real neat," Artie said. "She was a cheerleader."

Mrs. Colby glared at Shirley.

"You are not 'a Modjeski,' " she said. "You are 'a Colby.' "

It sounded like she was talking about breeds of cows, like telling someone, "You are 'a Holstein.' "

Shirley went on like she didn't even hear it.

"Well, Artie, Donna Modjeski is working in a defense plant in Indianapolis. Building airplanes. Isn't that exciting?"

"Sure! That's really neat!"

Mrs. Colby kept concentrating.

"No daughter of mine," she said, "is going to be a 'Rosie the Riveter.' "

"No one mentioned riveting," Shirley said. "I'm talking about *wiring*."

Mrs. Colby squinted.

"Factory work is factory work," she said.

"Listen to this!" Shirley said.

She grabbed a magazine off the couch that was folded to a certain page, and began to read.

" '. . . the work is exacting and tedious, but women's nimble fingers are adept at such jobs.' "

She held up the page of the magazine like it was evidence.

"That's *wiring* they're talking about!" she said.

Mrs. Colby sighed.

"Propaganda in Wartime is not only used by the enemy," she said.

Shirley flung the magazine onto the couch.

"It's not propaganda—it's the truth! It's also the truth that out of six hundred and thirty-two occupations essential to War Production, there are only fifty-seven of them that can't be done by women."

"There are some women who will do anything," her mother said. "There always were and there always will be."

"*Some* women! Mother, there are half a million women working in War Jobs."

"Heck, yes!" Artie said. "Miss Winger has this niece who works in a Navy Shipyard in Boston."

"I'm not surprised," Mrs. Colby said.

"Mother, you can't just stick your head in the sand. Things are changing."

"I bet Miss Winger's niece is as nice as Miss Winger," Artie said, "and that's about as nice as you can get."

"Times may change, but values remain the same," Mrs. Colby said, ignoring Artie's comeback. "Of course in Wartime, standards are lowered, and indeed there are women who are only too glad for an excuse to go around with dirty fingernails and no makeup."

"For Heaven's sake, Mother, don't you even read the ads?"

"I am not in the habit of perusing the Employment Section."

"I don't mean *those* kind of ads. I mean the ones for soap and hand lotion, where the women in War Plants tell

how they use Pond's or Hind's or something and stay looking nice to keep up their morale."

Mrs. Colby stood up.

"I won't hear any more of this nonsense. I'm going upstairs and lie down. And I don't want you hiking off somewhere with your little friend. I want you here when your
father comes home."

"We'll just be in the kitchen," Shirley said. "I want to
make Artie some lemonade."

Mrs. Colby walked out of the room like nobody else was
even there.

Shirley led Artie to the kitchen and he leaned against the
stove while she started slicing up lemons with brisk effi-
ciency.

"I've got to get out of here," she said in a low voice just
above a whisper. "Out of Birney."

"Because of Foltz, you mean?"

Shirley nodded.

"It's going too far. I care for him. Love him, I guess. I
can't help it."

"You mean you don't love Roy anymore?"

"Of *course* I do! That's why I want to get away from
Clarence."

"You mean you're in love with two guys at the same
time?"

"Of course not. I can't help loving Clarence, but I'm not
in love with him. "I'm *in love* with Roy. It's not the same
thing."

"I can make Foltz leave town. I'm going to tell on him."

"No! It'll just make a terrible mess. Besides, I *want* to go
to Indianapolis. I can live with Donna Modjeski and work
in the War Plant. I've got to do something *real* or I'll lose
my mind, I know I will."

"But your folks won't let you."

"If they won't give me their permission, I'm going anyway. I'm free, white, and eighteen. I've made up my mind."

"So what if he follows you? Foltz."

"I won't tell him where I'm going. I've made up my mind about that, too."

"When are you going to go?"

"Soon as I can. Next week, maybe. On the Greyhound." She started squeezing the lemons with grim determination.

"Wow," Artie said in the low, conspiratorial tone that Shirley was using. "This is really something!"

"Yes," she said. "Finally."

5

A RTIE stayed home on Saturday night instead of going to Ben Vickman's party. He knew darn well the whole "party," the records and dancing and Cokes and potato chips were just an excuse for playing spin-the-milk-bottle, and he sure didn't want to spend the evening watching Fishy Mitchelman smooch it up with Caroline Spingarn. Besides that, the kids were still kidding him about what happened at Caroline's party. When bigmouth Vickman invited Artie he said, "You can come if you don't tip anyone over—including yourself!" Everyone got a big yuk out of it, and at recess the guys grabbed each other when they saw Artie coming and pretended to "dip," making high-pitched screams that were supposed to be an imitation of Marilyn Pettigrew when she was felled by Artie's over-zealous embrace.

Artie told Vickman he was busy studying for a merit badge in Botany.

He told himself he had too many serious things on his mind, what with worrying about what was going to happen with Shirley, Foltz, Roy, and the War, to mess around with seventh grade social life.

He told his folks he had a crick in his back and just wanted to lie on the davenport and read through Mom's new magazines.

Mom and Dad had the radio tuned to "The National Barn Dance," and they were hopping and twirling around to the music of the "Barn Dance" regulars, Lulu Belle and Scotty, Arkie the Arkansas Woodchopper, and the Hoosier Hotshots. Mom and Dad were real giggly because it was Saturday night and they were having their Pabst Blue Ribbons along with a big bowl of popcorn. It used to make Artie feel kind of funny that his folks got a little bit tipsy on beer most Saturday nights, but then he saw this ad in a magazine where the Brewing Industry Foundation explained that "A cool, refreshing glass of beer—a moment of relaxation—in trying times like these, they too help to keep morale up," and he realized it was all right. It sure was better than the nights when they sat around after supper looking glum and worrying about Roy.

Artie was only skimming through the Ladies' Home Journal while his mind kept jumping back to wondering how the heck he could help Shirley convince her mother it was okay for nice girls to work in a War Plant. He knew she was bound and determined to do it anyway, but she'd feel a lot better if she got her mother to approve, so she wouldn't just have to sneak out and hop the Greyhound.

He stopped flipping pages when he came to this ad that showed a nice girl who was doing exactly what Shirley wanted to do. The ad, for Pond's hand lotion, told the story

of "Hilda," who said: "Dick enlisted two months before
Pearl Harbor—I wanted to be doing something necessary,
too, so I found *my* job helping to build planes. I get up at 4
A.M. and don't get back home till 4 P.M. It seemed *outlandish* at first, but now I like it. I do have to watch out for my
complexion, though . . ."

Artie figured Mrs. Colby might be impressed that
"Hilda" was still worrying about her complexion, which
meant she was being ladylike even though she worked in a
factory.

Artie ripped the page from the magazine, and Mom
turned around to look.

"Hey! You tearing up my new *Journal*?"

"Must be a pinup," Dad said.

"Not in the *Journal*," Mom said.

"Come on, it's just an old ad," Artie said, folding it
quickly and sticking it in his pocket so he wouldn't have
to explain anything.

Mom came toward him, holding out her hand.

"The ads have stories on the back of them sometimes,
and I haven't read this month's stories yet."

"There wasn't any story on it," Artie said.

"Then let me see."

"I swear."

Dad took a swig from his glass of beer and gave Artie a
wink.

"Some of those gals in the ads now, they got gams as
good as Grable."

"Aw, come on," Artie said, feeling his face get hot.

He hated when his Dad talked about gals and gams and
things to do with sex, especially when he winked.

Mom was still holding her hand out.

"Artie, I want to see what you tore out."

"I need it. For school."

"You can have it back as soon as I look at it."

"Novschmovzkapop," Artie said disgustedly, taking the folded page from his pocket and handing it over.

"No language, son," Dad said.

"That's from the funny papers, Dad. The guy who's always saying 'Novschmovzkapop.' It's the strip where the little girl holds the hanky up to her kid brother's nose and says, 'Now blow.' "

Dad took a swig of beer and rolled his eyes toward the ceiling.

"Carry me back to ole Virginny," he said.

Mom had unfolded the page and was looking it over, her brow furrowing in puzzlement.

" 'Dick enlisted two months before Pearl Harbor'?" she read out loud.

"It's just a crummy ad," Artie said, reaching to take the page back.

"Ad for what?" Dad asked, and came to look.

"Oh, brother," Artie sighed. "I guess it's a federal case now."

" '. . . so I found *my* job helping to build planes,' " Mom read.

Dad looked over her shoulder and continued, saying " 'I get up at four A.M. and don't get back home till four P.M.' Who is this, 'Rosie the Riveter'?"

" '. . . It seemed *outlandish* at first, but now I like it . . .' " Mom went on.

Dad grabbed the page away and said in a high voice, imitating a girl, " 'I do have to watch out for my complexion, though.' "

Mom grabbed the page back.

"Hey, you're messing it up!" Artie said.

"What's this got to do with school?" Mom asked.

"Lemme have it. Please?"

"I will if you tell me what it's for."

"Okay," Artie said. "It's for Shirley."

Dad put down his glass of beer and Mom turned off "The National Barn Dance" and came and sat down by Artie next to the davenport.

"Shirley wants to do what the lady in the ad is doing," Artie explained. "Work in a War Plant, making airplanes. So I thought I'd show it to her. That's all."

"All what?" Mom asked.

"All there is to it."

His mother kind of looked at him sideways, like maybe there was more, which of course there was. Artie had to be real careful not to give away the part about Shirley wanting to get away from 4-F Foltz, and he told his brain to be *on guard*. He figured he wasn't lying, he was telling the actual truth, but just leaving out the part that would ruin Shirley's life if anyone else knew about it.

"Where?" Mom asked.

"What?"

"Where would she work in a War Plant?"

"Wherever they have one. Donna Modjeski is working in one in Indianapolis, where they make planes."

"It's a pretty far piece to Indianapolis," Dad said.

"Anyway, her mother doesn't want her to," Artie said. "That's the whole story."

He was proud of his craftiness, telling the truth as far as it went, but leaving out the part about Foltz. He figured he could hold his own in an enemy interrogation, as long as they didn't threaten to beat his privates to jelly, and only wanted to match wits.

His mother put her hand to her mouth, covering a grin.

"Marcelline Colby must be having kittens," she said.

"Speaking of kittens, let's not get catty," his Dad said. "I doubt you'd be much more thrilled than Miz Colby if you had a daughter wanted to go off and work in a War Plant."

"I'd root for her, that's what I'd do. I'd pack her a nice lunch in her lunch bucket and send her off to make B-Seventeens."

"Not your own daughter, you wouldn't."

"Shirley's my daughter-in-law, or will be, and I'm behind her a hundred percent."

"In-law's not the same. Blood is thicker than water."

"Blood nothing. I'd do it myself it we had a War Plant here."

"You'd do *what*? Rivet?"

"As good as any 'Rosie.' "

"You'd get that pretty braid of yours caught in some machine."

"I'd wear me a turban. It's all the style now."

"Since when did you care a hoot about style?"

"If it kept my hair from getting caught in a machine."

"Well, you don't have to worry, they aren't gonna make any B-Seventeens in Birney."

"Maybe I'll just up and go off with Shirley to where they do. Couple of working girls."

"You already got your job, woman. And foolin' aside, I don't see Shirley Colby weldin' wings on bombers."

"Why not? Other girls do."

"Must be the kind built like a Mack Truck. Shirley, she's not only small, she's delicate-like."

"But, Dad, she'd be good for wiring," Artie said. "All the articles say 'the nimble fingers of women' are good at that, and you don't have to be big or anything."

Mom put her hand on Dad's chest and started tickling her fingers around.

"I got nimble fingers myself," she said.

"You just keep 'em busy on *me*, not some B-Seventeen."

He poked her and she giggled and then they were nuzzling again and Artie went back to the magazine figuring the crisis was past for now, and then the phone rang.

Everyone stopped to listen, counting two longs and one short, which was their ring, and Mom got up to answer.

Dad yawned, and rubbed his stomach.

"Wonder who's calling on Saturday night," he said.

"Hello? Yes, this is Mrs. Joseph Garber. Who's this?"

Her face went suddenly pale and she put her other hand on the phone, gripping it tightly.

"You want me to what?" she asked.

Dad stood up, squinting at her and cocking his head to one side like he was trying to figure out the call.

"Who is it wants something?"

Mom pressed the phone against her chest.

"The Red Cross," she said. "Wants me to sit down."

Then she fainted.

Dad sprang across the room to her and Artie jumped off the davenport and grabbed the phone off the floor.

"Hello, this is Arthur Garber, son of Mr. and Mrs. Joseph Garber, brother of Corporal Roy—"

Dad yanked the phone away from Artie with his left hand, still holding his right hand under Mom's head.

"This is Joe Garber. I'm already sitting down, so tell me whatever you have to."

Artie held his breath.

"*Wounded* in action," Dad said. "Then he's alive? He's all right?"

Mom opened her eyes and pulled herself up to her knees, holding on to Dad.

"'Shell fragmentation,'" Dad said. "Yes? . . . But he won't lose it? . . . Thank God. . . . When? . . . Yes, I understand. Fine. Thank you. Thank you very much."

Dad put the phone down and pulled Mom against him, holding her tight.

"It's all right, it's all right."

"How bad?" she asked, digging her fingers into Dad's back.

"He was wounded in the thigh. He won't lose the leg."

Dad took hold of Mom's arms and pried them away, so he could look at her.

"He's coming home. He's on his way to San Diego, to the Naval Hospital. He'll have some skin grafts, and then he'll be home."

"When?"

"Maybe only weeks. A matter of weeks."

"Wahoo!" Artie yelled.

Mom sank back on the floor.

Artie jumped up and grabbed a pillow from the davenport and lifted Mom's feet up onto it.

"What are you doing?" she asked, raising up again.

"Putting your feet up is treatment for shock. I learned it in Scouts."

"I don't need my feet up," she said, pulling her legs back and then sitting up on them. "I need to be on my knees."

"What's that for?" Artie asked.

"For giving thanks to God," she said.

She bowed her head, and Dad and Artie scooted around so they too were on their knees beside her.

The three of them knelt there on the living room rug, each one saying his own prayer in silence. After a while Dad reached out one hand to Mom and one hand to Artie and they were linked, together, in thanks, and then Dad quietly said, "Amen," and they all stood up and hugged.

"To think," Mom said, " 'a matter of weeks.' "

Artie suddenly rushed to the closet and yanked out his coat.

"I gotta go tell Shirley," he said.

Mom and Dad both started talking at him.

"Be careful how—"

"Button up before you—"

That was all he heard before he was out the door.

The ticket booth at the Strand was dark. Artie went in the lobby and looked around quickly. The only person there was the Usher, but it wasn't Foltz. Billy Shavers, this tubby kid who played snare drum in the Band, was stuffed in the red and black outfit, one of the gold buttons open at the stomach, letting the white of his shirt poke out. He was eating a Mars Bar and reading a Captain Marvel.

"Hey, Billy, you the Usher now?"

Without looking up, Billy pointed to his gold-buttoned, bursting jacket.

"I ain't Admiral Nimitz."

"So did Foltz leave town, or what?"

"All I know is Old Man Risley offered me Usher, four bits an hour."

"Hey, Billy, that's great! Congratulations and salutations!"

Artie figured it was all some kind of Wartime miracle, like a story in the *Saturday Evening Post*. Just as Roy is coming home a wounded hero, his 4-F challenger has skulked away in defeat. Probably he gave up on making out with a loyal girl like Shirley; maybe Shirley finally just laid down the law and told him to get lost.

"So Billy, did Shirley Colby go home? She's not in the booth."

Billy pointed a chocolate-stained finger to a coat hanging on the door of the ticket booth.

"Coat's still here."

"Maybe she's watching the movie?"

"Dunno."

"Well, is it okay if I go in and see the end while I wait for her?"

Billy shrugged.

"Madame Curie discovers radium is how it ends."

"Well, I'll go look. If you see Shirley, will you tell her I'm in there, and got something real big to tell her?"

"How big?" Billy asked, stuffing the last of the Mars Bar down his gullet, "Six inches?"

"You always got your mind in the gutter?"

"Takes one to call one."

Artie shook his head in disgust and walked into the darkened movie. He slid into the back row and sank down in his seat. Greer Garson was Madame Curie, working away in the laboratory, wearing a white coat like scientists and druggists have, and her husband, Walter Pidgeon, was helping her out. They both looked pretty pooped, probably from staying up all night year after year trying to discover radium. It was hard to get charged up about it if you missed most of the movie, so Artie just leaned back and looked at the screen, not even concentrating. He had run all the way over like it was the hundred-yard dash, and he figured he was even more pooped than Walter Pidgeon was in the movie. He closed his eyes.

Shirley Colby was wearing a white lab coat, and pouring some bubbly potion into a test tube. She wasn't in the radium lab, but the weird, secret kind with all the zigzaggy fiendish modernistic machinery where they always brought Frankenstein back to life again. There was a clap of thunder, a streak of lightning, and the guy who was strapped to the table broke his bonds and started stalking toward Shirley, but instead of being Frankenstein, the guy was Clarence Foltz. Shirley screamed, Foltz let out a yelp, and then the two of them were moaning and talking some kind of gibberish.

Artie blinked, and sat up. It was dark, and he was the only one left in the theater. Evidently Billy Shavers didn't even know yet the Usher was supposed to make sure that everyone was gone when the last show was over.

Or was it really over?

The screen was blank, but there were sounds coming from somewhere, much like the moans and gibberish he had heard in his dream. He pinched himself to make sure he really was awake.

He was.

The sounds seemed to be coming from up above where the movie projector was. Maybe Old Man Risley was playing some movie for himself with only the sound and not the picture.

Artie sat still and listened.

"Ohhhhhh," went the low voice.

"Noooo," said the high one.

"Huh?"

"*Here.*"

"Where?"

"Ohhhhhhhhh."

"Go—*on.*"

"Eeeeeeeeeee!"

"Wait!"

"Shir-leeeeeeeeee!"

Artie stuck his fingers in his ears. He got up, stumbling, and plunged through the door to the empty lobby. He blinked, looked around, seeing only the folding chair where tubby Shavers had been, and the wadded-up wrapper from the Mars Bar lying on the floor. Artie reeled out, and leaned against the building. He was breathing hard, his heart pounding. He couldn't think, didn't want to try. He just stood there, like a watchman or guard, holding the building up, his hands shoved deep and clenched in his pockets. The street was empty. Finally Shirley came out, alone.

"Where's Foltz?" Artie said.

"What are you doing here?"

"Is he still in there?"

"Clarence? He's closing up."

"How come, if he's not the Usher anymore?"

"He runs the projector now. Why? What are you doing here?"

"I heard you. And him."

"What do you mean? Where?"

"In there."

Shirley looked puzzled for a second, and then her face seemed to collapse. She covered it with her hands.

Artie just stood there.

Foltz came out.

He looked at Shirley and then at Artie, and sprang at him, grabbing his collar, yanking it.

"You goddamn little sneak!"

"Don't!" Shirley hissed.

She grabbed Foltz and pulled him away from Artie.

"Goddamn you," Artie said quietly. "Goddamn you both."

Shirley took a step toward him, like she was walking on ice that might break underneath her.

"I'm leaving tomorrow," she said. "Tonight was the last time—I mean, that I'll ever see Clarence."

"You won't see Roy then, either," Artie said.

Shirley flinched, like he'd slapped her, and then she took a deep breath, and nodded.

"You're going to tell him. What happened tonight."

Artie shook his head.

"No," he said. "Never."

"What do you mean then? That I won't see Roy. Artie? Artie!"

She fell to the sidewalk in front of Artie, grabbing him around the waist, squeezing so hard he thought she might crush his bones.

"Stop!" Artie yelled. "Listen!"

"Oh, Jesus God," said Foltz.

Shirley was sobbing and choking as she spilled out words.

"Don't tell me he's dead don't tell me they killed him don't tell me don't let it be true oh God oh please—"

Artie grabbed her arms and yanked them to keep her from crushing him.

"He's alive, he's only wounded in the leg, he's coming home."

"Oh my God oh my God oh thank God oh Jesus Christ in Heaven thank you—"

Shirley pitched forward, curling into a ball on the sidewalk.

Artie knelt down beside her and Foltz came and knelt on the other side and laid his hand gently on her head.

"It's all right," said Foltz. "I'm going. I'll go. Tonight. Now. Forever."

Shirley was trembling so hard her teeth were knocking together and Foltz quickly leaned down and kissed her, quickly, and then he stood up and looked at Artie.

"Forget I was ever here," he said. "I never will be again. I swear."

Artie nodded.

"Is that a deal?" Foltz asked.

"Yes," Artie said.

Foltz made a crooked smile, but it wasn't sarcastic, it was even kind of brave, and he straightened his shoulders.

"Semper Fidelis," he said, and then he turned and was gone.

Artie pulled Shirley up and hooked one of her arms over his shoulder and walked her home like someone wounded.

6

"Our Father, who art in Heaven, thank you for bringing Roy home today from the War, and let him not be too banged up in the leg or shell-shocked in the head. I pray that him and Shirley will have a swell time and be madly in love, and Roy will never find out about Foltz. Also, I pray that Foltz, wherever he is, will find a nice girl to love him so he can settle down and stop running all over the place. Thank Thee for all this stuff, Amen."

Artie opened his eyes and got up from his knees. He went to his bedroom window and made the Sign of the Cross, like the old Christian heroes did, just for good measure, vowing he would never slack off from worshiping God. There were bright streaks of orange in the sky, like banners, and Artie took it as a sign that this was going to be a great day and everything would go right. He had butterflies in his stomach, like you got from being nervous before a big ball game. Even though it was his brother and not himself coming home from the War, Artie felt this was the biggest day yet in his own life.

Artie had been at school when Roy called from the Naval Hospital in San Diego to say the skin grafts had been successful and he'd be coming home in one piece, with just a cane to help him walk. He said he had been the luckiest guy in the world because the shell fragments that hit him had missed "the femoral artery" so even though he bled a lot and had to have transfusions, he's come up smelling like roses. If everything healed right he'd eventually be almost as good as new, with just a big scar for "a souvenir." The best thing of all was he wouldn't be sent back to fight in the South Pacific; he'd be stationed at the Marine Base at Parris Island, South Carolina, to help train new recruits for combat.

The Garbers and Shirley got to stand in the place of honor on the train station platform to welcome Roy home, along with the High School Band, the VFW Fife & Drum Corps, and Alben Smalley, a dapper guy with a mustache who owned the Birney Lumber & Supply and was also the Mayor. School was let out and most of the stores on Main Street were closed so everyone could turn out.

> Off we go, into the wild blue yonder,
> Climbing high, into the sun . . .

The Band and Fife & Drum Corps were saving the "Marine Hymn" for Roy's arrival, so everyone was singing the "Army Air Corps" song along with them to get in the spirit of things. Shirley was all dolled up in a pink dress and a pair of white heels and matching hat like women wear to church, which showed she was really grown-up now and

not like the high school cheerleaders who were hopping
and prancing in front of the crowd in time to the music,
their beautiful bare legs twinkling in the soft April sun.

> Down we dive, spouting our flames from under,
> Off with one helluva roar . . .

Artie peeked back over his shoulder to look at the
crowd, wondering if Caroline Spingarn was watching him
be the brother of a hero. He couldn't see her right off but
he knew she was there; everyone was there, even Mr. and
Mrs. Colby were somewhere, probably way at the back,
being above it all. Mom had invited them to stand right up
on the platform along with Shirley, but Mrs. Colby said she
didn't think it was "fitting" and went on some more about
how Shirley and Roy weren't officially engaged like in
Emily Post. She didn't even think it was right for Shirley to
stand with the Garbers but Shirley put her foot down on
that one.

> We live in fame, or go down in flame,
> Hey!—Nothing can stop the Army Air Corps!

There were shouts and cheers when the song was over
and Mr. Goodleaf raised his baton again to strike up another one but just then the old familiar whistle of the 10:52
hooted out of the distance and everyone pushed closer to
the track, looking down the long line of rails to see the tiny
dot of the engine as it first came into view. Shirley grabbed
Artie's hand so hard he thought she might crush through
the bone.

"He's coming," she said.

"Darn tootin'," Artie gasped.

Steaming and hissing and clanging, the train pulled
alongside the station, its iron wheels screeching and grind-

ing to a stop. Mr. Goodleaf had his baton raised, waiting
for the moment Roy appeared. An old lady got off with a
basket, taking each step like it was the biggest deal of her
life, while the crowd strained anxiously to catch the first
glimpse of the hero. The old lady was followed by a gum-
chewing man with a briefcase who looked like some kind of
salesman. He grinned and waved at the crowd, like it was
all for him, and there were some nervous boos and hisses,
and calls of "Hey, Roy!" "Where's Roy?" "We want Roy!"

Shirley tightened her crunch on Artie's hand.

"What if he's not on it?" she whispered.

"He is—he's gotta be," Artie said.

"Maybe they have to carry him?"

The bell clanged and the whistle hooted; steam puffed
out from the belly of the train as it made ready to start
again. Artie's Dad charged up to the steps of the car that
the lady and man had got off of, like he was going on board
to see what had happened to Roy, but just then a figure
appeared at the top step, a tall, gaunt man with a cane,
wearing not the fancy dress blues with the red stripe down
the leg, but the plain forest green uniform of the United
States Marines. He was a Corporal. The Band struck up
"From the Halls of Montezuma," and the Marine came
down another step, and you could see his face. It looked
something like Roy, except it was so dark tan and weather-
beaten, and the eyes so deep and sunken and glazed that it
looked like the face of some hardened old veteran, a guy
who'd been fighting on far-flung beaches and storming up
enemy hillsides since he was born, an old guy at least thirty
if he was a day. For a second Artie thought the veteran
must have been the guy who was bringing Roy home, helping him down the steps with his crutches or something, but
then he came down another step and the corners of his
mouth moved; it wasn't really a smile but more like some-

thing hurt, and he looked around at the crowd and blinked, like he had made a mistake and was getting off at the wrong stop, but Mom yelled "Roy!" and Dad reached his hand up and the Marine took it and moved on down to the platform as the train huffed and rumbled, moving away, and it was Roy all right, or anyway, the guy who used to be Roy.

Mom and Dad hugged him and Roy held his arms out, still carrying the cane in one hand, bending slightly, like a puppet whose limbs were too stiff and straight to actually wrap in a hug but did their best. Artie ran up and grabbed Roy around the waist, just squeezing, and he felt the old familiar hand on his head, pushing back the wide-brimmed Scout hat, but instead of tousling his hair and rubbing the old knuckles in his scalp, the big hand lay flat and tentative, not even mussing the hair, just barely touching, the way you would hold your hand above a hot stove.

> . . . first to fight our country's ba-a-ttles,
> And to keep our honor clean . . .

Artie's hat fell backward and the hand pulled away from his head. He stepped down to get his hat, and saw Shirley standing there staring, not moving, her eyes wide and frightened, her hands holding the hat on the back of her head as if to keep it from falling off. Roy took a step toward Shirley. Then she ran to him, throwing her arms around him like she was going to tackle him, her body moving into his so hard he dropped his cane, and he pressed his stiff arms into the sides of her pink dress, managing to get his hands against her back, the two of them holding and rocking slightly so it looked like they both might tip over and fall in a heap but they held, standing, clutched.

We are proud to bear the ti-i-tle,
Of United States Ma-rine!

The crowd broke into a roar at the end of the song, and
the Birney cheerleaders bobbed out onto the railroad tracks
in front of the crowd, raising their arms and pulling the
words of the old basketball cheer down from the hard gray
sky:

He's a man, who's a man,
He's a mighty Bearcat man—
Garber! Garber! Garber!

Roy's face stared over the shoulder of Shirley's pink
dress, expressionless, his mouth a thin, straight line, his
eyes burnt-out, like they had stared straight into some fiery
explosion and never really focused again. He hadn't even
kissed Shirley on the mouth; he just kept holding on to her,
his hands hooked into her back, the knuckles hard and
white.

Alben Smalley cleared his throat and took a step toward
Roy and Shirley.

"The town of Birney is proud to welcome home its own
brave son, Roy Garber."

There were whistles and cheers, and Shirley pulled away
from Roy, not wanting to hog the moment. Artie rushed
over and picked up the fallen cane and placed the crook of
the handle in Roy's hand. His fingers squeezed around it
slowly, hard.

"We don't have a 'key to the city,'" Smalley said, "I
guess because we aren't even a city."

Smalley turned and smiled at the crowd, and there were
scattered laughs and some cries of "Go, Birney!" "Attaboy,
Roy!"

"But we do give you our hearts," Smalley continued, turning back toward Roy, "and our doors and homes are open to you, in gratitude, for your courage and sacrifice, to keep us all safe for democracy."

Cheers again.

"I know that all of us would appreciate any words you could bring us from the fighting front, to rekindle our own efforts here on the Home Front. Would you honor us with a few words, Corporal?"

Roy stared at Smalley a moment, puzzled, as if the guy had spoken in a foreign language. "Words?" he said. Then he looked around the crowd, which was hushed now, waiting.

"Greetings," Roy said.

It was almost a whisper.

Then Roy poked his cane ahead on the platform and started to walk, limping, moving right ahead through the crowd, Shirley and Mom and Dad and Artie following, and Mr. Goodleaf, realizing that was all Roy had to say, pointed his baton at the Band and the Fife & Drummers and they all struck up "Praise the Lord and Pass the Ammunition" and the crowd parted, letting Roy through, stepping back and aside from his path.

Artie sat in the back seat of the car with Roy and Shirley, racking his brain to think of stuff to say that would make his hero brother feel at home.

"I hope you're hungry," Mom said. "I made a roast."

"Yes."

"Plenty of Blue Ribbon on ice," Dad said.

Roy nodded. He sat with the cane propped between his legs, his hands folded over the top. He just stared straight ahead.

"Hey, Roy," Artie said, "Knock knock."

Roy didn't seem to hear, or maybe he'd forgotten

how to carry on the joke, so Shirley said, "Who's there?"

Artie leaned forward so he was looking at Shirley over the top of Roy's cane.

"Alby," he said.

"Alby who?" Shirley answered.

Artie took a deep breath and then sang with all his might, in his best "colored" accent:

> Alby down to getcha in a taxi honey,
> Better be ready 'bout a half past eight—

Roy, still staring straight ahead, said, "Good one."

Suddenly Dad took up the song where Artie'd left off, singing extra heartily:

> Oh honey, don't be late,
> Wanna be there when
> The band starts playin'—

Mom and Shirley and Artie joined in to belt out the last of the song, and Roy puckered his mouth like he was whistling along with them, but no sound came out.

"Your folks could just drop me off, Roy," Shirley said, "if you'd like to be home alone for a while, with just your family. I understand."

Roy turned and looked at her.

"What?"

"Maybe you'd just like to rest for a while."

Roy took his left hand off the top of the cane, and held Shirley's hand with it.

"Shirley Colby," he said.

She leaned her head against his shoulder and no one said any more as the car rumbled on to the Garbers'.

There was roast beef and mashed potatoes and gravy, creamed onions and stewed tomatoes, cornbread and biscuits, rhubarb and applesauce, and Mom was warning everyone to save room for dessert. Artie was afraid Roy might just pick at his food, the way he seemed so quiet and far away, but he really chowed down, taking seconds and thirds and almost gulping, and everyone seemed relieved by his hearty appetite, as if it was a sign he was really all right, and the others all pitched in and did the talking for him, laughing and chattering to beat the band, so there weren't any empty spaces.

"Mince pie and apple pie for dessert," Mom announced.

Roy looked up from his plate, staring at Mom with a little quizzical turn to his mouth.

"Mince?" he said.

"You want a piece of both, or just mince?" Mom asked.

"I forgot about mince," Roy said.

"Your mother's is the best there is," Dad said.

"*Mince*," Roy said again, like it was a foreign word he was learning.

"Whipped cream on it?" Mom asked.

"Last year I had coconut," Roy said.

"They had coconut pie over there?" Mom asked.

"No. A real coconut. Off a tree."

"Just imagine!" Shirley said, real perky.

"You've surely seen the world, son," Dad said.

Roy wiped his napkin over his mouth, slowly, and set it down, folding and smoothing it on the table.

"I've seen—" he said, and everyone stopped eating, waiting for him to say what it was. But he just sat there, staring at the napkin. His hands began to tremble, and he put them in his lap.

"Coffee?" Mom asked.

Roy gazed at the napkin, and spoke in a kind of chant. "I—have—*seen*."

And he burst out crying, bawling like a baby, shaking and sobbing right there at the table, the tears streaming down his cheeks onto his plate, and he made no effort to stop or even wipe the tears. No one got up to rush over and try to comfort him; it didn't seem right somehow, since none of them had *seen*. They all just sat at their places and bowed their heads.

7

For the first couple days he was home, it seemed like Roy was haunting the house. In his old high school clothes he looked even more the stranger, as if the dark veteran Corporal of the Marines who got off the train was trying to camouflage his years and his death-defying experience by wearing the casual costumes of youth. He walked noiselessly, seeming to float from one room to another, his dark face wreathed in the smoke of continual cigarettes.

Artie had to shoo away kids who came to gawk at the house, hoping to get a glimpse of the battle-weary veteran. He even had to give the brush-off to his own buddies, knowing Roy didn't feel like meeting some kid and shooting the shit with him, answering dumb questions about the War. Ben Vickman had the nerve to turn up, acting like he was Artie's blood brother or something, but Artie just gave him the brush-off. With Warren Tutlow it was harder; he came over to bring this terrific serving tray he had made in Shop especially for Roy. It was plywood, with a map of the South Pacific shellacked on it, showing the islands Roy had fought on outlined in red, white, and blue. Artie explained to Tutlow that Roy was trying to get his mind off the War, he thought, but he'd take it in and give it to him when the time was riper. Tutlow nodded solemnly, understanding the whole thing like a real friend.

Mom let in Iva Tully and some of the grown-up neighbors who came bringing pies and cakes, brownies and Toll House cookies, baked beans and cornbread, in case Roy was hungry for any of it. Roy was always polite, and sat there eating some of whatever anyone brought right away, but he didn't say much except "thank you," and ate all the stuff like it was the same thing, like he didn't really taste any of it. When the person who had brought the food left, Roy would stop eating and take what was left out to the kitchen.

When Artie came home from school on the third day Roy was back, there was music.

> Kiss me once, and kiss me twice,
> And kiss me once again—
> It's been a long, long time.

Roy and Shirley were dancing in the living room. You knew it was "dancing" because the record was playing, otherwise it just would have looked like a guy and a girl were standing there hugging each other, moving their feet about a millionth of an inch every once in a while. Artie didn't want to break up the clinch by saying anything, so he went straight back to the kitchen to pick around in the surplus food. Mom was there, bustling around in her going-out dress and shoes.

"Don't take your coat off," she said. "We're leaving in a sec."

"Where?"

"The Moose Lodge Catfish Dinner and Bingo for Bonds night."

"That's in Oakley Central."

"That's where we're going."

"All of us?"

"You, me, and Dad."

"What about Roy and Shirley?"

"Shirley brought over some records. They're dancing."

"I saw."

"Well. Let's shake a leg now. We're going to walk downtown and pick up Dad."

"Sure."

Artie knew better than to ask any questions. He was glad Roy and Shirley would get to be alone, especially inside instead of the back seat of a car. Roy had taken the car and gone out with Shirley both the other nights he was home, but it hadn't seemed to make him feel much better. Artie was dying to know what had happened, or hadn't happened, and if it hadn't, why. He wondered if Roy's wounded leg made it hard or impossible for him to make out with a girl. Even worse, he worried that the change in Roy, the unspeakable things he had *seen*, somehow prevented him from getting sexed up anymore, or maybe made sex seem unimportant, something that belonged to civilian life and was blasted right out of your mind by the War. But if that was true, Roy surely wouldn't be out in the living room clinching with Shirley in time to the music. Maybe it was something that took a little while to get back, like you have to get your circulation going again after you've been out in the cold a long time.

Mom grabbed her coat from the hall closet and swung it on as she stopped briefly by the door to the living room.

"Okay, kids, there's enough in the kitchen to feed an army, so have a good time."

Roy and Shirley broke out of their clinch, but each kept an arm around the other.

"Thanks," Roy said.

"We'll be fine," Shirley said.

"And don't worry if we're late, these 'Bingo for Bonds' nights go on to all hours."

"Heck, yes," Artie said.

Mom grabbed his hand and pulled him along out of there, as the Andrews Sisters crooned, "you'll never know just how much I miss you—"

"Bingo for Bonds Night" was actually over a little after nine, but Mom suggested instead of going straight home that they have dessert at Verna's, this great little truck stop joint on Route Nine. They had already had bread pudding and brownies at the Catfish Dinner, but nobody mentioned that. It was a night for not mentioning things, especially what was on anyone's mind.

They all had a piece of Verna's hot apple pie, while the jukebox played the same song that Roy and Shirley had been dancing to in the living room that afternoon.

"You'll never know just how much I *care* . . ."

Artie prayed that Roy and Shirley still cared for each other, still loved each other, and that love would make Roy be more like himself again, or the way he used to be, anyway. He hoped they had made out all the way while everyone was gone, but the one thing that scared him was if somehow while Roy was doing it with Shirley he could tell if she had done it with anyone else. You were supposed to be able to tell if a girl was a virgin or not, she bled all over the place if she was, but that would have happened way back before Roy went off to the War, when they first had done it. But what if there was some secret way a guy had of knowing whether a girl had done it with somebody else? If there was any kind of test like that, old Roy would know it, and if he found out Shirley'd done it with anyone else he'd probably go right off his rocker.

"Maybe we ought to get going," Artie said.

He was picturing Roy going stark-raving in the living room, pitching Shirley right through the door with some sort of deadly jujitsu he had learned from the Japs.

"Have some more pie," Dad said.

"I'm stuffed."

"What's the big rush?" Mom asked.

Artie squirmed in his seat.

"It's late is all."

"Tomorrow's not even a school day," Mom said.

"Well, I want to get up early, so if Roy wants someone to talk to. He gets up with the birds now."

"Best thing to do for Roy is not worry over him," Dad said.

Mom nodded.

"He needs time."

"Shoot, he's had most all afternoon and night," Artie said.

"I wasn't talking about that, for Heaven's sake."

"What your Mom means is, he needs time to get the War from his head, relax and recuperate. These things don't happen overnight."

"He's only got eleven nights left," Artie said.

"He'll have his whole life," Dad said.

Mom sniffed, and blew her nose.

"Even then, he'll have scars," she said.

"The one on his leg's not so bad," Artie said. "I saw it."

"Your Mom doesn't mean those kind," Dad said quietly.

"Never mind," she said. "Just pray those are the worst kind he has."

Artie was getting a headache. He figured there'd be

plenty of time to pray that Roy didn't get any worse scars than he had; right now he was worn out from praying that Roy hadn't found out anything about Shirley that she didn't want him to know.

When Artie and his folks finally came home, stomping and talking real loud as they went inside, Roy and Shirley were sitting on the living room floor playing Chinese checkers.

"Who's winning?" Mom asked real brightly.

"Oh, Roy is, he's really good," Shirley said.

Roy took one of his marbles and hopped it right over a row of Shirley's. Then he looked up and actually smiled, the way he used to.

"Haven't lost my touch," he said.

Shirley reached over and squeezed his hand.

Artie figured everything was fine.

The next morning, Roy wasn't up with the birds. He didn't even come down for breakfast, though the smell of waffles and syrup and sausage was as powerful as perfume all through the house.

"I think we should just let him sleep," Mom said.

Dad nodded as he dug into his waffle.

After breakfast Artie went upstairs and stopped at the door of Roy's room to listen. He didn't hear a sound, not even snoring. He had hoped that Roy would be up-and-at-'em this morning, maybe even like his old self again, after the time alone with Shirley. Maybe it hadn't been so great after all, maybe later on they'd had a fight when Roy took her home and now he was really down in the dumps, or maybe he'd had some terrible nightmares about the War and was trying to wake up from them and couldn't. Artie lifted his hand, hesitant, then rapped very softly on the door. There was no answer. Artie put his hand on the knob, turned it gently, and peeked inside.

The bed was all made and Roy was lying on top of it wearing just his skivvies and the dog tags that hung around his neck. You could see the red stitches on his stomach where they'd taken off skin to fix his leg, and the other stitches on the part of his thigh where he'd had the operation. He was smoking a cigarette, tapping it into an ashtray that lay in the hollow of his belly, and staring at the action photos of himself as a basketball and football star that hung on the opposite wall. Or maybe he was staring right through them; the way his eyes looked he might be staring through the wall itself, through the house, the Town, the whole country. The real smile of the night before was gone, the mouth a hard line again, so he looked like the older veteran who had stepped off the train, a stranger, and even more strange and out of place in this boyhood room with the pennants and sports pictures, the ribbons and trophies of high school games. The man on the bed didn't match the rest of the room.

"Roy?"

The man's body jerked up straight, the hand dropping the cigarette.

"I'm sorry!" Artie said, and rushed to brush at the sparks and ashes that had fallen on the bedclothes.

"Damn!" said Roy, whacking a spark out.

"Dumbo Garber, that's me," Artie said.

"Take it easy, kid. I'm the goof-up."

"I shouldn't have bothered you, that's all."

"Hey, I can't just hang in the sack all day, can I?"

Suddenly Roy smiled, and clapped a hand on Artie's shoulder, the first time he'd done that since he'd been home.

"Hell," he said, "I haven't even thrown you a pass yet. My leg may be gimpy, but there's nothing wrong with my throwing arm."

"Let's go!"

Roy swung off the bed, holding his wounded leg, and

Artie charged off to get the football. It was almost like old times.

In the next couple of days Roy was mostly like he used to be, but there were moments when he seemed to slip out of it and into the silent, far-off stare, not seeming to notice or hear anything going on around him, and then he'd snap back again, like going in and out of a trance.

Every day Roy would have a big breakfast with the whole family, and then he'd take the car and drop Artie at school and Dad at the station and go get Shirley for their all-day picnic at Skinner Creek. Evidently Shirley's folks didn't make any fuss about it. Artie guessed they must be impressed and maybe a little afraid of the grim new Roy who'd been seasoned and aged by the War, who was now in some ways older than anybody's parents.

One day when Artie came home from school Roy was asleep in a chair in the living room and Shirley whispered not to wake him; she was getting ready to walk on home by herself, but Artie insisted he'd walk her. He hadn't even had a chance to talk to her alone since Roy had been back, and he wanted to know if everything was going as good as it looked, and if there was anything he could do to make it even better.

"I wish these days would never end," she said dreamily, as Artie strode proudly beside her, protector of his brother's beloved.

"You're real happy, huh?"

"Deliriously. Except—"

Shirley's face clouded over, like she was in some dark trance of her own, seeing into depths of things.

"What? Except *what*?"

"Clarence."

"You're not still in love with him, are you?"

"Artie! I was never *in love* with him, I explained all that to you. I did love him, as a person, that I cared about deeply, that's all."

"But you still care? Is that it?"

"Of course I still care. I wish him well, wherever he is, but that isn't *it*, what bothers me so."

"What is, then?"

"That I was so weak, so carried away, that I—that we *did* it. While Roy was at War. It's like a dark cloud, over all this happiness."

"But he'll never know, will he? Roy?"

"If he ever did, it would be the end."

"But he loves you."

"He'd never forgive me."

"How do you know?"

"I know. He's a man."

"You mean men can't forgive, ever?"

"Not that."

"How come? How come you're so sure?"

Shirley stopped walking and put her mittened hand on Artie's arm, as if to physically convey the truth of what she told him.

"Artie. It's the way men are."

He nodded, Shirley took her hand away, and they walked on to her house in silence, weighed down by the burden of nature's stern law.

When Artie got home a car he'd never seen before was parked outside, and he hoped it wasn't some reporter come snooping around. This one old guy had come over from the paper in Moline the second day Roy was home and asked a lot of questions about "what it was like" on Guadalcanal and Roy's answers got shorter and his face got tighter till Artie was afraid he'd explode and finally he said he was sorry but he couldn't really say any more and the guy got ticked off and asked how the people on the Home Front were supposed to know what was going on if their own boys returning home wouldn't talk? Then Roy's tan had turned the color of a bruise and he handed the reporter his hat and said, "Tell 'em to read Ernie Pyle."

If any reporter was snooping around, Artie would give him the bum's rush and say, "Tell 'em to read Ernie Pyle."

It wasn't a reporter, though; it was Bo Bannerman, Roy's old teammate and pal who had gone with him and Wings Watson to see Bubbles LaMode the day of Pearl Harbor. Bo had been "rotated" back to the States after flying twenty-five missions over Germany as a ball-turret gunner on a B-17, and was stationed at Scott Field, right over in Rantoul, Illinois. When his folks wrote him Roy was coming home after being wounded, Bo had got a pass and come back to see his old pal. The two buddies were sprawled on the living room floor, drinking beer and whooping it up just like in the old days, while Shirley's record of "Besame Mucho," the Latin love song, was playing on the Victrola.

Artie took off his coat and went back to the kitchen, not knowing if he ought to intrude on the talk of the two heroes, who probably had stuff to say to each other that regular people weren't supposed to hear. Mom was whipping up a batch of Toll House cookies and she asked if Artie wanted to help, or would rather go listen to "the boys."

"They might not want me sticking my nose in," Artie said.

"I'm sure they won't be shy about telling you to scram if that's how they feel."

She reached up in one of the cabinets and pulled down a bag of potato chips.

"Here. Feed these to the lions."

She smiled, and twitched Artie's ear.

"Hey, thanks, Mom."

Artie ripped the bag open and went in to offer it to the guys.

"Grab some grub!" Roy said, reaching in for a huge handful.

"Don't mind if I do," Bo said, rummaging in the sack.

"Hey, Artie, you remember Bad Bo here," Roy said.

"Sure. How they hangin', Bo?"

"Loose as a goose, little buddy. Hey, the kid's hep, huh, Roy?"

"Whattya expect from my own brother?"

Artie, full of pride, took that as kind of an invitation to join them, so he sat on the floor and tried to sprawl out the way Bo and Roy were, like he was one of them.

Bo demolished the potato chips he had taken and reached for another fistful.

"Hey, Bo," Roy said, "don't they got potato chips over in England?"

"They got what they call 'chips,' but they're really french fries, not actual potato chips."

"And warm beer, I heard tell."

"You ain't heard nothin' about what England's got, *Keemosabee*."

"You tryin' to tell me somethin'?"

Bo tipped his beer can and guzzled down what was left.

"Chug-a-lug," he said. "You wanna hear some 'war stories'?"

"*Hear* some? I got some to *tell*."

Roy slugged down some more beer, and Bo took his empty can and bent it double with his bare hand.

"There more where this come from?" he asked.

Roy crushed his own empty can and winked.

"You better believe it, pardner. This is the *Home* Front."

"I'll get 'em!" Artie volunteered eagerly, and scrambled up from his sprawl. He started to run to the kitchen but Bo waved him back.

"Uh, Roy," Bo said in a low, secret voice. "Before we crack any more, is there someplace we can swap war stories without burning the ears off your Mom out there in the kitchen?"

"We'll beat a hasty retreat to my old room. Artie, how 'bout bringing us up that whole six-pack from the icebox?"

Artie snapped a salute and said, "Roger!"

"And Artie," Roy said, "bring up a church key with it, okay?"

"*Church* key?"

"You know—the opener. So we don't have to chew the lids off the cans."

So that was what you called the little metal gizmo that cut the neat little triangles in the top of the beer can. It wasn't an ordinary "can opener"—it was a church key! Elated at feeling even more a part of the manly world of the servicemen, Artie bounded off to the kitchen while Roy and Bo went upstairs singing raucously: "Off we go, into the wild blue yonder—"

When Artie brought up the beers he hesitated, then asked, "Is it okay if I stay?"

Roy took a can of beer and knotted his brows as he looked at Bo.

"Whattya think, Sarge? Is the kid ready?"

"If he's old enough to button his fly, and button his lip."

"I'll never tell, Scout's Honor!" Artie said.

"Okay, close the door," Roy said.

A thrilling tingle went through Artie's whole being. He felt he had been allowed entry into an inner sanctum of manhood such as he had never dreamed of knowing as a mere almost-thirteen-year-old kid. He was with a couple of veterans of the War, one from the European Front, one from the Pacific, about to exchange *war stories*! These were things that the brave fighting men didn't deign to disclose to inquiring reporters, the real stuff of battle too personal to spill to civilians, too gory and terrifying to reveal to girl friends and wives, parents and loved ones. He squatted on the floor, Indian fashion, concentrating totally, wanting to remember for the rest of his life the wrenching details of what it meant to face death and deal death to others.

As if all this weren't enough, Roy opened not two but *three* cans of beer, and handed one to Artie.

"You going to hear war stories, you might as well have a little foam."

"Hey, thanks!"

"Just button your lip about *that*, too," Roy said.

"Damn right!" Artie said, feeling grown-up enough to cuss out loud.

He took a swallow of the beer, and almost choked.

It tasted like soapsuds.

Artie smacked his lips, like he really loved it. He'd have gladly drunk horse pee if that's what the guys were having.

"Whoo-ee!" Bo exclaimed. "Let's tell a few tales."

Roy waved his beer can and stamped his feet.

"Roll me o-ver, in the clo-ver!" he sang out, croaking.

Artie was a little surprised, since he thought the sacred nature of the subject would make the guys somber, sad in a courageous kind of way, and something like reverent. But he realized that was dumb. Roy and Bo were carrying on just like a couple of death-defying RAF officers in those movies where they banged on the piano and got pie-eyed before going up on a mission to shoot down whole squadrons of Messerschmitts. You treated war and death lightheartedly, that was the style!

Artie squeezed his eyes shut and forced down another slug of beer.

"Let me tell you 'bout England," Bo said. "What they got over there, see, they got these country girls. Blond, rosy cheeks, bazooms on 'em like Howitzers, big, long legs, and ass—you never saw a beautiful sight till you saw one of those milky-white, firm big bottoms of an English country gal. And legs! A good English country gal makes Grable and them look like they're standin' on hatpins. I mean, these sweet English lassies are built for a man, and they appreciate a man. Roy, they got ways of showin' their appreciation that you never heard tell of."

"Country gals? I thought London was supposed to be the hot old town."

"Stay away from it. Sure, there's some of your sharpies there, but it's all grab and gimme, hustle and bustle, wham-bam, thank-you-ma'am. That's London. Gimme a hayloft out in one of them little 'shires' any day of the week."

"Like they say, you been making hay, huh, Bo?"

"Making hay when the sun shines!"

"Well, there's no hay to speak of out on the islands," Roy said, "but there's plenty of grass. And I don't mean just to roll around on. You ever seen a gal wearin' a grass skirt? The way it parts and moves back and forth when those legs come swishing out? It's one of the seven wonders of the world, ole buddy. And there's no grass at all on top o' course, just the beautifullest boobs God ever gave to woman."

"I guess, but hell, man, you're talkin' dark meat. If that's what you favor, or is all to be had, I guess it's okay, but—"

"Not 'dark' like you're thinkin' of, buddy. More like cocoa. Hot chocolate with a lotta milk in it. Creamy tan. And luscious."

"No bull?"

"Swear to God. But that's just the islands. A year ago, I got me a week of R'n'R in Pearl, and that is *Heaven.* I mean, the most luscious women in the world. Chinese, Native Hawaiian, mixes and strains of the best stuff made even better."

"So whattya do, talk pidgin to 'em? 'You gimme some nooky-nook,' all that palaver?"

"Hell, not on Pearl. On Pearl you got a very educated class of girl, the nicest kind of girl in the world, right in your convent schools—and when school's out, lookout, buster! There was this one, Marie—"

"Lemme tell you about this country gal called Nell—"

"I'll match you Nell with my Liana from Pearl any day."

"Liana? Thought you said Marie?"

"Hell, I had me Liana *after* Marie. Now listen to this—"

Artie lost track of the names and anatomies, the athletic exploits of wild hula girls of the islands and steamy English milkmaids. He kept forcing down the beer, not wanting to show how confused and surprised he was.

He had thought he was going to hear about the s̶ ̶ts of battle, the way it really feels to have a sneaky Jap come at you with a knife, the terror of a Messerschmitt diving at the turret of your B-17 while you hung there thousands of feet above the evil terrain of Germany. But that wasn't what "War stories" were at all.

When Bo and Roy finished off their first beers from the pack and opened more, Artie glugged down the rest of his can and took a second one to keep right up with them.

"*Ice* cubes!" Bo shouted. "You tryin' to pull my chain, Garber? What the hell she do with any ice cubes at a time like that?"

"Don't knock it till you try it, ole buddy."

"Well, *how*? I mean, *where*?"

The stories got so complicated that Artie didn't really understand them, or even think he wanted to. He was glad when they finished off the six-pack and Bo had to go home for supper. Artie wanted a chance to talk to Roy alone. His head was buzzing, but he felt real good in a new kind of way, in spite of the pukey taste of the beer. He felt like he almost understood the answer to a puzzle, and if only he could fit a few jagged little pieces into place he would solve the whole thing.

When Bo left, Roy flopped down on his bed and lit a cigarette. Artie stood up and went to the window. The sun was going down and everything seemed suspended, lifted out of time.

"Say, Roy, I was just wondering," Artie said.

"Yeah?"

"I guess if a guy is overseas, in Wartime, he gets to make out whenever he wants, even if he's married, or got a girl back home?"

"Well, sure, I mean, in Wartime, you never know which day is your last, so you just try to do whatever you want and that you'd like to do, see? It's like 'live for the moment,' 'cause that may be all you got."

Artie nodded.

Roy took a big drag on his cigarette and blew a stream of smoke toward the ceiling. Then he waved the hand with the cigarette and spoke in a funny, fake-English accent.

"Laugh, drink and be merry, for tomorrow you may die!"

"Sure," Artie said. "I get that part."

"What part don't you 'get'?"

"Well, what about the girls?"

"The girls back home, you mean?"

"No, I meant the girls overseas, that you guys do it with."

"What about them?"

"Well, they're not all whores or anything, I guess."

"Hey, there are whores in every country of the world, always will be, peacetime and War. But one thing your old brother can say, with his head held up to any man: 'I never paid for it.' "

"So the girls you did it with over there, they were really 'nice girls'?"

"Damn right they were. Some of those native girls, they don't really know too much, and o' course if they are nice you want to give them a chocolate bar or something. Even the Christian girls, those educated ones like Marie from the convent school in Pearl? Well, they appreciate a gift if you got PX privileges, a nice pair of nylons, something a lady anywhere in the world would like, but it sure is nothing to do with whoring."

"I don't mean whoring. What I don't get is, how can they be nice girls, if they do it with soldiers and all?"

"Hell, Artie, it's Wartime for them, too. Their countries are being bombed and invaded, their own men are off fighting and dying in the war. There's no tomorrow for them, either."

"So it's like in Wartime, people don't have to obey the sex laws and stuff and everyone agrees it's okay."

"Pretty much, I guess, yeah."

"And a nice girl whose guy has gone off to War and her country is at War and she does it with some other guy, she still is a nice girl?"

"Damn right! Now you take that Marie, in Pearl, the one from the convent school? Hell, I'd be proud to bring her right home here for supper. You sure are thinking this matter out, buddy."

"I just want to make sure I get how it is," Artie said.

Roy got up from the bed and took his shirt off. He went to his dresser and pulled out a can of talcum, shook some onto his hand and then slapped it under his armpits. He was getting ready to get dressed for supper, and Artie wanted to solve the puzzle before they went downstairs or he knew he'd lose the whole sense of it.

"Don't break your brain, ole buddy," Roy said. "Just ask the old Corporal here."

Roy mashed the cigarette out in an ashtray on top of the dresser, then pulled a fresh shirt from the top drawer and started putting it on.

Artie walked across the room and back, wobbling a little bit, but feeling like he was almost floating. He felt he was right on the edge of some beautiful solution, if only he could gather in his mind the exact right words.

"Okay," Artie said, straining his whole mind into one single focus of super concentration. "What if there's this girl whose country is at war, and the guy she loves has to go off and fight far away, and while he's gone, the girl makes out with another guy? If she still loves the soldier and wants to marry him when he comes back, is she a nice girl even though she made out with some other guy in War-time?"

"Hell, yes. If her country's at war, and her guy is off fighting the enemy, there's no tomorrow the night she makes out with another guy. Nice girls all over the world are doing it right now, be they French, English, Hawaiian, whatever."

"And no one could blame them?"

"No one who'd been around the block and knew which end was up."

"Especially a guy who'd been making out with lots of different girls of all different creeds and colors while he was off to war. Right?"

Roy was about to light a new cigarette, but he left it dangling in his mouth and squinted real hard at Artie.

"Are you asking about a particular guy?"

Artie's head began to throb, and he rubbed it real hard, trying to keep things in focus that seemed to be slipping away and spilling.

"Not exactly," he said. "I mean, if it's true what you say then it doesn't matter who the guy would be, does it? Or the girl?"

Roy lit the match he'd been holding, but he had trouble getting the flame to hold still at the tip of the cigarette. Finally he made the connection, and waved out the match.

"What girl?" he asked.

"The one who's the girl friend of the guy who goes off to War and makes out with lots of other girls."

"Is this the girl who makes out herself while the guy she loves has gone off to War?"

Artie felt like his brain was going to burst.

"Well, I guess it could be, yeah."

Roy took the cigarette he had only started to smoke and jabbed it into the ashtray on the dresser so it broke, and some sparks flew up.

"Let me get this straight now," he said. His voice got higher and faster as he spoke. "A guy goes off to fight in the War and risks his life and limb to keep his country safe, and the so-called 'nice girl' he leaves behind is fucking her ears off with every stud who comes down the pike."

"That's a lie!"

"You just said she made out while her boyfriend was gone off to War."

"I never said with every guy who came down the pike!"

"Oh, there was just a handful, a lucky two or three who hit the jackpot?"

"One! There was only one guy!"

Roy grabbed the front of Artie's shirt, twisting it.

"Who?"

Artie jerked away. Everything was spinning now, out of control.

"Hey, come on, you're getting me all mixed up," he said.

Roy grabbed his shoulder and pulled him toward him again. His hot, beery breath was in Artie's face, making him dizzier.

"Who was the sonofabitch who got in her pants?"

Artie pushed his hand against Roy's chest. "I was only talking about 'some girl,' that it might have happened to."

"I know who the hell you're talking about!"

"I never said Shirley!"

Roy let go of Artie and slammed his fist on the dresser so hard the ashtray jumped off and fell to the floor.

"That bitch! That dirty little two-timing bitch!"

"You liar!"

"*Me?* What the hell did *I* ever lie about?"

"You said it was all right for a nice girl to do it if her country was at war!"

"I didn't say *America*, for chrissake!"

"But America's at war—we're fighting the Japs and the Germans, you are yourself!"

"America is not getting bombed and invaded, it isn't at war like England and France and Hawaii, and you know why not? I'll tell you why not—'cause guys like me are over there getting blown to shit to protect our loved ones, while all the time they're home humping away like rabbits!"

"You mean if the Nazis had actually bombed Chicago, or the Japs had invaded California, then it would have been okay for Shirley to make out with a guy?"

"You got everything all screwed up, kid. I was talking about *foreign* girls, not *American* girls."

"American girls are different?"

"They're damn well supposed to be! What the hell you think we're fighting for, anyway? Haven't you ever heard of 'the American Way of Life'?"

"It's not fair!"

"Great. I come home and find out my girl friend is cheating on me and my own little brother is knocking the American Way of Life. Jesus. What am I fighting for, anyway?"

Roy went to the closet and grabbed his Windbreaker.

"All I meant was, it doesn't seem fair that you get to make out in Wartime all you want, and Shirley's not allowed. That's the part I don't get."

Roy rammed his arms in the jacket and yanked the zipper up. "Well, ole buddy, I'll make it real simple for ya. The fact is, I am a *guy* and Shirley is a *girl*. You got the picture now?"

Roy grabbed his cane and pounded out of the room.

"Hey, wait!"

Artie ran after him, scrambling down the stairs two at a time.

"Hey, Roy, please *don't*!"

Roy was already charging out of the door, hobbling forward with huge, lopsided strides.

"Stop!"

Artie hurled himself outside, careening across the front yard in a dizzy panic, throwing his whole body into tackling his brother around the waist, but Roy didn't even fall, he just kept on moving, pushing Artie away as he went. Artie held on for dear life, sliding down and grabbing hold of Roy's good leg.

"Please!" he yelled.

"Get away, go home."

"She wasn't in love with the other guy, she just felt sorry for him!"

"I can't wait to hear all about it, straight from the bitch's mouth."

"No!"

Artie still clung to Roy's leg but then Roy broke into a limping gallop and his heel came back and struck Artie in the chest. He let go of the leg and sprawled on the sidewalk as Roy hobbled off like fury down the middle of the street. The pain shot through Artie's body like sudden poison but was not as bad as the awful knowledge that he'd gone and ruined the lives of his two favorite people in the world.

Roy was drunk for three days and Mom and Dad couldn't do anything with him; he was like a wild man. He still wasn't all the way sober when he packed up and left for Parris Island before his leave was even up.

Everyone in Town knew the story.

Artie went to the Strand to find Shirley, but Patsy Ann

Paddington, the new Junior Prom Queen, was sitting in the ticket booth just like she'd always been there and always would be.

Artie got up the nerve to call the Colby house by putting a handkerchief over the phone to disguise his voice in case Shirley's mother answered.

Shirley's voice sounded like she was speaking from the bottom of a well about a thousand miles away. Artie begged her to meet him at Skinner Creek and he thought she said yes.

Shirley wore no makeup. Her face looked pale and startled.

"It's all my fault," Artie said.

He blew his nose to keep from crying.

"Don't blame yourself for my mistake," Shirley said.

She took his hand and they walked along the creek.

She told him she was going to Indianapolis to live with Donna Modjeski and work at the Curtiss-Wright airplane factory.

"Can I see you off at the Greyhound?" Artie asked.

"My parents are going to drive me."

"Oh."

He was glad she had a ride, but sad because it seemed like her mother had proved it was right that in the end she could only depend on her own family.

"Will you come back home when the War is over?"

"We'll see," was all she would say.

It seemed like she was one of the casualties—a person who was wounded in the War, and might or might not get well again.

They sat on the bank of the creek and Shirley smoked a cigarette. It didn't seem right to talk. Artie thought of how long ago it was that they used to walk home after cheerleader practice singing "The White Cliffs of Dover" and he had to blow his nose again.

He walked her back to the corner of her block and then turned and ran home and shut himself in his room.

The day after school was out the Allies invaded the beaches of Normandy, France, and Tutlow came over with some homemade explosives to celebrate D-Day. The aspiring little scientist was blinking eagerly behind his thick glasses, anxious to blast off his improvised arsenal, but Artie just shook his head.

"No, thanks," he said.

"What's wrong? You still in a funk 'cause your big hero brother got two-timed?"

"Oh, go blow it out your ear," Artie said, and walked in the house.

He snitched a Pabst Blue Ribbon from the icebox and drank it alone in his room, listening to the senseless clangor of church bells and firecrackers. The beer still tasted awful to him, like soapsuds, but he liked that it made him belch. Belching seemed lowdown and grown-up, which was how he felt instead of like a kid who got a kick out of setting off homemade explosives. He even liked knowing the beer was bad for him.

Even though Roy was back in the States, it seemed he was actually farther away now than when he was halfway around the world. He wrote back a postcard after he got to Parris Island, saying he was settled there and everything was fine. Now that he didn't have a girl to write home to, the family knew they wouldn't be hearing much from him, but Mom tried to look on the bright side. She said they'd be *seeing* more of him now; he'd probably get to come home for Christmas, and maybe even Thanksgiving. After all, he was only in South Carolina, not the South Pacific. Artie didn't say anything, but he knew in his gut that Roy wouldn't come back home till the War was over.

Artie got a postcard from Shirley, too. It showed a pic-

ture of the Soldiers and Sailors Monument in the center of
Indianapolis. She said she was working hard and loved it.
The card was signed "Rosie the Riveter," and didn't have
any return address.

Artie felt like that was all he had left of his two favorite
people.

Postcards.

V

1

ARTIE sure was relieved when America dropped the Atom Bomb on Japan.

The most important thing it meant was that Our Boys wouldn't have to die invading the stronghold of the evil yellow Empire. Before the Bomb was dropped, the papers were saying it would cost about 175,000 American lives to capture the "Home Islands" of the Japs, where every last fanatical man, woman, and child would fight to the death and fall on their swords. But even the crazed Warlords knew there was no use battling the A-Bomb, so it saved the lives of those hundreds of thousands of American boys who'd have been killed in the invasion.

It also meant Roy would finally come home. Like Artie suspected, he hadn't come back to Birney for the holidays, even though he could have taken a train from South Carolina. Instead he sent presents to the family, U.S.M.C. souvenirs of Parris Island, and a card that said he was going to spend Christmas with a real Southern Belle on her family's gigantic plantation. But now that the War would be over he wouldn't have any more excuses to stay away. He'd have to come home, and Artie and the folks could help him adjust and begin his new life in the Post-War world.

Artie hoped Shirley would come home too, and maybe she and Roy would patch things up and live happily ever after, but he knew that was probably a pipe dream. For all he knew, Shirley had married some old guy she met at the airplane factory, or a serviceman at the U.S.O., or maybe some race car driver from the Indianapolis 500. At least with the War over anyway, she wouldn't have to keep working at the factory; that was just something women did in Wartime, and after the national emergency was through they were supposed to get back to being regular women again. Maybe Shirley would go off to college and become a terrific schoolteacher beloved by generations of students.

In the secret, most selfish part of his mind, Artie was glad the A-Bomb had ended the War because he was sick and tired of it. He knew he'd "remember Pearl Harbor" the rest of his life, but it seemed now part of his childhood, along with the patriotic songs and the drives for Bonds and scrap, the rationing stamps and Gold Stars hung in the windows of homes where boys would not return. All that seemed like a dream already, and Artie was ready for the real things of life, like high school and girls.

Everything had started happening real fast in the spring, like the whole world was getting ready to clean up the mess it was in and be ready for the opening of high school in the fall. In just a couple of weeks around the time of Artie's fourteenth birthday, F.D.R. died, the Germans surrendered, and, as if swept along by the tides of change, Artie decided to work at his Dad's filling station all summer instead of going back to Camp Cho-Ko-Mo-Ko. It seemed a more grown-up thing to do, and that was what Artie was in the mood for, now that his voice had cracked and turned from alto to low tenor, and his height had shot up to five-six-and-three-eighths according to the orange crayon marks on the door of his room. To add to these thrilling changes, he had also grown manly hairs under his armpits, around his privates, along his legs, and even a few on his chest. He liked to walk around the house with his shirt off, flexing his push-up-strengthened biceps and singing the great new popular song:

> Gimme land lotsa land under starry skies above—
> Don't fence me in . . .

The song really said how people felt now. They were tired of the years of rules and regulations, of counting rationing points and pennies, of staying home to save gas and eating oleo to save butter. They wanted to break the shackles of caution and duty ("I can't stand hobbles and I don't like fences") and roam out free across the rich, big land that was theirs by the grace of God and the rightness of destiny. They had fought for their freedom and wanted to enjoy it.

Besides those things, the song had another, more personal meaning for Artie. It seemed to say how he felt about finally growing up, the feeling of newfound freedom that he just was beginning to experience, like a cowboy let loose on the open range and knowing it all lay before him, the life ahead that seemed as glorious and spacious as the land itself; and now, just getting the first clear glimpse of it, knowing the excitement of it, he wanted more, he wanted it all.

Artie loved working on cars in the greasy hot garage of the filling station, sweating and wearing only his dirty old dungarees and clodhoppers but Dad made him put on a T-shirt to wait on customers out front at the pumps. Even then he rolled up the short sleeves of the T-shirt clear to his shoulders so his biceps showed, and he kept tugging up the front of it to scratch at his stomach and admire the manly new hairs curling out around his belly button.

When the feisty, tough little President Harry Truman dropped a second A-Bomb on one of the Imperial Japanese strongholds the Nips at last gave up and America proclaimed "Victory Over Japan" which was celebrated as a great new national holiday, "V-J" Day. Dad closed down the filling station and Artie rushed home and took a shower, anxious to keep his date for this historic occasion with Caroline Spingarn.

She owed him one.

Back in the spring when Germany surrendered and America declared "Victory in Europe" Fishy Mitchelman had rushed onto Main Street and tried to kiss some lady who was carrying a bag of groceries to her car. When she screamed and dropped the groceries, Fishy just threw back his head and shouted "V-E fo' me!" and started to chase two girls across the street who shrieked and ran for cover in the Odd Fellows Building when they saw him coming. When Artie saw Fishy go berserk like that he figured maybe he'd taken some kind of musical dope and was on a rampage of sex and terror, so he took him into Damon's to try to calm him down with a rainbow Coke.

"You got to get hold of yourself," Artie said in his manly new voice, which he tried to make even deeper so it sounded like the ad for Lifebuoy soap when the bass voice warned against getting "BO," which stood for "body odor."

"Got to celebrate the big V-E," Fishy protested. "Don't you listen to the box?"

"Sure, I heard about V-E Day on the radio, but what's that got to do with chasing girls?"

"Says on the box in Chi, New York, Frisco—soldiers and sailors all smoochin' the skirts in the streets to celebrate."

"You're not a soldier or sailor, though."

"Any guy's got patriotism can kiss the girls."

"That's in the *city*, fella. People do anything in the city."

"Foog. Maybe I'll roll up to Chi."

"It'll be all over by the time you get there. The kissing part, anyway. They can't just keep doing it, even in cities. Otherwise, you couldn't have traffic or anything."

"Foog and double foog."

"Well, I gotta go see a man about a horse."

Artie got up all the sudden and left a dime on the table to pay for the Cokes. Fishy had given him a great idea, but he didn't want to let on about it.

He went straight to Caroline Spingarn's house and asked if she wanted to dance.

That's what you did now if you wanted to make out. You danced. Everyone had seemed to realize all at once that spin-the-bottle was just a little kids' excuse for necking, and the more mature, grown-up thing to do was put on a nice record so you could press your bodies together and go from there.

Caroline looked kind of suspicious at first when Artie showed up on her doorstep in the middle of the day asking to dance, but then she brightened up and said it just so happened she had a neat new record of "Swinging on a Star" if he wanted to dance to it. They went down to her basement game room, plugged in the Victrola, and Artie did a few jitterbug steps to the music before he pulled Caroline right up against him and planted one right on her mouth.

Caroline hauled off and slapped him one.

"What's the big idea?"

"Don't you even know? It's V-E Day. Everyone's kissing everyone, unless they're unpatriotic or something."

"Well, why didn't you say so?"

"I figured you heard it on the radio."

"I heard about V-E, but not about kissing."

"Well, they're doing it. New York, Chi, Frisco, everywhere."

"I don't know," Caroline said, and went and turned off the record.

"Don't know what? You don't believe me?"

"I believe you."

"What's wrong, then?"

"It doesn't seem right to go whole hog when just *half* the War is over."

She folded her arms across her waist.

"Well," Artie said, "you got to keep up morale to win the *other* half."

"It doesn't seem like the thing to go around kissing when Our Boys are still fighting and dying to beat Japan. You of all people should understand that. I mean, your own brother was wounded over there."

"Yeah, I guess."

Artie felt pretty crummy when she brought that up, but then he found something good about it.

"When we beat Japan, I guess *then* is the time to go whole hog."

"At least then the *whole* thing will be over, not just part of it."

"Right! Listen, I'll see you V-J Day!"

One hot August night after supper Artie was lying on the living room floor reading *Knute Rockne, All-American*, this book about the life of the greatest football coach in the history of the world, when suddenly he heard banging on the front door like someone was trying to break the house down.

"Hold your horses!" Artie yelled, and hurried to the door, scratching at the hair on his belly.

Fishy Mitchelman was standing there all decked out in his zoot suit, holding his gym bag. Before Artie could say anything, Fishy pointed at him and started singing:

> Get your coat and get your hat,
> Leave your worries on the doorstep . . .

Artie opened the door, but instead of coming in, Fishy did a little jiggle step away and motioned like he wanted Artie to follow him.

"Just di-rect your feet—" he sang.

"What's up? You going somewhere?"

"Rollin' up to Chi. Wanna come?"

"Why? What's goin' on?"

"V-J Day! Smoochin' in the streets!"

"Hey, don't joke about something like that. The Japs have got to surrender first."

"Laid down the foogin' sword five minutes ago, said so on the box."

As if to confirm the story, a fire siren started to wail, and the church bell began ringing.

"Wa-haaaaaa!" Artie yelled at the top of his voice.

"Grab your taps, Gates. Train to Chi at ten."

"You really goin' to Chicago, right now, at *night*? Your Mom's letting you?"

"Trixie? She's comin' too. Let's perambulate!"

"Fish, I can't just go to Chicago. I never even been there."

"Do anything now, the War's over!"

"Look, you go ahead, have a good time."

Fishy shrugged, lifted his right hand and wiggled his finger as he pranced down the steps toward the street, singing.

> Saw an old man who danced with his wife
> In Chicago—

Artie tried to call Caroline Spingarn, but the line was busy. Probably everyone's line was busy all over America, people calling all their friends and relatives to talk about the war being over. Suddenly Artie remembered Roy, and was ashamed that his first thought was making out with a girl instead of giving thanks that his own brother had come through the War alive. He went to his room and closed the door, getting down on his knees by the window like he used to do, like he hadn't done since way back last winter. He thanked God for ending the War and keeping Roy alive all through it, and prayed that now everything would get back to normal and life would be like it was supposed to be again, with everyone working hard and having a swell time. After his prayer he lay down on his bed and examined the hairs on his chest, looking for new ones. He pulled on the ones that were there, figuring that might make them get longer. Caroline had never even seen the hairs on his chest, so she didn't know he was really becoming a man. Maybe tomorrow instead of just going by her house and trying to grab a V-J kiss in the basement dancing to some jivey record he'd invite her to go for a picnic and swim out at Skinner Creek. They could have a long philosophic talk about the War, the plans for Peacetime, and the meaning of Life. And all the time he'd be wearing his bathing suit and she could see the hairs on his chest.

Caroline lay on the rock in her bathing suit, sunning herself. Her eyes were closed, and she looked like one of those starlets that the guys overseas were always voting The Girl I'd Most Like To Be Under A Palm Tree With. That was great, but Artie was disappointed that she wouldn't go in swimming.

"I can't," she said.

"How come?"

"Artie, there are certain things a girl can't do at certain

times, when she gets to be a certain age, and certain things happen."

"Oh," he said. "I get it."

She was riding the rag. That's what the guys called it, anyway, when girls were having their curse. He didn't actually know what it all meant or why it happened, except it showed a girl was growing up and could have babies, and that meant she could go all the way. He never knew it had anything to do with swimming, but he tried not to let on. He just hoped not being able to swim didn't have anything to do with not being able to kiss, but he couldn't figure why it should. Caroline looked perfectly normal, lying there on the rock in her shiny blue bathing suit, in fact if anything she looked better than normal.

Artie cleared his throat, making his voice go as deep as the "BO" ad on the radio.

"Well, I guess we'll remember this day the rest of our lives," he said.

"What? Why?"

Caroline blinked her eyes open and raised up on her elbows, looking surprised, like a horsefly had bit her.

"Caroline, this is V-J Day!"

"Oh," she said, "I thought you were talking about you and me, in particular."

She sank back onto the rock and closed her eyes again.

"Well, I was in a way, since here we are being alone together, you and me, on the day of Victory over Japan and the end of the Second World War, the biggest war in the whole history of mankind."

"Mmmm," she said.

She looked like she was falling asleep.

Artie checked the manly hairs on his chest and then crept over on his hands and knees and put his mouth down on Caroline's.

She jumped.

"Artie!"

"What's wrong?"

"What do you think you're doing, anyway?"

"Giving you the V-J Day kiss you promised me back on V-E Day, that's all."

"I did? Promise you that?"

"Caroline, you turning into some kind of teaser or something?"

"Sticks and stones," she said.

"Caroline, we're not just kids anymore."

"I'm certainly glad you're aware of that."

"I'm aware of you told me you'd kiss me on V-J Day, when you wouldn't do it on V-E Day. What are you waiting for now, the United Nations?"

"I don't just go around kissing people."

"You went around kissing Fishy Mitchelman last year."

"That was at parties."

"That's not all, according to Fishy himself."

"He's a boy."

"What's that got to do with the price of eggs?"

Caroline sat up again and glared at Artie.

"*Boys lie*," she said, and then turned over on her side, so her back was to Artie and his hairy chest.

"All boys aren't like Fishy," he said.

"That's right. Fishy has rhythm. Most boys don't have any at all."

"You still stuck on him or something?"

"Fat chance."

"You sure are in a lousy mood for V-J Day."

"Artie, I told you it was a certain time of month. Besides, I don't think it's such a neat thing to go around celebrating dropping Atom Bombs and wiping out thousands of men, women, and children."

"They're Japs!"

"They're human beings, too!"

"Wow. Some people sure forget easy. V-J Day isn't even over and you're feeling sorry for the Japs."

"Why don't you go swimming? Just because I can't doesn't mean you can't."

"What's that got to do with the Japs?"

"Nothing. Nothing in the world."

"Okay. I think I will."

Artie stood up and walked to the creek. He waded in, and then flung himself into the water, diving down, holding his breath and moving fishlike over the rocky bottom, not coming up till he thought he would burst. He went and dried off, looking at the hairs lying flat and bedraggled on his chest.

"I sure will be glad when high school starts," he said. "Everything will be different then."

"I hope so," said Caroline.

"You and me both."

Artie went home and sneaked a beer up to his room. He didn't feel like washing up or changing for supper and he went down to the table just wearing his bathing suit and a grungy old khaki T-shirt.

Dad looked at him sideways and said, "This isn't Camp Cho-Ko-Mo-Ko, son."

Artie made a grunting sound and splatted some potato salad onto his plate.

"I wonder how long it will take the boys to come home now," Mom said.

"Soon enough," Dad said. "Let's just be thankful it's over."

Artie scratched under his left arm and then raised it, searching through the new hairs of his armpit to see if he could find a chigger bite.

"If you mean Roy," he said, "I'll bet he waits till the last."

"The view of your armpit is not exactly appetizing," Mom said.

Artie put his arm down and let out a terrible belch. The odor of Pabst Blue Ribbon and potato salad spread through the room like gas.

"P-U!" Mom said, grabbing her nose with a finger and thumb.

" 'Scuse me," Artie mumbled.

Dad threw his napkin down on the table.

"That does it," he said.

His face was furious red, and Artie felt his own ears get hot.

"I *said* 'excuse me'!"

"Go to your room."

"My *room*! For cripe's sake, I'm fourteen years *old*!"

"Maybe that's the trouble," Dad said. "Now *move*!"

He really meant business.

Artie threw his own napkin on the table, noisily shoved the chair back, and slouched to his room, slamming the door behind him.

He was crouched on his bed, examining the cracks between his toes to make sure he didn't have athlete's foot, when Dad opened the door.

"You and me are going fishing," Dad said. "Saturday. Up to Lake Minnekewanka."

"Okay," Artie said.

"Now go and apologize to your mother and see if she'll give you some supper."

"Yes, sir."

They hadn't gone fishing since Roy went off to War. The whole family used to go for a week every summer and sometimes just for a Saturday, up to Minnekewanka or Crystal Lake or the Reservoir, the four of them sitting in a rowboat holding their long bamboo poles over the side and "drowning worms" as Mom called it. The fishing wasn't too great in Illinois, and sometimes you sat for a couple of hours without even a strike before pulling up the anchor and rowing to some other spot that looked like it might be a good place to hit a whole school of bass, but most times anyway you got enough bluegills or sunfish or perch to cook up a batch for supper. The main point though was to have a good time being out in the open, on the water, under the sun, together. Maybe that's why without talking about it they hadn't gone fishing since Roy had gone away; it would have been too sad out there in the rowboat with him missing.

Now since the War was over and Roy was safe and would be coming home before the year was out anyway, fishing seemed okay again, and besides, this wasn't a family outing, just a man-to-man kind of thing with Artie and his Dad.

The lake was like glass, not even a breeze stirring. Artie and his Dad wore old straw hats with big brims to keep off the sun. They had sat in the same place for over an hour without saying a word. That was the nice thing about fishing; you didn't have to talk just to hear yourself, you could just sit and keep your eye on the red-and-white bobber that dunked down into the water when you got a bite, and you didn't even have to think about stuff, you could just be still and let your mind go blank.

When Dad spoke, his voice was low and soft. It was all right to talk, as long as you weren't so loud you scared the fish away.

"You're growing up now," Dad said.

"I guess so."

Another good thing about fishing was that you didn't have to look at the other person when you talked, you could just concentrate on watching your bobber, so you never felt as embarrassed about stuff as you would if you had to stare into somebody's eyes all the time.

"It's not all peaches and cream. You got to make some effort. Otherwise, you're liable to get off on the wrong foot for your whole life."

"Sure."

"Lots of fellas, along about your age, they get sneaky. Then it gets to be a habit. Like snitching beers. You can have a beer now and then, it's no crime. Just be out in the open about it. Don't go hiding in your room, or out in some bushes, be it beer or anything else."

"Yes, sir."

"How you act at home is how you get to be. That's why you want to have some manners, even if it's just family. Sure, you want to relax and kick off your shoes sometimes, that's what home is for, but you don't want to act like you're out in the barn."

"No, sir."

"You'll be all right, you just keep your head on."

"I'll try."

"I know you will. I know you'll try specially hard when Roy comes home. We all got to."

"You think he'll be sad?"

"He was wounded. More ways than one."

"You mean Shirley?"

"They both got hurt, the two of them. Things like that happen in Wartime. It's a shame."

"Darn right it is."

Artie felt proud, and manly, sitting there talking over deep stuff with his Dad while they fished.

It was quiet again, an almost perfect stillness, like the

world was in just the right balance. After a while Dad squinted up at the sun and then looked around the lake.

"Maybe we ought to try over there in that little cove, where the willows hang down. Looks like it might be a spot for a nice school of bass."

"Good idea," Artie said.

2

THAT fall was a season of victory.

The countryside flared with the red and gold blaze of the turning leaves, and the land was lush and ripe for harvest. Apples hung fat and heavy on the trees, and pumpkins lay like orange treasure in the fields of farms. The air was sharp, tinged with the scent of leaf smoke and cider, and at night the autumn skies were lit by the victory glow of football bonfires. The long War was over, and life was full.

Artie was part of this grand new season, following right in his brother's footsteps as quarterback of the freshman team. His arms and chest were ringed with the gold and black stripes of Birney, and the fact that the jersey was faded and torn only made it more glorious, part of the tradition. The freshman team got the hand-me-downs of

the old varsities, so the smudged numerals and raveled
sleeves were like badges of honor, the ragged emblems of
former battles fought by the valiant troops of the Bearcat
past.

Barking signals in his best new "BO" Lifebuoy voice,
Artie in his pads and cleated shoes and battered leather
helmet was a leader, guiding his team down the ordered
stripes to the goal line, the score, the victory. They were
tied with the freshmen of DeKamp 6–6 in the first game of
the season when Artie hupped the call, got the snap from
center, pedaled back to survey the flow and pattern of attack and defense, spotted his favorite receiver cutting
down the sidelines, grasped the seam of the leather oval,
set, cocked his arm, and snapped his left wrist forward to
send the ball spiraling like a shot to the waiting arms, the
trained sticky fingers of the fleet-footed future All-Star end
who was also now his best friend—Ben Vickman!

They were a team. Not just the starting eleven that Frosh
Coach Ray Spinezzi was molding into a finely tuned gridiron machine with its own fighting spirit and character, but
within that, a shining part of it, was the dynamic aerial duo
of Artie Garber and Ben Vickman, a quarterback and end
who were pounding along in the footsteps of the great grid
combinations, Birney's own answer to Cecil Isbell and Don
Hutson of the Green Bay Packers! Well, anyway, they had
clicked for a total of three complete passes, which really
was fiery stuff for freshmen, who usually just gave the ball
to the biggest guy on the team and hurled themselves forward like a pack of wild elephants, or passed by throwing
the ball up for grabs and saying a prayer.

It showed how wrong you could be about a guy. Ben
Vickman was the last human in the world whom Artie
would have ever imagined he'd ever team up with for anything. Back at the start of the summer when he wanted to
practice up on his passing he tried to get Warren Tutlow to

work out with him. Artie figured that even though Tutlow
was small, and wasn't growing very much, he might learn
to leap for the ball and become some kind of circus-act
receiver, a jack-in-the-box who popped out of a pack of
enemy defenders and nabbed passes with surprising skill
and timing. But when Artie got his spiral down and was
throwing real bullets, they either bounced off Tutlow's tiny
chest or the impact popped his glasses off. When Tutlow
tried without his glasses, he couldn't see the ball till it was
almost right up to him, and after a couple of times when
he turned for the pass, squinting and blinking, and it caught
him right on the nose, he gave up.

"I don't think football's my game," he said.

"Maybe you're just not an end," Artie told him. "Maybe
you could be a 'watch charm guard.'"

"There's other things than football," Tutlow said.

"I guess."

After that they didn't look each other in the eye for a
while and Tutlow turned to his chemistry set, trying to
develop a gas that would make people giggle against their
will.

For a while Artie tried to train Fishy Mitchelman to use
his long, flailing arms and lanky body to the good purpose
of catching a football, but every time Fishy went out for a
pass, he'd wiggle his hands in the air and snap his fingers,
singing some dopey jive stuff, and forgetting where the ball
was. Then he'd yell "Foo-ball!" and do a little dance step.

"I guess you'd rather be in the Band," Artie finally told
him.

"Woody Herman's band!" Fishy croaked, throwing his
head back and snapping his fingers.

Artie took an old tire home from the filling station, hung
it with a rope from the limb of a tree in the backyard, and
practiced throwing the football through it every Saturday
morning. One day Vickman came by on his bike, watched

for a while, and said, "You wanna play 'doughnuts' or football?"

Artie spit on his hands, rubbed them together and said, "You wanna go out for one?"

Vickman dropped his bike to the ground right on the spot and went charging across the yard, holding his arms out. Artie cocked his wrist and put his whole arm and body into throwing Ben Vickman the hardest bullet pass he could ram right into the gut of the wise guy. There was a grunt as the ball struck home, and Vickman wavered a moment but held on to the ball and fell backward with it. Artie went running over to him, and extended a hand to help him up.

"Nice catch," he said.

"Not a bad toss," said Vickman. He spit from the corner of his mouth and stood up.

"Now gimme a bullet," he said, "if you got one."

They practiced the rest of the day, and Vickman stayed for supper.

Only a handful of kids came to freshman games, mostly girls. They did not include Caroline Spingarn, who had ambled down the hall of high school the first day of class right onto the arm of Scooter McShea, a Junior who was Central Region State Low Hurdle Champion and sixth man on the basketball team. Artie had to laugh. Ha. He bet Old Scooter didn't have to wait for any Wars to end before he got a kiss off her, and he probably got a lot more than that, being a Junior and a low hurdle champ, but Artie preferred not to think about the details. There was this real nice new girl who had moved from Wisconsin, Gay Ann Fenewalt, who came to the opening freshman game and cheered like crazy, her thick gold braid bouncing against her back, her apple cheeks glowing in the late September sun. At school the next day she told Artie he was a wonderful passer, and he realized she was a genuine person, not the kind who was impressed by guys just because they were upperclassmen.

Not just in Birney but all over the country Sports was now as important as War used to be (the papers predicted the greatest "Sports Boom" since the Golden Days of the 1920s) and the homecoming heroes lost no time in trading in their Service uniforms for the combat gear of gridiron and diamond. Detroit pitcher Virgil Trucks got home in time for the World Series, and only one week out of the Navy he pitched the Tigers to a 4–1 win over the Chicago Cubs as his team went on to take what the papers called "The Thrill Series," saying the 1945 baseball championship was "stuffed with more thrills than anything since the War started!"

Artie was itchy for Roy to get back and be part of it all. He wanted his brother to see him playing quarterback for the freshman team, and maybe even go with him on a double date. Roy could drive, and Artie would get to sit in the back with Gay Ann Fenewalt, maybe even unhook her bra and place his eagerly trembling hands on her bare boobs. In the meantime Artie worked hard at football and school, and even helped out his Dad on the weekends.

One Saturday morning Artie was pumping gas at Joe's Premium when a beat-up old Plymouth coupe rolled up. Artie wiped his hands with the greasy rag that he wore jauntily in his hip pocket, and went around to lean on the driver's window.

Some girl was behind the wheel, and she smiled at him.

"Fill 'er up?" Artie asked.

"You sure have grown, Artie."

He blinked, and looked at the girl again.

"Shirley?"

"I guess I've changed too," she said.

Her hair was cut so short it looked like a tight black cap pulled down on her skull. Her beautiful bangs were gone, and she wore almost no makeup. For a second, Artie thought of those women in France who had their heads shaved because they had made out with German guys during the Occupation, but he realized Shirley had probably cut her hair like that so it wouldn't get caught in the airplane factory machinery. Her cheeks had a hollow look and she seemed a lot older, but still real pretty, especially when she smiled.

"Hey, this is great!" Artie said. "Can I buy you a rainbow Coke at Damon's? I get off in an hour."

"I'd love it. In the meantime, give me a dollar's worth of Regular."

It was almost like old times, having the Cokes at Damon's. But the times were new, and the two friends were different now. It was sort of spooky, but exciting, like people who had known each other years ago at some summer camp and now were grown up.

Shirley had bought the coupe she was driving with her own money she'd made at the War Plant, and she'd even saved up some more to go to college. She wanted to do it on her own, and not have to take from her folks when they could use it themselves. She was going to start Urbana the first of the year, and in the meantime, get some reading done and have a long visit with her parents. She had planned to wait to come home till after Thanksgiving, but everyone got laid off because of the War ending.

"What about Donna Modjeski?" Artie asked. "Did she get laid off too?"

"Donna got married," Shirley said. "To a man she met in Indianapolis. He's older. But very nice."

"What about you?" Artie said.

Shirley held up her left hand, which was bare of any jewelry, and wriggled her fingers.

"No wedding ring," she said.

She smiled, and put her hand back in her lap.

"Didn't even fall in love," she went on. "Met some nice

guys, though. I dated some. Decided I was pretty normal, after all."

"You're not!" Artie burst out. "I mean, you're *better* than normal."

Shirley laughed, smiling.

"Well, at least I'm not worse, anyway."

Artie sucked up the rest of his Coke, and leaned back in his chair.

"Well, you're home from the War now. That makes about everyone, except Roy. He's still down at Parris Island."

"How is he?"

"Okay, I guess. I mean, we really don't know. He never was much at letters. Except to you."

Shirley's cheeks turned as bright as if she had rouge on them, and she stirred the ice at the bottom of her glass.

"I was such a kid," she said.

"You want to see him again?"

"I doubt that he wants to see *me*. Anyway, I'm not expecting any miracles. That's not what I came home for."

"No, I didn't mean you did."

"It sure was nice seeing *you*, anyway."

Shirley smiled, and stood up. Artie offered to walk her home, forgetting she had her own car now. It was probably just as well. They might get real sad, thinking about the old walks, realizing now the Bluebirds were finally over the White Cliffs of Dover and the world was free, but other things hadn't turned out like they thought.

3

WHEN Roy finally came back home from the War the parades were over. The biggest parade of all had been for the first guy home, and it turned out to be Burt Spink! He hadn't even got overseas, but was stationed at Fort Riley, Kansas, where he was only a private in the Quartermaster Corps, which meant he probably just helped get the other guys' uniforms clean, but he was the first to get home so he got the best parade. A few weeks later a whole crowd from Oakley Central came up with the High School Band to welcome back some of their guys who had fought in the tanks with Blood 'n' Guts Patton, but after that mostly just the family and friends of the guys who got back went down to the station to greet them. You couldn't keep having parades all the time, they got old just like everything else, and besides, people were busy now going about their new Post-War lives.

Artie knew that was the way Roy wanted it. He hadn't even come straight home from Parris Island, but stopped off with one of his new Marine buddies who lived in Atlanta to "have a little R'n'R," as he said on the postcard he sent. When he finally got home one day in late October, the town just went on about its business. Artie got an excuse Mom wrote so he could get out of school and go to the station with his folks. The only other people waiting for the train were the Minnemores, and that was just because they were going to Chicago.

When Artie saw Roy, he was just as glad the bands and cheerleaders and everyone weren't there to greet him. His uniform was rumpled, like he'd slept in it on the train. His face was puffy, and there were deep purple blotches under his eyes. The eyes didn't seem to focus exactly, and the grin on his face was kind of crooked, like he was just coming out of a pileup in a football game.

Roy didn't carry his cane, but he swayed a little when he walked to the car.

"How's the leg?" Dad asked.

Roy slapped his thigh.

"Good as gold," he said.

When he got in the car he unbuttoned his jacket and loosened his belt, and his stomach bloated out like an inflated innertube. He patted it and belched, and the car smelled like some kind of stale, sweet syrup.

When they got home and Mom brought coffee out for everyone in the living room, Roy took a half-pint bottle from his hip pocket and splashed some in his cup.

"Coffee Royal," he explained.

"Good whiskey?" Dad asked.

"The best. Real bourbon. Sour Mash, from Kentucky. Try a splash?"

"I'm just a beer man," Dad said.

"Well, whatever Roy wants," Mom said, "he deserves it."

Dad nodded.

"There is a time to plant, and a time to reap," he said.

"And a time to rest," Mom added.

"I had me some real good R'n'R in Atlanta," Roy said. "The best. All I need's a little sack time, and I'm ready to roll. Go out and get me a piece of that Post-War world."

"There's plenty of time," Mom said.

"You gave some good years," Dad said. "Hard years. We're grateful to you, son. And thankful you're home."

Roy nodded, took a slurp of coffee, spilling some in the saucer, and then jumped up.

"*Snafu!* I left your presents in the car!"

Roy had gone shopping in Atlanta and bought a lavender sachet for Mom, a hand-painted tie for Dad, and a fountain pen for Artie.

Everyone was real excited with their presents, and thanked Roy a lot.

He laughed in this sharp, mocking kind of way that didn't sound happy or funny.

"The 'Spoils of War,' " he said.

Then he poured some more of the Sour Mash into his coffee cup.

The second day Roy was home he got out his cane, and used it to walk down Main Street. He even used it walking around the house, and Artie asked him about it.

"How come you're using your cane?"

"Sometimes the old wound acts up again."

"I thought it was healed, though. You said you were good as new."

Suddenly Roy tore off his belt and yanked down his pants and even his underpants and stood in the middle of the living room in broad daylight with all his sex hanging out and he gave an angry slap to the outlining of stitches on his thigh.

"See it? There it is, buddy. It's *real*."

"Hey, I know, I'm sorry," Artie said.

Roy stared at him almost like he hated him and then he pulled up his pants and buckled his belt back and picked up the cane and stalked off to the kitchen, pounding the cane on the floor as he went. Sometimes he used the cane and sometimes he didn't, but Artie never mentioned it again one way or the other.

Roy was really different from the time he'd come home before from the War. Instead of being quiet and staring a lot like he was thinking deep thoughts, he talked all the time and cackled his sharp, mocking laugh. Artie invited Vickman and some of his other new pals from the freshman team over to talk to the hero whose exploits they all had heard about, and Roy told them lots of War stories—this time the "War stories" were really about battles and enemy attacks and dodging bullets instead of stuff about making out with girls. The guys were really impressed at first, but then Roy started telling some of the stories over again and Vickman said he had to get to bed early because of being in training and the other guys agreed and said they had to go home. Roy asked if they'd like a shot of bourbon and they said they couldn't because it was during the season.

"Hell," Roy said, "when I was a freshman we drank the varsity under the table."

The guys just shrugged and went home.

Artie was kind of embarrassed for Roy, and then he felt guilty for feeling that way, so when Roy asked him to sit awhile out on the porch with him he did, even though he really wanted to get to bed early himself.

"Hell," Roy said as they sat out in the dark, "looks like your team's a bunch of pantywaists."

"They're okay," Artie said.

"Looks like I better come over to practice some day and show 'em a thing or two about the game of football."

"Sure," Artie said, without much enthusiasm.

Roy mainly slept late and hung around the house drinking bourbon. After supper, Artie would sit out on the porch with him before going to bed.

Roy complained that most of his buddies were gone, and there wasn't diddly-squat to do in this one-horse town. Bo Bannerman and some of the guys had already gone off to college on their G.I. Bills, or up to Chicago or Detroit to get jobs.

"Don't know what they're in such a rush about," Roy said. "The rat race starts soon enough."

"I guess," Artie said.

It made him feel down in the dumps that Roy thought grown-up life was a "rat race," but that was the kind of crummy mood he was in since he came back home.

"I wish to hell Wings Watson was here," Roy said. "Now there's a guy who'd have liked to live it up a while before he got stuck in the groove."

"It's a shame about Wings all right," Artie said.

"All the guys are gone, one way or other."

Roy took another swallow from his bourbon bottle.

"Hey, Roy," Artie said, "You know who's home?"

"I give up."

"Shirley."

"Who?"

"Shirley Colby."

Roy made his harsh little laugh, and spit through his teeth.

"She's going to college next semester," Artie said. "To Urbana. She saved up a lot of money when she worked at the War Plant."

Artie had written to Roy about Shirley moving to Indianapolis to work in the airplane factory, but Roy had never mentioned it.

"Speaking of hot stuff," Roy said, "whatever became of Beverly Lattimore?"

"She married some guy she met at the U.S.O. in Moline. A Seabee, I think. From Pittsburgh."

"Just my luck."

Roy took another belt of bourbon and then stood up.

"Guess I'll hit the sack," he said.

Artie went up to his own room and prayed to God that Roy would feel better.

Dad asked Roy to give a talk to the Moose Lodge about fighting the Japs in the South Pacific, and Roy kind of perked up and put on his dress blue uniform with the red stripes down the pants.

Evidently Roy's talk to the Moose was a big hit, and it seemed to give him a real shot in the arm. He started getting up early and going to help out Dad at the filling station, and Sunday he put on his dress blues again and went to church with the rest of the family. Monday he dropped by freshman football practice and gave the backfield guys some tips on passing.

"Thanks a lot for coming to practice," Artie said when he walked home with Roy.

"Hell, I got a real kick out of it."

"That was great, what you showed us. I bet you'd be a great coach, you know?"

"Ah, I was just horsing around," Roy said, but Artie could tell he was proud. Maybe that's what he would do in life, be a great football coach, the greatest since Knute Rockne. It made Artie feel good, thinking it might happen.

The whole family was in a great mood for their first big outdoor barbecue. Dad had decided to splurge and buy one of the new barbecue grills like people all over America were getting so they could enjoy the new life of Post-War leisure and home entertainment. It was pretty darn chilly, but the whole point of having a barbecue grill was so you could sit outside and eat in the fresh air, so everyone put on jackets and went to the backyard while Dad put the steaks on. They didn't have a backyard picnic table yet like the kind people had in the magazine ads, but Mom spread a blanket on the ground and they sat around like it was a picnic, eating steak and corn on the cob and potato salad and drinking Pabst Blue Ribbon out of the can, except for Artie who just had a Coke because he was still in training.

"Well, this sure is 'The Life of Riley,' " Dad said.

"That's for me," Roy said. " 'The Life of Riley.' "

That was the name of a new radio show with William Bendix, and everyone talked about "leading 'The Life of Riley,' " which meant enjoying yourself and having all the good stuff to do it with.

"You fellas can be 'Riley,' " Mom said, "and I'll be 'Queen for a Day.' "

That was another popular new program, where regular housewives from all over America could compete to be "Queen for a Day" and win all kinds of terrific prizes, like a thousand dollars in cash, fur coats, jewelry, and free trips to nightclubs.

"The sky's the limit these days," Dad said. "They used to tell us 'Prosperity is just around the corner,' but I never thought I'd live to see it. Now it's here."

"Thanks to Roy and all the boys who won the War," Mom said.

"You better believe it," Dad said.

He raised his can of beer toward Roy, like a toast, and Artie did the same with his Coke bottle.

"Ah, hell," Roy said, being modest.

"I just want to see you get your piece of this Post-War world," Dad said. "You deserve it."

Roy slugged back a big gulp of his beer.

"A guy just has to pick his spot," he said. "I'm in no rush."

"No need to be," Dad said. "Plenty of new opportunities out there that won't go away. Things we never dreamed of."

"Shoot, yes," Artie said. "I read in *Life* they already got radio shows you can *see*, in New York, and pretty soon they'll have these little picture tubes in everyone's living room, like little movie screens."

"I don't know if I'd want to *see* Stella Dallas," Mom said. "I already have her pictured in my own mind."

"Don't worry," Dad said. "I'm not running out to buy any picture tube. We just bought us the barbecue grill."

"Not only that," Artie said, "*Life* says there's going to be 'machines that think like men.'"

Roy made a harsh little laugh.

"Where does that leave the men?" he asked.

"Don't worry," Dad said. "Any machine, it'll take a man to run it."

"That'll take 'Whiz Kids,'" Roy said. "Math brains."

"You have the brains, Roy," Mom said. "You just have to use them."

"What's that supposed to mean?" Roy asked.

"That we have all the confidence in you," Dad said quickly.

Roy finished off his beer and squeezed up the can with his hand.

"Well, like I said, I'm not rushing into anything."

"Nobody wants you to," Dad said.

"If you ask me, you'd make a great football coach," said Artie.

"I was just horsing around," Roy said.

"Yeah, but I mean, if you wanted to—"

"If I wanted to, they'd tell me to go get a rinky-dink college degree in Phys. Ed."

"You have the G.I. Bill," Dad said.

"But I don't have my high school diploma, so go ahead and say 'I told you so' and get it over with!"

Dad shook his head.

"I wasn't going to say that at all."

"You'd only have to finish up your last semester," Mom said.

"If you think I'm going back and sit in a class with a bunch of kids, you've got another think coming."

"I bet you could make it up at a college," Mom said. "There's probably a lot of G.I.'s doing that."

"You could probably do it right at Urbana," Artie said.

Roy took his beer can and heaved it as hard as he could in the neighbors' yard.

"Will everyone get off my back?" he said.

"Roy, you know you're welcome to come in with me at the station," Dad said, "if that's what you want."

Roy jumped up, his fists clenched and his face flushed red.

"It's not what I goddamn want. I don't want a goddamn thing. I want to be left the hell alone!"

He turned and ran in the house.

"Dear Lord," Mom said.

Dad put his hand on her arm.

"Don't worry. He'll find himself."

Artie didn't say anything, but he understood something. Roy was afraid.

He was scared to death of what in the world he was going to do with his own life.

Artie got up and started collecting the paper plates and steak bones.

That was the end of the family's first outdoor barbecue.

Roy came home drunk that night. He had got in a fight at the Purple Pony. His right eye was swollen, and his shirt was ripped. Artie helped Mom and Dad put him to bed, and afterward he sat in the kitchen with them.

"We've got to do something," Mom said.

Dad sighed and shook his head.

"You can lead a horse to water but you can't make him drink."

"We can't just sit back and watch him go to pieces," Mom said.

"No," Artie said. "We can't."

Mom and Dad stared at him, but he didn't say anything else. He just gave them each a hug and went up to bed.

He knew it was up to him.

And Shirley Colby.

"You're the only one can help him," Artie told Shirley over Cokes at Damon's Drugs.

"He doesn't even want to see me."

"He's scared is why."

"I saw him one day on Main Street, on the other side of the street. I waved, and he turned away."

"Do you still love him? I mean, are you still *in love* with him?"

Shirley took the straw from her Coke and twisted the ends together in a little bow.

"I always will be," she said.

"He will with you, too. No matter what he says."

"In my heart, I believe it. But I don't know what to do about it."

"You got to be alone with him some way."

"Well, I can't go tie him to a tree."

Artie put his Coke glass down and leaned across the table.

"That's it!"

"Artie. Be serious."

"I don't mean the part about tying him up, I mean trees. The woods. The old place, where you went to be alone."

"If only—"

"I'll get him there."

Artie stood up, and Shirley went around the table and hugged him, right in the middle of Damon's Drugs.

4

O N Saturday morning Artie took a cold bottle of milk
up to Roy and woke him from his latest hangover.

"What the hell?" Roy said, blinking.

Artie handed him the bottle of milk.

Roy started gulping it down and then stopped to take a
breath and looked suspiciously at Artie.

"Who are you supposed to be? Florence Nightingale?"

"I got to talk to you."

"Go ahead. I'm listening."

"Not here. Not in the house."

"Uh-oh. Girl problems, huh?"

"Yeah."

Roy finished off the milk, and flopped back on his pillow.

"Well, if you give me a chance to shower, we can take a
little hike around the block."

"That's not enough."

"Ohhhhhh. You 'got it bad and that ain't good,' huh?"

"Yeah."

"Well, I guess we can take a spin out in the country, if the old man'll let me touch the car again."

"No. I mean, I'd just like to walk out to Skinner Creek, to the rock. You know? Where we used to go and talk."

"That was the good old days, kid."

"Well, it's still there. The rock."

"Hell, it's November."

"The sun's out, though, and it's way above freezing. Anyway, I'll build a fire."

Roy sat up on his elbows, squinting.

"Jesus wants me for a sunbeam," he said.

"It's really important."

"Okay, okay! Put on some coffee, anyway. Then we'll go freeze our tails."

Artie grabbed the empty milk bottle and hustled downstairs.

They were almost to the rock but not in sight of it yet when Artie stopped.

"Hey, Roy, you go on," he said. "I gotta see a man about a horse. Be there in a shake."

"You hurry up and start that fire, Mr. Boy Scout."

"Sure! Be right there!"

Roy walked on and Artie unzipped his fly and faced toward a tree. He even tried to pee, to make his lie more realistic, but he couldn't. He just stood there, holding himself.

He didn't hear any noise from Roy walking, and wondered if he was waiting to hear the sound of peeing, maybe suspecting something was up. Artie squeezed his eyes shut and concentrated everything on trying to make the water come, but nothing happened. He even made the sound of "pssssss" to himself like he used to do when he was a kid to get himself going, but that didn't work either. Finally he put it back in his pants and zipped up his fly, figuring Roy had either got to the rock by now or was waiting on the trail to catch Artie in his lie, but either way it was too late now to pretend anymore. Whatever was going to happen would happen.

Artie would have given a cool million to go and sneak a look at what was happening, but he'd given Shirley his sacred word of honor, not as a Boy Scout but as a man, that he wouldn't spy on them. He realized anyway that spying was kid stuff, something that belonged to his childhood. Next April he'd be fifteen, and that fall he'd be a Sophomore and a varsity man. He was not a little kid anymore, and he didn't do kid stuff. He had done his part of the job, which was getting Roy to the rock, and now his only duty was to get the hell out of there. Still, he just stood where he was. Then he bowed his head and prayed.

"Dear God, make it all right with Shirley and Roy, and give me the willpower to go home now."

He took a deep breath and started walking out of the woods when he heard the sound and stopped.

It was Roy, laughing.

It was scary.

The laugh was the harsh, croaked, bitter kind that Artie was used to hearing from Roy all the time since he came home from War, but this time it was worse, like it came from way down inside him and was being yanked out like a part of his guts. It was almost crazy, and Artie wondered if maybe Roy really had cracked, and might do something terrible.

To Shirley.

"Forgive me, God," Artie whispered.

Then he turned and got down on all fours and started crawling toward the high rise of ground that gave a view of the rock. The smell of dead leaves, like an odor of fear, filled his head. When he got to the rise he stopped without crawling up to look. At least he wouldn't break that part of his pledge. He would only listen.

The horrible, wrenching laugh came again, and then Roy was shouting.

"I surrender! You win! The dumb vet fell for the trick! Oh, brother—if the old platoon could see me now! Ambushed by a kid and a broad!"

"Will you listen to me, please?" Shirley said real calmly.

"You got a speech? Go ahead—deliver! 'Friends, Romans, countrymen—lend me your beers.'"

Then the awful laugh again.

Finally it stopped, and turned to racked coughing, and then there was quiet.

"I don't have any speech," Shirley said quietly. "I really just have one thing to say. I hope you can hear me."

"I may be dumb, but I'm not deaf."

A wind came up, stirring dead leaves. Then the woods were silent.

"I love you, Roy Garber."

"Love!" Roy bellowed. "Oh, good, just great! I am melting, look, I am melting into a little pool of butter, just like Little Black Sambo, that's all I'll be, a little pool of butter on the ground."

"You're afraid," she said. "You're a coward."

"Now, you listen to me, little lady. I may be a lot of things, I may be no-good and worthless and a goddamn drunk, but I did not get the Purple Heart and a game leg by being a coward."

"I know you're not afraid of dying," she said.

"So what am I afraid of? You?"

"Yes, I hurt you."

"I managed to survive, thank you, ma'am."

"So did I."

"You want the Purple Heart, too, or something?"

"I want you. I need you. And you need me even worse."

"Don't flatter yourself, baby."

"I don't. I'm a coward, too. But I'm a loner. I can make it by myself. I have. I don't think you can. Not very well, anyway."

"Thanks for the vote of confidence."

"I'm sorry if the truth hurts."

"So what if it's true? So what if I'm not a loner? You think you're the only fish in the sea?"

"No. But I'm the best one for you."

"You have really got some gall, sister."

"I hope so. Anyway, you don't want a girl who's like you. I'm your opposite. That's what you need."

"That doesn't make sense."

"Yes, it does. We fit together."

"Oh, yeah? Well, let me tell you something. I been with a lot of women. 'All cats are alike in the dark.' "

"You know that's not what I'm talking about."

"I don't know *what* the hell you're talking about."

"Us. We could have a life together."

"Like I said before. There's plenty of fish in the sea."

"You're afraid. You know that, don't you?"

"Get off my back."

"There's plenty of fish in the sea for me, too."

"So why don't you go fishing? Hell, you'll be up at Urbana in a couple of months, you can hook a real world-beater. Some Whiz Kid who'll make a mint. Restore the family fortunes, make your folks happy."

"I want *you*."

"Why? Is it a challenge or something? Save the no-good kid who has no future?"

"See? You're afraid. You're not just afraid of me, either. You're afraid of just about everything but bullets. And death. Those are easy. Am I right?"

"You bitch. You goddamn bitch."

Roy started crying. It was soft at first, like a baby, and then it grew into sobs, and then yelps, like a wounded animal. Then it died down, then stopped.

"I love you, Roy."

Artie held his breath in the silence that followed, praying without any words. Then Roy's voice came, different now, low but clear, with a steady, simple calmness to it.

"Help me," he said.

It was quiet again, and Artie started to crawl up to where he could peek, but then he remembered he was not a kid anymore. With stern determination he turned away, stealthily crawling on all fours, moving as quietly as possible over the matted leaves till he came to the path. Then he stood up and breathed deeply, filling his lungs with the fresh, bracing air, and ran toward home, leaping and bounding, stretching his arms to the limitless sky. He did not look back.

LUCIANO'S LUCK

1943. Under cover of night, a strange group parachutes into Nazi occupied Sicily. It includes the overlord of the American Mafia, "Lucky" Luciano. The object? To convince the Sicilian Mafia king to put his power—the power of the Sicilian peasantry—behind the invading American forces. It is a dangerous gamble. If they fail, hundreds of thousands will die on Sicilian soil. If they succeed, American troops will march through Sicily toward a stunning victory on the Italian Front, forever indebted to Mafia king, Lucky Luciano.

A DELL BOOK   14321-7 $3.50

JACK HIGGINS

bestselling author of *Solo*

BREAD UPON THE WATERS
BY
IRWIN SHAW

"A rare novel of substance. Shaw hits the top of his mark in this novel about gratitude and the entangling relationship of giver and receivers. A crackling story of happiness, tragedy, bathos, unkindness, failure to communicate, hope, selfishness, and minor revelations."
—*The Houston Chronicle*

"Vintage Shaw. He is addictive and immensely enjoyable. Shaw captures the uneasiness, the dark night of the 20th century soul."
—*The Boston Globe*

"A breakthrough—surely his best novel. One is caught up in it, mesmerized. This is a gripping story about the interplay of changing relationships."
—Clifton Fadiman, *Book-of-the-Month Club News*

A Dell Book   **10845-4**   **$3.95**